Merciless Havoc

Merciless Havoc

Montana Mayhem
Book 3

Millie Copper

This is a work of fiction. All characters, places, and incidents are products of the author's imagination or are used fictitiously. Any resemblance to actual people, places, or events is entirely coincidental.

Technical information in the book is included to convey realism. The author shall assume no liability or responsibility to any person or entity with respond to any loss or damage caused, or allegedly caused, directly or indirectly by information contained in this book of fiction. Any reference to registered or trademarked brands is used simply to convey familiarity. This manuscript is in no way sponsored or endorsed by any brand mentioned.

Written by Millie Copper

Edited by Ameryn Tucker

Proofread by Dianna Bradley and WMH Cheryl

Cover design by Dauntless Cover Design

Also by Millie Copper

Montana Mayhem Series

Havoc in Wyoming Series

Nonfiction Books

Join My Reader's Club!

Receive a complimentary copy of *Wicked Havoc: A Montana Mayhem Prequel*. As part of my reader's club, you'll be the first to know about new releases and specials. I also share info on books I'm reading, preparedness tips, and more. Please sign up at:

MillieCopper.com/Wicked

Who's Who

The Monroe Family: Skinny and malnourished, Leanne Monroe and her two children were last-minute additions to the group making their way from the safety of the ski lodge outside of Bakerville, Wyoming, to their homes in Montana. Eight-year-old Sebastian has a ready smile for everyone, while his older sister, Sadie, keeps to herself. Leanne is cantankerous, often speaking her mind and going out of her way to be difficult. What their traveling friends don't know is the family's keeping a secret—a secret their safety has hinged on.

Donnie McCullough: A bit of a rebel, Donnie is determined to help Leanne Monroe and her children make it to their aunt's home. When their journey began, Leanne seemed to only tolerate Donnie. Now the soft touches and lingering glances suggest something more.

The Hoffmann Family: Kimba and Rey Hoffmann, along with their three children—Nicole, Nate, and Naomi—fled Denver after the bridges exploded. They are invaluable members of the group and are committed to helping the other families in their quests.

The Dosen Family: Away from home when the attacks started, Jennifer and her three sons are determined to return to their small ranch outside of Great Falls, Montana. Eighteen-year-old twins Atticus and Asher, along with sixteen-year-old Axel, have all trained with the militia alongside their mom. Will a few months of training be enough to see them safely home?

The Dawson Family: After her husband's atrocious acts made her family an outcast, Victoria Dawson and her two sons, Brett and Jameson, need a fresh start. They'll be joining the Dosen family in Great Falls—if they can make it there.

Rochelle Bennet, PJ Cameron, and Robyn Sorensen: When the traveling group reached Lockwood, Montana, Robyn Sorensen, who was injured from being under water for too long after slipping into a cold creek, was handed over to the care of the military and her parents.

Rochelle and PJ headed off on their own in search of Rochelle's son, who was away at summer camp when the attacks started.

Tamra Nicholson: A twice-widowed mom of two daughters, thirteen-year-old Beth and seven-year-old Debbie. Her first marriage was built on love and trust—her second one, convenience and security which was needed at the end of the world. Turns out, what she thought was security was nothing more than a lie. After traveling for two weeks with Sadie and her group, they're safe in the small town she grew up in.

Sadie's Story

Chapter 1

June

My mom, Leanne, shoots me a smile and a wink. "Sadie? Why don't you and Sebastian come with me on a walk. It'll be good to stretch our legs. Wes, will you join us?"

My mom's brother, Uncle Wes, gives a nod as my little brother, Sebastian, scrambles to his feet. Even after a full day of traveling, with him and me riding in a much too small cart being towed behind the mountain bikes, Sebastian's energy never seems to waver.

I glance toward the family of four we've been traveling with the past few days: an older man in his seventies, his son in his late forties or maybe older, the son's wife, and their boy in his early teens—thirteen or fourteen, I'd guess, but I haven't asked, and no one has said. While the boy seems nice enough, we'll only be together a few more days, until they head east and we continue north.

There's no reason to become friends. Mom and Uncle Wes decided it'd be safer to travel with them—safer maybe, but I certainly don't feel welcome.

I glance to the woman. She has her head on her chest, a grimace of pain crossing her face. She's been having stomachaches, which causes her to be grumpy and rude to everyone. Mom said it's probably because of the diet we're eating while on the road.

With no fresh fruit or vegetables available, our food is things we trap or snare: squirrels, rabbits, small rodents, and birds. I don't even think we should be eating some of the stuff. The rabbits and rodents all have bugs on them. I mean, it's bad enough to think about eating a squirrel or a mouse, but to see bugs jumping off them . . . it's really pretty disgusting.

1

My body gives an involuntary shudder. Yuck.

Tonight's dinner will be cold rabbit and partridge, leftover from earlier today when we were in a rural area and able to cook without fear of being discovered. Tonight, we're camped closer to a town. We know we're not the only ones hungry, eating bug-laden small game, and we fear someone will smell our cookpot and come investigate.

We don't want that. It's better to stay hidden.

Even before we met up with the others—who we found by smelling their cooking and took a chance they were friendly after watching them for about an hour—we were careful, choosing to avoid threats and dangers as much as we could after leaving La Grande, Oregon, on our way home to Spokane, Washington. Well, not Spokane proper, but a little community less than a half hour north.

"Baby girl?" Mom reaches her hand for me.

I furrow my brow. I wish she'd stop calling me that and acting like I'm a young child. Those days are long past. I open my mouth to object.

She lifts a shoulder and gives me a kind smile. "Sorry. Sadie."

"Fine," I mutter before shooting my eyes back to the woman.

Her husband gently rests a hand on her shoulder. She shrugs it away, mumbling something that sounds less than kind. And I'm sure I hear my mom's name.

The woman, Clarice, is not happy we're with them. I heard her last night, talking much too loudly from inside their tent, as she told her husband, Ben, how annoying my mom is. She said she's too cheery and too religious. Both are true statements. Even with everything that's gone wrong, Mom still keeps a smile on her face and sends praises to God, saying He'll get us through.

As we step from the small clearing we're camping in to the lush forest, Sebastian says, "My stomach hurts a little, too, Mom. Do you think I have the same problem as Clarice?"

Mom lets out a small laugh. "I suspect we're all going to have stomachaches at some point on this trip, not only because of the food we're eating but because of everything that's happened along with traveling."

"But she's just riding on a motorcycle!" Sebastian throws out his hands. "It's not like her husband and the grandpa—or you and Uncle Wes—who pedal the bikes."

"Shh. Don't judge, Sebastian. None of us have it easy. Since the terrorist attacks and the bombs— "

"I can't believe they actually saw the bombs." My brother's eyes are wide. "And the . . . the clouds. What are they called?"

"Mushroom clouds," Uncle Wes says. "They happen after the detonation of a nuclear bomb, when the fireball rises into the air."

"But not all nuclear bombs, right?" Sebastian asks. "Not the kind that made the cars stop working?"

"Right. That one didn't hit the ground. It exploded in the atmosphere, the sky, somewhere high up."

"And it doesn't make that bad stuff, the radiation, so we're safe from that?"

"We pray so," Mom says. "Keep in mind, honey, we don't really know what's happening, just what people think and what a few have seen, like Ben and his family."

At least Ben and his dad, Bart, seem happy to have us with them. The boy, Liam, doesn't act like he cares either way. But Clarice . . . I get it. Mom can be a lot. Even before the bombs and other attacks, she could be annoying.

We step out of the trees to a bubbling creek. I breathe in the fresh scent of the water combined with the earthy aroma of the forest. I wish we could camp here, right near the water. It's so peaceful—the smells, the sounds. I can almost forget the troubles of the last couple of weeks, troubles that started with deliberate plane crashes at five different US airports and escalated from there.

At first, we didn't worry much about it and just continued what we were doing. Mom was in La Grande for a conference, and the organizers decided to continue it. By the time everyone realized just how serious the attacks were, we were stuck and were unable to drive after the EMP ruined our car.

Not that there was any fuel available anyway. Part of the terrorist attacks included blowing up gas refineries and launching a cyberattack that wiped out electricity. Even if there was fuel, neither Mom nor Wes had any cash left, and the cyberattacks took out the banks and ATMs. It was a mess.

And Mom smiled and praised God through all of it.

One of the church pastors helped us find sturdy mountain bikes and the trailers so we could begin the two-hundred-mile-plus journey home. Over and over, Mom said what a blessing it is I'm so small, how it was part of God's plan so Sebastian and I could ride.

Sebastian and Wes kneel by the creek, looking at small fish darting along the edge.

"Maybe we should go back and ask Ben if he has some fishing line," Wes suggests. "Didn't he say he brought some?"

Mom shakes her head. "I don't know. But if he did, I'd think he'd be here now, trying to catch something to eat."

"No one's catching anything out of our stream," a harsh voice says loudly.

Mom and I spin around, coming face to face with the huge barrel of a long gun. Mom reaches for my hand.

"You two by the water, get up and move over there," the man says.

"No problem," Wes agrees with a quiver in his voice.

Once the man has us lined up, two other guys, who are also carrying guns, step into view.

"Well then, guess we've found ourselves some poachers," a man with overly bushy eyebrows says, waving his gun at us.

"Can't have 'em catching our fish," the first guy agrees. "Gotta putta stop to it."

"We're not fishing." Wes lifts his hands. "We were just, um, talking about it."

"Thinking about stealing is the same as stealing!" Bushy Brows declares. "You stealing our food—well, that's a problem."

The trees rustle. I dart my eyes toward the sound and catch a glimpse of Bart, the older man in our group. He turns quickly, disappearing back into the woods.

"Hey, you!" the third guy calls out. "Get back here!"

"Go after him," Bushy Brows says. As the two men take off, he turns to Wes. "How many are with you?"

Wes clears his throat. "That's it. Just the five of us."

Mom looks to Wes with wide eyes. Sebastian tilts his head at him. Wes quickly places a hand on my brother's shoulder.

"Don't get any wild ideas," the man says. "This shotgun will take out the lot of you at this distance."

My stomach sinks to my toes. I don't know anything about guns, but I have no reason not to believe him. And from the look on his face, I believe he'd do it. For what? For fishing? Not even fishing, just talking about fishing.

"Hey, man," one of the other men yells at Bart. "We've already seen you. Why don't you come on out here and join your family?"

It's several seconds before a voice responds. "Okay. No problem. I'm coming out."

Mom lets out a loud breath. The voice isn't right. It isn't gravely enough to be Bart. It's less than a minute until Ben—not his dad—steps out of the forest with the men behind him, pointing the gun at his back.

"Should we tie 'em up?" one of the men holding the gun on Ben asks as they near the creek.

"Don't think we need to," Bushy Brows says. "They'll behave, won't you? Or else the kids get it first."

I feel my mom tremble beside me.

"We'll take 'em with us."

The guy who was first to hold the gun on us says, "Why we bothering with that? Let's just take their stuff and send them on their way."

"You see their camp?" Bushy Brows asks.

"Nope. But I bet they have one."

"Go on, see if you can find it. Louie and me, we'll take 'em to the farm."

"I still don't see why we're bothering with holding them."

"That's why you're not in charge, Reggie," Bushy Brows says, pointing the gun in the direction of the guy. "Stop mouthin' and do what you're told."

Reggie, the original guy who pulled the gun on us, lifts one of his hands. "Whatever you say." He shakes his head before spinning toward the forest and stomping off.

I want to yell out, to warn Bart and the others to go. *To hide.* I look to Mom, who gives a slight shake of her head. Tears dot her eyelashes as she reaches for my little brother's hand and then takes mine.

Bushy Brows and the other one, Louie, march us along the creek to the main road. Though the walk isn't long, the sun's already setting when they guide us down a long driveway toward a ramshackle house and several sorry looking buildings.

"Where should we put them?" Louie asks.

5

"That shed over there. It has a padlock on it. Should hold 'em."

Once we're inside the dark and dusty shed, which smells heavily of mold, Mom pulls Sebastian and me close. "We're okay," she tells us over and over as we rock back and forth. After a few minutes, she says, "God will protect us."

I let out a snort.

"He will, Sadie. I'm . . . I'm sure of it."

Sebastian and I sit next to each other, leaning against a clear space on a wall. He draws designs and shapes in the dirt floor with his finger while the adults talk in low voices, trying to figure out why we've been captured and how we can get away. I want to join the discussion but instead choose to listen and stay quiet.

After a while, Sebastian leans his head on my shoulder and falls asleep. I must also drift off because the next thing I know, there's light streaming in through the cracks of the rickety shed.

"Have some water, Sadie," Mom says, gently jostling my arm. "They brought water and food a few minutes ago."

"Food?" I ask, sitting up.

Sebastian is already awake, shoving something in his mouth. "It's cow," he says around a bite. "And it's really good."

"Beef," Mom corrects. "But he's right about it being good."

"They wouldn't let us fish, but they're giving us meat?" I ask, shaking my head.

"Crazy, huh?" Uncle Wes nods around his own mouthful of food.

The meat and water are all we get until later in the day when a guy I've never seen before brings a fresh jug of water and more meat.

After the night's meal, Mom and Wes start talking about God and how He'll bring us through this. Sebastian, who's way too much like Mom and is always saying and doing churchy things, joins in the conversation. Ben says nothing, and I respond only when it's expected of me.

The food and water delivery continues the next day, but on the third morning, Bushy Brows shows up with only water. "You folks are draining our supplies. We're cutting your rations to once a day until we can figure out what to do with you."

"You could let us go," Ben says.

"Humph. You know, I've considered it. But at this point, if I let you go, it'll undermine my authority. You folks have become a status symbol of sorts. And a bargaining chip."

6

"A bargaining chip?" Wes asks.

"Yup. Seems there might be another group nearby who's interested in having help in their fields and homes. Might just trade you for a few goods and things."

"Like slaves?"

Bushy Brows just lifts his shoulder and leaves.

A few hours later, someone shows up with meat, about half the amount we were previously given.

Ben divides it into five equal portions. Mom and Wes offer Sebastian and me a little more from their amount.

"Don't do that," Ben says, his voice harsh. "We need to get out of here. We'll need to fight. You need your strength."

Chapter 2

It's been three days since they reduced our food amount. While they do bring water several times throughout the day, the lack of food is taking a toll on all of us. That along with the overwhelming heat and the stench of this shed. There's no bathroom, so we've made a privacy screen in one corner and use a bucket. It's disgusting.

We don't talk much, just sit and wait—wait for more water and a few morsels of meat. Wes paces sometimes, which causes Mom to snap at him to sit down. She's stopped smiling, stopped spouting Bible verses and insisting God will rescue us.

Sebastian, though, has stayed faithful, sure we're going to be fine. He talks about different Bible stories, like Daniel in the lion's den or Shadrach, Meshach, and Abednego who were thrown in the fiery furnace. And he's told us over and over about David killing Goliath by slinging a stone at him. In preparation of being a modern-day David, Sebastian has collected five rocks from the dirt floor and fashioned his own sling out of an old red shop towel and a couple lengths of twine found on one of the shed's shelves.

Ben, Mom, and Wes also scoured the shelves for things to help us escape or things we'll need after we're out. Although it's mostly a bunch of old, dusty junk, they do find a few things: a forgotten piece of rebar and a few empty water bottles—one that Wes filled with dirt and tied a piece of twine around the neck of, making his own sling-style weapon.

I'm almost asleep, trying to nap in the sweltering heat, when the lock on the door rattles. I crack an eye to see who's bringing us water this time. It's a new guy, slightly overweight with strawberry blond hair and an ugly scowl. One of the others, a creepy guy who's brought food before, is behind him. But neither are carrying water.

"You— " the new guy points to Mom " —grab the girl and come with us."

My eyes shoot open.

Mom steps in front of me. "I'll go with you." Her voice is low and has a slight quiver to it. "But my little girl, she's not feeling well."

"Don't matter. She's coming with us."

"Please. She's just a little girl. Only . . . um, she's only twelve. I'm sure whatever you have planned, I'll be . . . " A slight choking noise escapes her. "I'll be enough."

"Twelve?" the creepy guy mutters. "That's too young, even for me."

Mom shoots me a quick look, giving me a slight shake of her head.

Tears fill my eyes as I whisper, "No, Mom."

Wes moves in front of Mom. "She isn't going with you either. They're both staying here."

The new guy's fist slams into Uncle Wes's chest. The other hand quickly pops him in the nose, sending my uncle to the ground.

"Stop!" Mom yells, as Ben gets to his feet. "I'll go. I won't . . . I won't fight you."

The new guy sneers. "I don't mind if you fight a little."

A whimper escapes my mom. She turns her head to meet my eyes. Instead of their usual loving, soft glow, they're hard and unyielding. Angry. "Take care of your brother and mind your uncle."

"Shut up and get out here." The man grabs her arm, flinging her through the door. He looks at me, curling his lip. "Too bad you'll miss the party. We would've showed you a good time."

"Leave her alone," the other guy says. "You heard the mom, she's just a kid."

"Yeah, well, she's too skinny anyway . . . and ugly at that."

The door slams with a bang. Sebastian bursts into tears as the lock catches. I pull him close to me, my own hot tears of sadness and anger dropping on his head.

Ben helps Uncle Wes from the floor and then their heated words fill the room.

Sebastian lifts his head, his eyes searching mine. "Will they bring her back?"

I bite my lip.

He lets out a long breath. "We'll pray. We'll pray, and God will take care of her." Sebastian immediately begins his petitions, begging his God to keep Mom safe and bring her back to us. We stay huddled together as Uncle Wes paces and Ben sits leaning against a wall, deep in thought.

It seems like forever, though it's probably only half an hour, when the lock rattles and the door opens. Mom is tossed back into the room, landing in a heap on the ground. The sleeve of her shirt is ripped, and she has a fat lip and a cut by her eye.

"Mom!" Sebastian cries, scurrying to her.

"I'm okay." She gives him a smile that resembles a grimace. She picks herself up from the floor, straightening her shirt as best she can.

With her jaw set, she turns toward me. "We're okay, Sadie." She rests a hand on Sebastian's shoulder. "We're okay." Then she turns to where Uncle Wes is standing near Ben. "We need to get out of here. Now. They aren't going to wait for the limited food to do its job."

"They told you that?" Ben asks.

"He bragged about it," Mom spits out the words.

"I thought they were trading us?"

"Guess that didn't work out." Mom runs a hand through her tousled hair.

"What can we do?" Wes looks to Ben.

Ben motions for all of us to move close. With our heads together and our voices low, a plan begins to form.

A plan even Sebastian voices as dangerous. "We definitely need God now."

"Humph," Mom scoffs.

Sebastian gives her a strange look. "Mom?"

"You just do what we've said, Sebastian. You too, Sadie."

Ben has us put the treasures we've found in our pockets. I have a length of twine and a shop rag dotted with holes. Waiting is hard. *Stressful.* Sebastian complains about his stomach hurting. I rub his back and offer soothing words.

When the lock rattles, Mom motions us to move against the wall. She'd already told us to keep our eyes closed but to be ready to do what she says, when she says it. Sebastian grips the red cloth, with his largest stone in it—his David weapon.

There's am *oomph* and then a scuffle. I slit open one eye to see one of the guards go down when Ben hits him with the rebar.

"Now." Ben orders as he takes the pistol from the guy. "Let's move."

Sebastian and I spring up and out the door. Another guy is on the ground, his face bloody, Uncle Wes's dirt-filled water bottle now tattered. I watch as Ben hits him in the nose with the of the butt of the man's own pistol.

"Go!" Ben says in a harsh whisper. "Head for the trees."

10

I put an arm over my eyes; the bright sun hurts after so many hours in the dim room.

"Run!" Mom gives me a slight shove. "Don't look back."

A gunshot causes me to yelp.

"Go! Go!" Sebastian grabs at my hand.

"Run faster," Uncle Wes yells.

I turn back to look at him as another shot sounds. He falls to the ground. "Uncle Wes!"

"Keep going, Sadie!" My brother pulls on my arm.

Ben fires the pistol he grabbed and looks down at Uncle Wes. His eyes meet mine. "Keep going."

We get to the cover of the trees. "Move behind that stump." Mom points to a fallen log.

As soon as Ben reaches us, he asks, "Why'd you stop? This isn't safe."

There's yelling and shooting coming from the farm. Men are running in this direction.

"Wes?" Mom asks Ben, her voice shaky.

"I'm sorry. It was instant."

Mom gives a stoic nod as she gets us moving again. There's no time to fall apart, no time to grieve. With tears streaming down her face, Mom urges us forward, deeper into the woods.

After a few minutes, Ben motions to a clump of vines. "There."

We shimmy into the bushes. Thorns rip at my arms, my hair.

Ben winces when he grabs a piece of brush to hide where we entered. He motions us to sit. Seconds later, we hear the men crashing through the forest, their heavy footsteps and breathing giving them away.

Mom puts a finger to her lips. After the noise subsides, I offer Ben the holey shop towel. He wraps it around his hand to stop the bleeding.

We stay put, hidden until full darkness. The men have circled us many times, cussing and cursing, questioning where we went. The last time we heard them, someone said it was too dark to keep searching. That was at least an hour ago.

"Let's go." Ben's voice is quiet. He moves the brambles to let us out.

We stumble through the dark, putting distance between us and the farm. We move as quietly as we can but know that if the men are

11

nearby, there's no way they won't hear us. Finally, Ben says we've gone far enough and we'll find a place to rest for a while.

Instead of in a thicket of thorns, this time he moves us to a depression in the ground, a cross between a hole and a crevice.

"Leanne, you and the children sleep. I'll keep watch. I'll need you to switch with me after a bit so I can rest too."

I'm exhausted, numb even. Uncle Wes is dead. I glance to my brother. Even in the dark, I can see his tears. "You okay?" I whisper.

"Don't whisper," Ben says. "Talk quietly, in your normal voice, but don't whisper."

"Why not?" Sebastian asks.

"Because it makes hissing sounds. Some people think it's easier to hear those sounds, where normal tones blend in better."

I remember reading something about that. A whisper is a higher frequency than a regular voice. That and the sibilants, those hissing sounds, cause people to hear the whispers clearer than regular voices, which can blend into the background.

"Where's that red shop towel?" Ben asks Sebastian.

My brother's face falls. "I left it where we were hiding before."

"You're sure? You didn't drop it along the way?"

"N-no . . . I think I left it. I looked for it not long after we got out of the thorns. I think I left it behind."

Ben runs a hand through his sparse blond hair. "We don't want them to have a way to track us."

"I can go back for it."

"Go to sleep, Sebastian," Mom says. "You too, Sadie. Ben and I will discuss what we need to do."

I give a weary nod as I pull my brother toward me.

Chapter 3

The following May

Deep breath. Flip off the safety. Another breath. Let it out slowly. *Focus, Sadie.* Aim at the body—the kill shot. Another deep breath. Exhale slightly. Now hold. *Squeeze the trigger.* Gently. Steady, even pressure. *You can do this.*

I'm shaking, shaking so hard the stupid sight is bouncing up and down, like a boat bobbing around in the ocean. I reposition myself, trying to connect better with the ground for a steadier rest.

His little nose wiggles.

I drop my shoulders and shake my head, passing the rifle off to Atticus.

With hardly any hesitation, he lifts the lightweight weapon to his shoulder and squeezes off his shot. The rabbit falls effortlessly to the ground.

"Sorry," I mumble. "It was different than shooting at a target. He was so . . . "

"Yeah, Sadie, I know. The first time isn't easy. Taking a life *shouldn't* be easy."

"It's a rabbit."

"Doesn't matter. A life is a life. I try and remember God gave us dominion over the animals, and with this responsibility, it's important to recognize the humanity of it. Quickly ending the animal's suffering is imperative. God gave us animals to sustain our lives. Especially now."

"I know that." My tone carries more impatience than he deserves. "And we need the food. If it wasn't for you— "

"Don't beat yourself up. You're new to shooting. And you're still young. Tell you what, I won't make you shoot again until you turn thirteen." He gives me a wink.

I roll my eyes at him. "Gee, thanks."

He responds with a crooked smile. Eighteen-year-old Atticus Dosen is seriously cute. I can't help but like him. I like his twin brother, Asher, and his younger brother, Axel, too.

With confusing names all beginning with the letter A, many in our traveling group refer to them as the *A Team* or the *A Boys*. Atticus has taken on a role of leadership in our group, especially as a mentor of the younger children—or those he *thinks* are children.

Out of the three brothers, sixteen-year-old Axel is the cutest. All are tall, brawny, and blond with blue eyes, but Axel has a slightly more chiseled look to his face, giving him an almost movie star like appearance.

Like many in today's world, the brothers—along with their mom, Jennifer—were overweight before everything fell apart. Forced rations and a massive increase in physical activity just to provide for day-to-day needs has left each of the boys looking totally buff.

Asher, Atticus's minutes-younger twin, is my favorite. He and Atticus are fraternal twins, so they look similar but aren't exactly alike. Where Atticus is serious, Asher occasionally jokes. And he has the best smile, still crooked like Atticus's, but . . . more. When he smiles, his entire face lights up.

Like the others, Asher treats me as though I'm his younger sister. They're all kind and protective of my little brother, Sebastian, also. Sebastian is eight, and everyone thinks tomorrow is my thirteenth birthday.

But they have no idea that, at my mom's insistence, I've been lying about my age. Tomorrow *is* my birthday. But instead of turning thirteen, I'll be sixteen, only a few months younger than Axel.

Barely a younger sister. *More like girlfriend age.* That won't happen, though. I can't let them know I've been lying.

Unlike the tall and bulky boys, I've always been small for my age—too short and too skinny, even before we almost starved to death over the winter. My body hadn't even really started to develop, and with everything that's happened, it seems to have not only stalled puberty but maybe reversed it. At least some parts of it.

The nurses at the ski lodge even had a name for it: amenorrhea. My extremely underweight mom has the same problem. I guess when a person is super malnourished and exercises too much, such as walking from Oregon to Washington and then to Wyoming, it happens.

14

With the way I look, it's been easy to make people believe I'm only twelve. Add in the fact that I'm clumsy, socially awkward, and ugly . . . it's certainly believable.

Pretending to be younger than I am is smart. It's no longer safe for a sixteen-year-old girl in today's world—not safe for my little brother or for my mom either. That's already been proven.

It's broken her—the things that happened, the things she's seen. What my brother and I have seen and experienced has been hard, but Mom has shielded us from most of it.

I've watched as the amazing and dynamic woman she was, friendly and outgoing, whittled away to the shrew she's become. With each terrible event, it's almost like a little more of her soul has disappeared.

Before, she considered herself something of an evangelist. She worked full time at a pregnancy center, telling people how much God loved them, how they needed Jesus, while helping the women find alternatives to abortion.

We were at one of Mom's conferences, where she was talking in some church about saving the unborn, when the terrorist attacks started. That's how we ended up with Ben and his family, then captured by those crazy men who murdered Uncle Wes. I've been thinking about those days a lot lately, especially since we're hiking again. This time, we're traveling with a group from where we met up with some of Ben's friends in Wyoming to go to my Aunt Karla's place in Lewistown, Montana.

We didn't plan on going to Wyoming. After we escaped, Ben said he'd help us get home. It took several months, and when we finally arrived, we found my Grandma Jackie and Grandpa Martin dead. By that time, my mom's transformation from the person she'd been to how she is now was nearly complete.

Finding them dead was the end of the mom I once had. Her mom and stepdad, who'd been married since before I was born, had been beaten and then killed before their house was ransacked. Mom lost it and totally went on a rant, yelling at God and telling Him how much she hated Him. Now she's gone from hating Him to denouncing His very existence.

That doesn't really matter to me. I knew God was fake long before the lights went out. I just went along with pretending He existed because it was expected of me. I went to church but never really paid attention to what was going on. I had no problem living my life without God in it.

But it's not the same for my mom. The person she's become . . . I don't like her much. Of course, I still love her. But there's really not much to like.

The last few weeks, after she got a bad case of pneumonia, she's softened a little. She was so sick, we thought she might die. The only reason she didn't was because a pharmacist just happened to be traveling the same route as us and had antibiotics with him.

Yeah. I couldn't believe anyone would have medicine with them and be willing to share. The people we're traveling with called it a miracle.

Even with the medicine, she's still weak, but the hacking when she coughs is less. And she's nicer, more like the mom I used to know.

"You want to take care of it?" Atticus asks as we walk toward the kill.

Do I want to? *Nope.* Not even a little bit. Even though I've done it more times than I can count, gutting and skinning still grosses me out. Especially with the fleas and bugs that cover the carcasses in the warmer weather. Atticus says we shouldn't even be hunting them this late in the year because May's weather is too warm, which is exactly why there's bugs on them.

But just like when we first met Ben a year ago, food is scarce, so we take what we can get. At least it's still early in the day and the morning is cool. Even so, everyone agrees our rabbit hunting days should come to an end until it freezes again.

By then, my family will no longer be with this group. We'll be settled in with my mom's aunt. At least that's the plan.

"Yeah, I'll do it." I hold back a sigh. "Do you still have gloves?"

"Just wear one on the hand you do the eviscerating with." Atticus hands me a single latex glove. "And watch the knife. The last thing you want is to slice your finger."

Making a face, I cut off the legs at the joints. Atticus hands me a pair of heavy-duty scissors from his pack, and I cut the skin up the inside of the legs. I roll and peel the skin to the chest, then stop to remove the guts. Another minute and the skin's on the ground next to the gut pile.

"You're pretty quick at that." Atticus gives an approving nod. "Did you learn how in school or while you were on the road?"

I lift a shoulder in response. "Can you pour water over my hands so I can get this off?"

"Let's just get them wet, then you can rub dirt to use as soap. Works better that way."

As I scrub my hands, I think of Ben Ferguson and how he kept us alive on our journey from Oregon to my grandparents and then on to Wyoming.

Mom was such a wreck after finding the bodies of Grandma and Grandpa. She was barely functioning. Ben made the decision for us to join him on his journey to Wyoming, where he thought he'd find safety at the house of a friend and be reunited with his wife, son, and dad after we were all separated.

When we finally reached his friend's Wyoming home, on a cold day in February, his wife and son were there, but his dad had died along the way. Ben was, of course, overjoyed to be reunited with them.

My mom's anger and bitterness increased immensely that day. It was like whatever little bit of humanity she had left in her—whatever part God might still be dwelling in—was completely gone. She was still good to me and Sebastian, but everyone else was like something awful she stepped in and was stuck to her shoe.

"How do you think it's going to feel to be a teenager?" Atticus asks as he places the cleaned and skinned rabbit in a fabric bag.

Pretty much the same as it's felt the last three years. "Fine, I guess."

"You know something I've discovered about teenage girls?"

I answer with a shrug.

"They talk more than twelve-year-olds. I predict, when you wake up in the morning, you'll go from being quiet and pensive to chatting up a storm." He lets out a small chuckle. "Whatcha think? Want to prove me right?"

I feel the color creep up my neck. He's right about me being quiet. While I've never been overly chatty, I've grown more solemn in the days since everything changed. When Uncle Wes died, it tore me to the soul. And just like my mom, finding my grandma and grandpa dead was another jab. Add in being in constant danger while traveling, so much danger even talking was risky, it just became easier to not say anything.

Our camp is within sight when Atticus says, "Hey, I was just teasing. I don't mind that you're quiet. None of us do. We understand you've been through a lot."

I give a nod. "Would you rather I say what's on my mind like my mom does?"

He lets out a hearty laugh. "Nope. That's fine. Quiet is good. More than good."

Chapter 4

Walking in the rain is terrible—beyond terrible, even. It's been overcast and drizzly since we woke up. We briefly discussed taking the day off, but with the weather like this more often than not, we'd never get anywhere.

Jameson Dawson threw a complete hissy fit over the rain, no surprise there. Out of everyone in our group, he's the biggest pain. At fourteen, he acts more like a spoiled two-year-old. At least his older brother, Brett, isn't a total jerk. He's more like Atticus and his brothers, trying to help and treating the rest of us decent.

Not Jameson.

Nope. He's awful. And his mom, Victoria, isn't much better. They're both unbelievably annoying. I know my mom is about ready to totally lose it with them. I could see it this morning. Her eyes flared, and a pinched look took over her skinny face.

Just as she opened her mouth, Donnie McCullough, who's only traveling with us because he has a thing for my mom, said, "Knock it off, kid, before I really give you something to complain about."

My mom lifted her chin at Donnie—about the closest she comes to a *thank you* these days. Things between Mom and Donnie might be friendly now, but they weren't always. They certainly met under uncomfortable circumstances.

She held a gun on him and his brother while taking their horses away.

After we made it to Wyoming with Ben and met up with his wife, we were surprised to find his friends had left their home and moved away with almost all of the rest of the town. Too bad the entire town didn't move away. Those who stayed behind were all killed by marauders.

We thought Donnie and his brother participated in the killings, or were at least up to no good. That wouldn't be too much of a stretch to believe. It's rare to find people in today's world who don't want to use or abuse you in some way.

Ben and his wife finally believed the McCullough brothers, but only after their friend arrived at the house. Once everything was sorted out, we went with Ben's friends to the mountain ski lodge they were staying at for the winter.

I'm not going to lie, I loved it there. It was finally a place of peace and quiet. We didn't have to walk all day every day, and we had regular meals and a warm fire. I wanted to stay, to have a normal life without the continual threat of being shot, without having to walk miles and miles each day in the cold and snow or wet and drizzly weather.

And did I mention the regular meals? When we were on the road before, we'd sometimes go for a day or two without eating. Mom started to have us drink pine needle tea to give us some vitamins and nutrients. Ben took to calling them pine shakes because they were just evergreen needles soaked in warm water. But it did little to fill our stomachs.

We didn't know then just how nutritious pine shakes could be. When the pharmacist was treating Mom, Sebastian brought up the pine shakes we drank over the winter. The guy got all excited, saying not only did they have vitamin C but they could also help with congestion. We're all drinking pine shakes now to try and stay healthy.

After meeting the pharmacist, we also learned about peeling bark from willow trees to use as aspirin. When we left the ski lodge, they gave us a small first aid kit with a few painkillers. With Donnie getting shot, not once but twice, along with other injuries in our group, they were used up quickly.

The willow bark tea helped relieve some of the body aches Mom had with her pneumonia. Sometimes we don't even bother making tea and just chew on the bark to get the pain-relieving properties released, then spit out the pulp.

Our food is better than when we were traveling with Ben last winter when rabbits, marmots, squirrels, and even starlings were almost a delicacy. When we lived at the ski lodge, we feasted on elk, beef, pork, chickens, and goat.

Feasted is not at all an exaggeration. When we arrived, skinny and malnourished, the town nurses gave us an exam and put us on special diets. We even got milk with each meal! I tried to be nonchalant about it, pretending the food wasn't a big deal, but it was amazing to not be hungry for a change.

When Mom decided we were leaving with the people going to Montana—everyone either trying to get back to their homes or on a specific mission—I wanted to cry. Leaving was the last thing I wanted to do. Even though I didn't know any of those people, they were nice to us, and the safety was amazing.

I glance at my mom. I want to be angry at her for making us leave. I want to yell, scream, and tell her how selfish she is.

She catches me looking at her and scoots next to me. With her mouth near my ear, she says, "Not the best way to spend your birthday."

"It's fine."

She places a hand on my shoulder. "Maybe we can stop early today and give you a proper birthday celebration."

I shrug. *Yeah, sure, Mom. You have a cake for me?*

Stopping early doesn't happen. We keep slogging along until late afternoon. At least the drizzle stopped, and everything is just wet instead of getting wetter.

"The place over there looks promising." Kimba Hoffmann points to a house well off the highway.

"Atticus, Brett," Kimba's husband Rey says, motioning with his hands, "you're with me while we check it out. Everyone else, stay frosty."

We're traveling north on US Highway 87 after leaving Billings, Montana, two days ago. It took three days just to get from Lockwood, which is south of Billings and where we separated from some of the people we'd been traveling with—Rochelle, PJ, and Robyn—to the northern edge of Billings.

The weather was terrible, cold and wet. Sometimes the rain even felt like snow. We only traveled a short distance each day, going from one military established campground to the next.

Billings was particularly stressful, with the military roaming around and checkpoints set up along the way. The only good thing about it was they had what they called *aid stations* in their campgrounds, where we were able to get a decent meal while drying off.

We'd planned ahead, expecting food to be limited in the city. The preparations for the journey, which started before my mom decided we'd be leaving, included killing a couple of deer and drying the meat. All along the way, in the unpopulated areas we traveled, we continued with harvesting animals and preserving as much meat as possible in order to sustain us through the city.

Sustain.

21

That's a word Atticus's mom, Jennifer, is extremely fond of. Of course, she's usually referring to God or Jesus when she says it. "Cast your burdens on the Lord. He'll sustain you," or, "He sustains all with His powerful word." Yeah, sure. *Whatever.*

You know what was sustaining the people of Billings? Until the military arrived, not much. We heard rumors the deaths were as high as seventy-five percent of the pre-EMP population. We also heard disturbing things about what people were doing to survive. Not only is the human population low, but there are no animals, no wildlife at all. We didn't even see any cats or hear any dogs bark as we traveled through.

After a less than celebratory birthday dinner of dried meat softened in boiling water to form a stew, Kimba jumps to her feet. "Party time, Sadie. We know this isn't anyone's idea of a perfect thirteenth birthday, but . . . " She gives a shrug and a smile. "We love you, and we want you to know it."

"That's right," her husband Rey adds, his slight British accent apparent even in those two words. "While we can't give you a birthday party fitting for becoming a teenager, we've planned a few things."

I glance at my mom. She gives me what she believes passes as a smile. "Happy birthday, sweetheart." Her voice is hoarse with emotion.

"Too bad you can't get a car for your birthday," Sebastian says.

I flare my eyes at him.

"I mean . . . wouldn't it be great? We could get a car and drive the rest of the way. I'm tired of walking."

"I'd kill for a car," Jameson Dawson declares in a tone that makes me believe he probably *would* kill.

Donnie shakes his head. "The problem isn't just finding a running car. But finding fuel for a car, now that's the challenge. All those cars sitting on the side of the road we see day in and day out, they're not only dead from the EMP but most were running on fumes from the gas shortage. Me, I'd rather we had enough horses for everyone. If you all had horses like my Gordie, it'd be much easier."

Though Donnie's close enough to join us, he's officially on watch. Axel Dosen is also on watch, standing guard in the detached garage with one of our two walkie-talkies. Kimba has the second one on her

22

belt. The rest of our group, fourteen not counting Donnie, are sprawled around the living room.

"Horses would be nice," Mom agrees.

"Sorry," Kimba says. "We don't have a car or a horse for you, Sadie. But I think we do have a few little gifts. Leanne?"

Mom reaches in a pocket, pulls out a ball of fabric, and hands it to me. "I know wool socks aren't too exciting, but they're practical. Sorry they aren't a match."

I reach for the soft cloth. "Thanks, Mom."

Wool socks are actually an awesome gift when walking across the state. Mom insists we pay attention to our feet, making sure to rinse out our dirty socks and put on a fresh pair each morning. And on days like today, when we've been trudging along in wet boots, we change our socks as soon as we stop and set out our shoes to dry.

Sebastian and I each started with three pairs of socks. One of mine got a hole in them a few weeks back. Jennifer Dosen helped me sew it up, but it's still not comfortable when walking. I only wear those socks as a last resort.

As I unfold the mismatched ankle socks, I recognize the purple one as a sock we found scrunched up under the bed in the house we stayed in when Mom was recovering from pneumonia. The other, striped in various shades of blue, is from a different abandoned house along the way. I breathe out another quiet thank you as travel-size shampoo and toothpaste fall out of the socks.

These were undoubtedly found along the way too. We squirrel away anything we may have a use for in the future. We have to be careful, though. Traveling by foot means most of our supplies are carried on our backs.

We do have a multi-tier utility cart we found that holds a good amount of gear. But the heavy-duty wheels are already breaking down, and we all wonder how much longer we'll be able to use it. We also have a large homemade wagon loaded with goods. We constructed it to carry Robyn when she was injured. Like the utility cart, its days are numbered.

Wheels, socks, and shoes don't last long when walking up to ten miles a day. Brett Dawson has a hole in one of his shoes; it's being held together with duct tape. We found a single shoe in his size, which he'll start wearing once the pseudo repair gives out.

That'll look great.

Mismatched socks are one thing. Mismatched shoes . . . no thanks. Plus, it'd be super uncomfortable. The pair he's wearing resemble hiking boots. The one he found is an athletic shoe. I hope my shoes hold out for the hundred or so miles we have left until we get to Mom's aunt's house.

"Our gift isn't practical in the same way," Jennifer says. "The boys and I, along with Victoria and her boys, thought you might like it. And it can be a reminder for you. Asher?"

Asher hands me a gray fabric-wrapped package.

"The shirt's for you too," Asher says. "We figured it could double as wrapping paper."

"Thank you." I unfold the fabric to reveal a T-shirt. It's a faded gray color with a small grizzly bear on the top left side and *Montana* written underneath it. I recognize it as one of the shirts being handed out at the aid station set up at MetraPark Arena back in Billings.

Inside the shirt is a piece of wood. "Um . . . " I mumble as I lift the smoothly sanded flat chunk out.

"Here," Asher says, shining a small penlight toward the gift.

Burned into the wood is a design and words. *He will make your paths straight. Proverbs 3:6.*

"What is it?" Naomi Hoffmann and Sebastian ask in unison.

I lift it up. "A saying."

"A verse," Jennifer corrects with a kind smile on her face. "A reminder."

"It's beautiful," Kimba says. "How'd you do it?"

"It was Asher," Jennifer answers.

I look to Asher, who gives me a slight nod. "It's called pyrography. A man at the ski lodge taught me it."

"What do you use?" Mom asks, rubbing the smooth wood.

"Hot nails and pieces of rebar, or anything else that you can use as a poker. That's another name for it. Pokerwork. The trick was not burning myself in the process."

"It's beautiful." Mom gives Asher one of her pitiful smiles.

Asher returns his own brilliant smile. "I enjoy doing it, gives me something else to think about."

"When do you work on it?" Sebastian asks. "I don't think I've seen you do anything but whittling and sanding."

"Here and there." Asher shrugs.

"Thank you," I say again.

"Give her yours." Asher lifts his chin toward Sebastian.

"Okay . . . but it's not as nice. Here you go, Sadie. I made it for you." Sebastian shoves a little figurine in my direction. "It's an owl."

I take it in my hand, caressing it gently. "It's very nice, squirt." It really is. I could tell it was an owl without him saying so. "Did you do this?"

He lifts a shoulder. "Mostly, but Asher and Axel helped me a couple of times."

"I love it."

"It has your name on the bottom of it. I didn't do the fancy burning like Asher did—he didn't tell me about that—but I carved your name."

"It's great. Thanks."

"We have something else for you." Atticus hands me a package, the paper around it crinkling.

My eyes go wide, and I let out a gasp.

Chapter 5

"Where . . . how?" My hands are trembling slightly as I take the small package from Atticus.

He chuckles. "Back in Billings at the Metra. Seems some of the military guys have chocolate as part of their rations. I met a guy who doesn't like chocolate, so he trades with travelers. I have two more for the rest of us to share . . . you know, since we don't have a cake for you. That little bag, it's all yours."

I caress the small, fun-sized package of coated button-shaped chocolates. I blink rapidly as tears sting my eyes. Crying over a small bag of chocolate is dumb, but it seems I'm doing it anyway.

"One more gift." Kimba's voice is bright and cheerful. "Then we'll feast on chocolate."

"Righto." Rey fumbles in the backpack at his side. After a moment, he carefully pulls out a knife nestled in a leather sheath, the mostly white handle almost glistening under the candlelight.

"Now, we asked your mom about this, and she agreed." Rey hands it to me. "Proper training is part of the gift. We'll make sure you know how to use it and use it well. My wife's a great teacher."

"Go ahead, take it out of the sheath." Kimba motions.

I unsnap the strap holding the knife in place and gently pull it out. It sticks a bit, so I exert a little more pressure. The slightly rough handle feels amazing in my hand.

"It's a fixed-blade knife. We found it in one of the houses we went through and thought it might be a good one for you."

"It's a lot like mine," Nicole, Rey and Kimba's seventeen-year-old daughter, says. "We'll be like twins."

Jameson makes a snorting noise.

Nicole shoots him a dirty look.

I agree with Jameson on this. Nicole is tall, blond, and beautiful, just like her mom. Not too skinny, too short, dull haired, and mousy like me.

"That's not all," Kimba says. "Now that you're thirteen, we'll start introducing you to more of the weapons than just the .22 rifle and teach you how to handle them all."

26

I drop my eyes. I guess Atticus didn't tell her I couldn't shoot the rabbit. I'm not sure I want to learn how to operate anything more than the light rifle.

"We'll go through them one at a time," Rey says, then points to his son. "Nate, you'll learn alongside her."

"I already know— " Nate interrupts.

"Some." Rey nods. "It's time to learn more. We'll start with the tactical rifles Kimba, Atticus, and I carry and then move on to the long-range hunting rifles, making sure you're proficient in a variety of stances. Then the shotguns and finally the handguns. You know most of our handguns are 9-millimeter semi-automatics, so they'll all operate similarly."

Rey makes eye contact with me and then his son. "Carrying in the same caliber makes things easier for ammo. We also have a few revolvers, like that monster Donnie wears."

"Hey now," Donnie says. "My little friend ain't no monster." He caresses his sidearm, a giant revolver. At first, he didn't want anyone to touch it. But after a shootout near the Montana and Wyoming state line, which left him with a bullet hole in his hand, he agreed it was smart for cross-training on all the weapons.

"Sure, okay." Rey laughs and lifts his hands, then turns to me. "You'll learn how to shoot everything from that bad boy to the small pistols. I think you'll be surprised. Although Donnie's looks like a big scary gun, it isn't any more difficult to shoot than the tiny little Beretta Nicole carries. It's easier in some ways. Nicole's small size is great if you're carrying concealed, which was common before, but there's no free lunch. A super small lightweight 9-millimeter like this one can be challenging to shoot accurately. Like Kimba said, we'll start your training with mostly dry firing— "

"You know about dry firing," his daughter Nicole says. "That seems to be all we do."

I move my head slightly. I've heard Nicole has not only the semi-automatic pistol that's on her hip but also a second gun, a revolver, that I haven't seen. She was part of the militia when we lived at the ski lodge and is proficient not only in shooting but also trained in hand-to-hand combat.

"Muscle memory, love. We're developing muscle memory."

"Yeah, Dad. You've told me. And I know we're conserving the ammo in case we need it."

"Not just that," Kimba adds. "But we take a risk every time we fire. Someone could hear it. It's a calculated risk to go hunting, but shooting at targets over and over . . . " She shakes her head. "It's not smart. We'll get you trained and comfortable, introducing you to all the different weaponry, especially your new knife."

"I'm surprised you're giving her a knife. You really think she's ready?" Victoria Dawson asks in a snotty tone, her southern accent overly pronounced.

"She's ready." Kimba makes eye contact with me. "Ready for the knife and more. We've talked many times about how everyone needs to be able to protect themselves. You too, Victoria. We can train you along with her on all the weapons." Kimba gives Victoria a smile.

"No. I'm not at all interested in guns, you know that. I think it's odd there're so many of them floating around. Says a lot about the kind of people in Wyoming."

"Self-sufficient?" Jennifer asks with a smile. "It's the same in Montana. We like to take care of ourselves."

"No shortage of guns in Wyoming," Brett Dawson says. "Ammo, though . . . "

"Right," Kimba agrees. "We figured that outfitting all of us with 9-millimeters made the most sense. It was such a popular cartridge and easy to find. One friend of Rey's used to joke that if he was short on ammo, he just took off the couch cushions and found a few rounds."

"Speaking of," Jennifer says, "let's make sure we do a thorough search of this place before we leave in the morning. I think we were all so excited about getting out of the rain we've failed in our scavenging efforts."

"Not just excited about getting dry," Naomi Hoffmann, the youngest of Rey and Kimba's children, pipes up. "But because of the party. Birthdays are fun. Whose birthday is next? Nate's?"

Her older brother lifts his hands. "I'll turn fourteen at the end of August." He glances around the room.

People call out birthdays or say something like, "Sounds like you're next." With a satisfied smile, Nate says, "I hope there will be a bag of chocolate for me too."

After the gift part finishes, Asher doles out pieces of candy to everyone. I hand him my bag so he can include it in the sharing, but he doesn't allow it. I make a tiny hole at the seam, just large enough to get out a single candy. It's amazing. I let it sit on my tongue until the candy coating melts away. Then, when the chocolate hits my taste buds—wow. It is . . . amazing. Just amazing!

We sit around talking while everyone munches on candy. Jennifer says how much fun it is to have a reason to celebrate. "We should do it more often. Even if it's not someone's birthday. We need to remember how blessed we are just to be alive."

The party is pretty much perfect. I mean, as far as a birthday party can be while squatting in a house in the middle of nowhere during the apocalypse. It doesn't even really matter much that they think I'm thirteen instead of sixteen.

"I'm going to take a look through the bedroom we're staying in, see what kind of goodies they have stashed that no one's found yet," Victoria says to Jennifer as the party breaks up. "The chocolate's hitting my blood stream and giving me a burst of energy. Might as well use it."

Jennifer stands and stretches. "I'll help. We don't want to take too long. Energy or not, it'll be time to settle in soon. I'm on last watch, so . . . " She lifts her hands.

Everyone except Sebastian and Naomi are included in the watch schedule. When we're walking, we're all on watch, trying to stay alert and aware. It makes the miles we put in even more challenging since it's not just a physical exertion but is also mentally taxing.

Reclining against the wall in the living room, I allow myself one more piece of candy. Even though Asher said they're all mine, I'm going to share them with Sebastian and Mom at least. And give a couple to Axel since he wasn't in here when they shared the other two packages. Everyone else is spread out in the house, doing their own thing.

I'm giving myself a birthday present. Although showers and baths aren't possible, unless you count walking in the rain, my skin needs a good scrubbing. I'll take a washcloth and a little warm water from the woodstove and have the best sponge bath known to man—or woman.

I remove the lid on the shampoo Mom gave me and inhale the citrusy sent. It's going to be fantastic. Then, after I'm clean, maybe there will even be enough daylight to read for a bit.

I boost myself off the floor and gather my gifts. It should all tuck nicely into my backpack, which is in the room Victoria and Jennifer are rifling through.

I'm almost to the slightly ajar bedroom door when I hear Victoria say, "It's her birthday, and she was barely cordial when thanking us for her gifts."

I stop walking, focusing on her words.

"She should've acted more grateful. But what should I expect? She's just like her mom. Rude. I don't know how that girl will ever survive in this world. She's going to need a man to take care of her, but no one's ever going to want her."

My hands go to my mouth as I step away. Victoria is only with us because she was basically driven away from the ski lodge—with good reason. A few weeks before my family arrived, her husband tried to take control of the place. He and his group of followers killed several townspeople before being stopped. He was killed in the process.

Many believed Victoria, and possibly even her sons, Brett and Jameson, were part of the plot. Maybe she was, maybe she wasn't. But there's definitely something odd about her.

But Jennifer's in there with her. She's always been nice to me—nice to everyone, even my mom when she definitely didn't deserve her kindness. She let Victoria say those things about me and didn't even try to stop her. Even though I didn't hear Jennifer agree with her, I'm sure she does.

She pretends to be nice to everyone, even makes a point of saying we should treat others the way we want to be treated. The Golden Rule. She says it's from the Bible. But she's obviously a fake. A lying fake.

I shouldn't be surprised.

Mom was the same way. She pretended to believe in God, to follow Jesus. She was always spouting off about how Jesus loved all of us, how He died for us, and how God knew us before we were even born.

She was so dedicated to her work in the pregnancy center, saying God didn't want any babies to perish, and also believing it was the church's job to help the mothers—whether they were married, widowed, or single.

She was so passionate about helping the women after they had their babies, she'd been instrumental in several area churches setting up nonprofits to help needy women and families.

But when things went bad, she blamed Him for all of it. If she were a real Christian, she'd never have turned her back on God.

30

Of course, if there really was a God, He wouldn't have turned His back on us either.

Chapter 6

I dreamed of my dad last night, of the way he was before he became too sick. In my dream, he was bouncing Sebastian on his knee, making him laugh. Mom and I were in the living room too. I was sitting on the floor in front of Mom's chair as she fixed my hair, giving me two braids. She laughed, too, saying how silly her boys were.

The dream felt so real. As I woke, I could feel the smile on my face. It was a glorious, happy dream. And I felt so loved—*knew* I was loved.

Taking in a deep breath, I look around the room. With a scowl on her face, Victoria meets my eyes. The hateful things she said come rushing back.

She quickly contorts her face into a fake smile, then in her annoying twang says, "Good morning, Sadie. I trust you slept well."

I answer with a curt nod as I remember a conversation between Axel and Brett. Axel said something like, "Hey, when I first met your mom, I never noticed she had a southern accent."

"Yeah," Brett responded. "She's from Tennessee, but she's lived up here since before I was born and worked really hard to sound like everyone else. It was better for my dad's business and . . . um . . . political ambitions for her to sound like she was born in Wyoming. He hoped to be Governor someday."

Brett let out a snort of laughter. "It was bad enough he was running for county commissioner before everything fell apart. I can't even imagine him being in charge of the entire state. Especially not with . . . anyway, I guess she's decided it doesn't matter how she talks now."

Victoria, still staring at me in the early morning light, raises her eyebrows. "Speak up, child. Use your voice."

I mumble a response before scurrying to my feet, then grab my pack and dart to the bathroom.

Closing the door, I lean against it. I'm going to show Victoria Dawson. I might be too small, too quiet, and too skinny. Maybe I'll never have a boyfriend or a husband. Fine. Who cares?

I don't need anyone to take care of me.

32

I flash back to hunting with Atticus and how I couldn't even shoot the rabbit—food we need to survive. No more. I'm done being a weakling. I'm going to have Atticus take me hunting again, and I'll do it this time. I swear I will!

And that's not all. I'll learn how to use the new knife Kimba and Rey gave me. And she said they'll start teaching me more about guns.

I know they were reluctant to teach me how to use the .22 rifle, especially thinking I was so young and weak, but when Mom got sick and Robyn was injured, we needed more people on watch. Even a skinny twelve-year-old can help watch for bad guys.

Besides training with guns, we've been learning self-defense martial arts. At the ski lodge, even the little kids learned how to defend themselves if they were attacked.

Sebastian and I learned a few of the basics after we arrived, but not a lot since everyone decided we were too sick from our journey to do much of anything physical. The trainers showed us how to get away if someone grabbed us by the wrist or put us in a bear hug. We were even taught the basics of doing a leg sweep to trip someone.

Kimba and Rey teach us that stuff and more. Kimba's shown us how to not only fight off an attacker with a knife—she used a fake knife made out of wood that Asher whittled for her—but also how to attack.

When we were getting our gear together for this trip, everyone was given a knife from the community storehouse. Sebastian and I each have folding pocketknives. We practice opening them so we can do it with one hand, but we know the little knives are really limited for defense. This new knife, though . . . I smile as I caress the smooth, slightly worn handle.

With this new knife, I'll better be able to defend myself. Kimba even said it can do some serious damage. I slide the brown leather sheath through my belt. Standing straight and tall, I examine myself in the mirror. It looks fine. The knife hangs a little low but still looks good. Tough.

A frown covers my face. While we've had some training on how to defend against knives, and a few lessons on using a knife to attack, I'm not really interested in cutting someone with it. I'll happily wear it and enjoy the way it makes me feel, but I don't want to use it on a human.

I spend more time in the bathroom than I should. Someone left a jug of water, and I use it to wash up—what I wanted to do last night. Even though it's only a sponge bath and the water's not exactly warm, it's almost glorious. Any opportunity to get even a little bit clean is wonderful. I eyeball the water, trying to decide if there's enough to wash my hair.

The memory of my dream floats over me. I can almost feel Mom running the brush through my hair. She was so gentle. I see Dad's smile and hear Sebastian's laugh.

Dad found out he was sick before Sebastian was born, but neither he nor Mom told me about it until much later, when he couldn't hide it any longer. By then, everyone knew he was going to die. Everyone except me.

My tenth birthday was his last good day. The next day, he woke up with a terrible pain in his ribs. A few days later, he went into the hospital and never came home.

I close my eyes and drop my head. Our life would be a lot different if Dad wouldn't have died—even now. Mom didn't work until he died, not really anyway. She volunteered one day a week at the pregnancy center, but being a volunteer was different from working full time.

She said it was a blessing. The pregnancy center was in the process of creating a full-time position while Dad was sick. After the funeral, they told Mom the job was hers if she wanted it.

Dad had medical insurance through his job at USPS, plus his military retirement, which covered most of the medical bills, and he had life insurance too. Even so, there was no way Mom wouldn't need to work. I think the pregnancy center probably created the job specifically for her, knowing she'd need it once Dad was gone.

I grab my comb and work on my hair. It's getting too long, and it's starting to feel like dry grass, especially at the ends. All the rain we've been having makes it frizzy, which just makes it look worse. Peering in the mirror, I narrow my eyes.

What's on the tip of my nose?

I move closer to the mirror and let out a groan. A pimple, a new one to go along with the one on my jaw that's just beginning to fade. *Great.* Just what I need. My nose is already ginormous, and the pimple will just make it look bigger, more pronounced.

I touch a hand to my ear; it sticks out too much. Both of them do. A girl back home had her ears pinned, pulling them closer to her head. She looked great afterward. I wish I could've done the same.

I told Sebastian once about how my ears were awful, how they were too big and stuck out. His response was, "You're lucky! I bet you hear really good with those huge ears."

Thanks, little brother. That didn't make me feel any better.

I jump at the pounding on the door. "Hurry up in there."

After loading my things back in my bag, I crack it open.

"'Bout time," Jameson sneers. "You know, you're not the only one who wants to use the room. 'Sides, no matter how much time you spend in there, it isn't going to help." He lets out a hoot of laughter before pushing past me.

"Don't listen to him," Nicole says, standing down the hallway and also waiting for the bathroom. "He's just a jerk. He's like that to everyone."

I drop my eyes and rush back to my room.

He's not like that to her. Nicole is gorgeous, with bright blue eyes and shiny blond hair that never looks frizzy or brittle, unlike my boring brown mess. And I'm sure she's never woke up with a pimple.

And I know Jameson likes her. All the guys do. And not the way they like me, as a little sister. She's not only beautiful, she's also fun and friendly. Atticus would never tell her she doesn't talk enough. Not only does she talk when she should, but she knows just what to say. She's never awkward or embarrassed.

Mom looks up from shoving things in her pack. "Sadie? What's wrong?"

I shake my head. "Just . . . the usual."

She reaches out to touch my arm. "The usual, huh?"

I look toward the door, then lower my voice. "Jameson. He's . . . he's so annoying."

"He's picking on you again?"

"He's just being the way he is, so . . . superior."

Mom gives a slight laugh. "At least he thinks so. He has yet to realize how a real man behaves."

"When will he realize it?"

"Hard telling. But if he's bullying you— "

I raise my hand. "I can handle it."

She lifts her eyebrows.

"Seriously, Mom. I can."

"Remember how he was with Rochelle and his mom?"

I drop my chin. I do remember. When we were stopped outside of Billings, Jameson slapped his mom and then shoved a lady that was traveling with us.

"I think it'll be okay."

Mom puts a finger on my chin, gently lifting my gaze to hers. "Talk is one thing. But if he puts his hands on you . . . " She gives me a pointed look.

"I know."

There are several beats of silence before she says, "You better get packed so we can get going. Oh, I almost forgot. Kimba found a stash of books. She put them on the dining room table, thought you might like something new to read."

"I would, thanks." Before the world fell apart, reading was my favorite pastime. Even since then, I've tried to find books as we've traveled. Finding the time to read while hiking across the country has been the bigger challenge.

When we first left the ski lodge, in the middle of March, my family rode in the back of a wagon pulled by two horses. Bundled against the cold, reading was a fabulous distraction from the many miles we traveled.

Now I can sometimes read a little before bed, provided there's enough daylight. With the scarcity of batteries, candles, and other artificial lights, it isn't possible to read after dark.

The drizzly rain is gone for the moment, but it's still overcast and threatening to start again.

"Don't worry," Atticus says as we start walking up the gravel drive. "It's going to burn off and the sun will come out."

"You think?" Brett asks, glancing around. "Looks like another storm's coming in."

With a lift of his shoulder, Atticus says, "Won't make it this far. It's going to get stalled on the mountains. I'd be surprised if there isn't sunshine and burning heat by lunchtime. But not for long. We'll get the rain back tomorrow."

I figure Atticus is right. He always seems to know these things. Mom calls him a walking weatherman. She says it with awe in her voice, like she wishes it was a talent she had.

36

It's definitely useful in a world without radio or TV telling us what to expect. Not that it matters. We walk in all but the worst of weather.

One night, after we'd walked in a light snow all day, Mom said we were like the old post office motto: *neither snow nor rain nor heat nor gloom of night stays these couriers from the swift completion of their appointed rounds.*

Sebastian got a kick out of that and thought maybe he should have a uniform to wear, like our dad when he worked for the post office.

Mom gave a soft laugh—not the real kind she used to give, but at least it was something—then said, "You'd look mighty handsome in a uniform."

"I think I'd like Dad's Army uniform better, though," Sebastian said after a moment of quiet. "And it'd make more sense now. People would think I was able to help them more than if I was wearing a post office uniform."

"Maybe so," Mom agreed. "Now settle in and go to sleep."

Chapter 7

When Sebastian was going on and on about the Army helping, we had no idea the military was finally organizing in our area.

Before leaving the ski lodge, we heard the president on the radio say he was starting efforts to rebuild the US. But we didn't know it was happening in Montana. We thought they'd start with much bigger cities than Billings, which was only a little over a hundred thousand people.

Of course, after all the bombings and other destruction, maybe the bigger cities are gone?

We'd been on the road about a month when we first heard about planes and helicopters flying around. I thought maybe things would soon get back to normal. We needed normal. Mom already had pneumonia by then, and I was preparing for the worst, expecting her to die and leave Sebastian and me orphans.

I overheard Mom talking to Jennifer, begging her between coughs and gasping for breath to take care of us, to make sure we reached Aunt Karla's. Jennifer said she would and, if Karla couldn't take care of us, we'd be a welcome part of her family. After hearing her and Victoria last night, I know she was lying.

Anyway, Mom got better. And when we got to Billings and saw all the military vehicles—Marines at first and then Army in a different area, along with some different volunteer units—I thought we should just stay there and not bother going on to Aunt Karla's. Mom was better but still not completely well. And maybe it'd be safe with the military.

Kimba and Rey plan on getting all of us where we're going—us to Lewistown and the rest to Great Falls—then they're moving on to Bozeman, Montana, where some friends live. After checking in on their friends, they plan to return to Billings and help with the reconstruction efforts. They used to work for the government, Kimba in the United States and Rey in England, and they think it's their duty to help rebuild America.

Donnie says they're nuts, that the military was probably in on everything that's happened, and maybe even the president was part of it, and they have zero intentions of putting things back the way they were. He keeps talking about a Great Reset and how, all along, they wanted to kill off most of the people so a few elites could flourish.

I asked Mom about that later, what she thought of Donnie's theories. She shook her head and said, "He has a wild imagination for sure. But I'll admit, some of his thoughts make sense. I've always wondered why we didn't strike back. When the attacks first started, there should've been some talk of retaliation."

"There was, remember? The president said that as soon as they found those responsible, we'd get revenge."

She shrugged. "I guess. But it seemed rather . . . weak."

I don't think it really matters where we go to retaliate anyway. Seems something like that would just result in more people dead. Soldiers, Marines, Navy, and Air Force people are needed to help get the cities back together. We don't need them going to some foreign country to get revenge. What good would come of it?

Besides, at one of the camps in Billings, we heard the entire world is now at war. In addition to the EMP, we know that there were actual nuclear bombs on both the east and west coasts—ground strikes resulting in unknown casualties and destruction.

But we didn't know other countries had nukes detonated also; there was nothing said in the announcements we heard over the ham radio from the president. We've also heard there are lots of border skirmishes and countries trying to take each other over.

It sounds like it's a mess everywhere. I wonder how well the reconstruction efforts will work here if the whole planet's in trouble. Donnie asked someone if it was World War III, but the guy said nothing has been made official. Official or not, it sounds like it may be.

Rey later said we shouldn't put too much stock in rumors, that maybe there are problems in other countries, but until we hear it through official channels, we should take it with a grain of salt.

Mom later whispered to me he was probably just upset, thinking about family and friends in other countries and how they could be in the same mess we are. I don't know what the truth is.

And I really don't know if it matters. Beyond what's happening to us here, nothing else seems to be of much importance.

~~~~~

As usual, Atticus was right. By noon, the sun is high overhead and hot.

By three o'clock, I'm a sweaty, miserable mess. I'm not sure which is worse—being wet from a cool, drizzly rain or wet from a hot, sweltering day. At least, when it's raining, we're more likely to find water.

Mom was worried about this section between Billings and Roundup. She'd driven the road before and remembered it being like a desert until closer to Roundup. But with the wet weather, there's been lots of water in the ditches along the road and even several ponds.

The water is gross, but we let it settle, strain it through a bandanna, then purify it with iodine or chlorine tablets. The big fear is the tablets won't do what they're supposed to and we'll get sick.

We finally stop late afternoon. There's no house to squat in tonight, but Rey sees the tips of trees behind a berm that's well off the highway, and we head for them.

When we camp, we always make sure to move away from the road. Ideally, we camp behind a row of hills or another divider so we can't be seen by other walkers or the rare vehicle.

We've seen cars and trucks in a few towns we've gone through—lots in Billings, mostly military but some not—and we heard one when we were near a junction of two roads but never saw it. We do know it's possible someone could come driving by.

We talked with one of the military guys back in Billings, and he said at some point they'll be going north toward Roundup, where we're headed, but that's probably a few weeks or months away.

They're concentrating on opening up Interstate 90, which runs from east to west, so travel will be easier for them and everyone else. Then they'll move to the smaller US and state highways.

This spot is nearly perfect. There's a small hill between us and the highway and a skinny, fast-moving creek running through the trees. Beyond the tree line, the landscape changes drastically, becoming almost barren and desolate, with several high rock outcroppings and rocky hillsides.

"Those look interesting." Donnie points to one of the rock-covered cliffs. "Back home, we'd expect to find pigeons roosting in places like that."

"Let's go see," Atticus says. "We can take the shotguns and use the turkey rounds."

"That's fine. The .22 will work, too, but you gotta be accurate. Either way, we don't have ammo to waste, so whether we use the shotgun or the .22, we need to be sure of our shots."

"The rock formation should help with dampening the sound too."

"Yep, good call."

They used the shotgun for goose hunting during the winter when we were traveling along a river and old fields. There were so many geese, we didn't worry at all about being hungry. It was amazing to eat almost as much as I wanted. We got deer, turkey, and small birds, too, along with rabbits.

Mom said many times how shocked she was by the amount of food available. She also kept reminding us that the abundance wouldn't last forever. Either the animals would run out or the ammunition would.

"I could go with you," Nate Hoffmann says with hope in his voice. "I can use my slingshot to help save on ammo."

"Don't think so." Donnie shakes his head. "They won't be close enough. You set up another box trap and stake it out, get us a grouse or something that way."

Nate gives a sad nod.

We've been collecting boxes, which we flatten for traveling, along with other things for setting up a simple trap to catch birds. At the ski lodge, part of the school day included survival training, including making primitive weapons.

Of course, the things they were teaching were things we'd been doing in order to stay alive: making friction fires out of found items, building shelters out of nothing, fashioning weapons out of trash. Even so, we still learned a few new skills.

Before my family arrived at the lodge in the middle of February, the students made slingshots. Nate's is pretty impressive, so beautiful it's almost a work of art.

And he knows how to use it. He's provided food with it many times, usually by setting up a box trap and taking a shot when a grouse, pheasant, or something similar goes after the food.

When we were getting ready to leave, another kid gave Sebastian a slingshot as a parting gift. My brother isn't as talented with his as Nate is, but he's working on his accuracy.

Sebastian also made another slingshot like the one he fashioned out of the red shop towel and twine he left in the brambles when we were hiding. This one's made out of paracord with a leather pouch.

Thanks to one of the old, retired military guys at the ski lodge, he's become quite proficient with it. Not to the point Nate is with the slingshot, but he's really good.

Donnie, Atticus, and Brett take off in search of pigeons. Kimba and Rey say they'll take a perimeter walk to make sure this spot is as secure as it seems. The rest of us set up the tents, then refill or collect and purify drinking water.

"I've never eaten pigeon," Jennifer says while we're working on water. "Have you?"

I shake my head.

My dad wasn't a hunter. He didn't even particularly care for guns, said he had enough of them in the Army. Mom met him after he'd already served twenty years and was working at the post office. He used to joke that he was in for twenty years and two minutes, and that was two minutes longer than he should've been.

At the time, I didn't really get the joke, but I'd laugh anyway.

Mom said his last few years were difficult and he was just done. Her mom, my Grandma Jackie, was less than happy about Mom dating Dad, especially since he was only a few years younger than my grandma! Dad was almost forty when they met. Mom wasn't even twenty-one and had just dropped out of college.

Dad had been married before, when he first went into the Army, but it only lasted a couple of years. He said as soon as he saw Mom, he knew there was something special about her. They only dated about five months and then were married. I was born a little over a year later. They wanted another baby right away, but things didn't work out.

Mom had a miscarriage and then didn't get pregnant again until I was seven. Sebastian being so much younger than me meant he was more like a little doll than a brother when he was born. I'd help change and dress him, like I was his little mom.

By the time I was ten or eleven, he was just annoying. When I was thirteen—for real, not the fake thirteen I am now—he was a total and complete pest. But now . . . I guess I don't mind him as much.

Even when things were really bad, when we didn't have any food and were so weak and tired we could hardly move, he never

42

complained. I don't know if he really knew how bad things were, but he kept telling Mom not to worry, that we'd be okay.

We were with Ben then, but he'd been missing for a few days. He left us holed up in a house while he went out to hunt. Before he left, he made sure we had a roaring fire in the stove and what he thought would be enough wood to last us until he got back.

A storm came in while he was gone, and Mom thought the worse. The wood was rapidly dwindling. Mom went out in the storm after more. She trudged through the snow, bringing in wet, broken limbs and small pieces. We put them near the fire so they'd dry while we burned the furniture.

The storm finally cleared, and the next day Ben came back, dragging a deer behind him. He looked awful. He could barely walk and had a cough. But he was dedicated to making sure we ate; he didn't even stop to rest until the deer was skinned and the meat was cooking.

Turns out he had frostbite on one of his feet. He ended up having to have several toes taken off. Mom says he was lucky he didn't die. The lady who did the surgery—not a doctor but some lady who'd studied herbs or some such thing—said it was God watching over him, watching over *all* of us.

Mom had already rejected God and all He stood for by then.

But Sebastian nodded vigorously in agreement. "I was praying the whole time Ben was gone. I knew he'd be okay, that we'd all be okay. And I know we're going to get to Wyoming."

"How do you know?" I asked.

"God told me," Sebastian answered with a shrug. "When I was praying, I heard . . . well, maybe I didn't hear with my ears, but I know everything will be fine until Wyoming."

"What happens after we get to Wyoming?" Mom asked.

"I don't know yet. But I'll ask Him later."

When Mom was sick, Sebastian knew she'd be okay. Now he keeps saying we're going to see Aunt Karla soon. I want to believe him.

As we're finishing the water, a strange noise sounds in the distance. I look to Jennifer. Her eyes are wide as she shakes her head. "Horses?"

"You think? It sounds . . . strange." We listen, barely moving, until the noise fades away.

Shortly after we return to camp, Rey and Kimba reappear from their scouting mission. "Did you all hear the horses and wagon?" Kimba asks.

"Is that what it was?" Jennifer asks. "Sadie and I weren't sure."

"Sound can distort in areas like this," Rey replies. "But, yep. A team and wagon, well loaded and heading toward Billings."

"Did they see you? Or our camp?" Mom asks.

"I don't think so, but I'm not sure if they heard the shotgun. It went off shortly before we saw the wagon. They weren't looking around, so . . . " Kimba lifts her hands.

The hunters bring back six pigeons. We pluck them and then made a spit out of green limbs to cook them over our small fires. Rey insists we only make small fires, producing as little smoke as possible, to help from being discovered by other travelers.

"This is good eating," Donnie says, wiping his mouth with the back of his hand. "We're going back right before dark to see if we can get a few for breakfast."

"You ready to start working with your knife?" Kimba asks me.

I lift a shoulder in response.

"Can I drill with you?" Nicole asks.

"Absolutely, but let me spend a few minutes just with Sadie, introduce her to her new friend. Then we'll all work on hand-to-hand combat. Since the ground's dried out, we might even do some of the judo and wrestling moves. It's always important to know how to get off the ground."

"Not me." Jameson crosses his arms. "Go ahead and waste your time with it, but I'm not interested."

"That's fine, mate." Rey nods. "You can go with Donnie and bring back more pigeons."

Donnie glares at Rey. "If he's coming with me, I expect him to keep his trap shut and do what I tell him."

"I'm not going with him either." Jameson puffs out his chest. "I'm going to bed."

"Jameson," his mom whines. "We've talked about you needing to help out more, like everyone else."

"How is what Kimba's doing helping?"

"Do you really not get it?" his older brother, Brett, asks. "We train so that if we're attacked and need to defend ourselves, we don't die."

Jameson smirks. "Maybe we don't die right away, but we'll never win. Why bother? Mom knows this too. She doesn't even carry a gun since she knows there's no use in fighting back." He drops his head and mutters, "Not that she'd fight back anyway."

I glance to Victoria.

She's staring at the ground. "I just don't like the sound." Her voice is a weak whisper.

"Why do you think there's no use in fighting back?" Kimba asks Jameson.

"Because it's true. Look at us. You and Rey might know what you're doing. Maybe Donnie with his big gun, too, even though he's already been shot twice, so . . . " He lifts a shoulder. "I guess Atticus has some knowledge. But the rest of us aren't trained soldiers. We're just women and children."

Donnie's gunshot-mangled hand goes to his head. His finger traces the hairless groove left by a bullet when we were attacked at the barricade of Bridger, Montana.

"It's true, we're not trained soldiers," Jennifer agrees. "But most of us did have some training. All my boys do. And I would like to point out, at eighteen, Atticus and Asher shouldn't be considered children. And Axel, Nicole, and Brett have been doing the work of an adult for almost a year now. I don't think many would consider them children. You've been asked to be treated as a grownup, right? To be allowed to make your own decisions?"

"That's right." Jameson juts out his chin. "And *my* decision is I'm going to bed."

Donnie makes a growling noise. "Get off your lazy— "

Jennifer loudly clears her throat.

"Let's get a move on it, kid." Donnie stands. "You're coming with me. Make yourself useful."

Chapter 8

After considerable grumbling, Jameson leaves with Donnie and Atticus to try and get more pigeons for breakfast. Brett stays behind this time, saying he'll do drills with us. I've noticed the Dawson brothers tend to avoid each other.

Where the Dosen brothers are often doing things together and seem to enjoy each other's company, Brett and Jameson often snap at or ignore each other. Understandable, with the way Jameson acts toward everyone, including his family.

And their mom does nothing about it. Many times, my mom or one of the others have asked Victoria—told her, even—to break the arguments up. But she rarely realizes on her own there's an issue. She's so often off in her own little world.

"Sadie?" Kimba gives me a smile. "Let's spend a few minutes while everyone's getting ready."

Because of the knife training we've been through before, she doesn't take much time showing me defensive or offensive moves. Instead, we work on smoothly pulling my knife from the sheath at my waist.

"It's a little tight," she admits. "Maybe Asher has something in his little packet of tools to fix where it's rubbing. I'll talk with him and see. You ready to practice?"

She claps her hands to get everyone's attention. "Okay, gang. We'll start with self-defense. Naomi and Sebastian, you're with us. Victoria, do you want to work on a few moves?"

Like Jameson, Victoria has little interest in training with us. Once in a while she'll try a few things, but she usually works around camp or disappears to her tent when we're training.

"Not today." She waves a hand. "I'll clean up while you all go off and have fun."

"Maybe next time," Jennifer says with a smile, always the one to try and keep the peace.

We start with some easy warm-ups. We get plenty of exercise each day by walking ten or so miles, but Kimba insists we need to stretch before we start.

"Let's work on escapes tonight," she says after she's determined we're suitably limber. "We haven't done those in a while. Everyone partner up."

Nicole gives me a smile and signals we should be partners. I make my way toward her. My mom, who's usually my partner, matches with Jennifer. Sebastian is with Naomi, the only one close to his age and size. Kimba partners with Rey so they can show the moves, then they'll walk around to each team to make sure we're doing it correctly.

Once everyone's ready, Kimba says, "We'll start with single wrist grabs. We've shown you two separate escapes for this. Who can demonstrate one?"

"Me! Me!" Naomi raises her hand and jumps up and down.

"Go ahead. Sebastian, grab her wrist. Remember, Naomi, no contact. You're just showing us how to do it, not touching or trying to hurt your friend."

Sebastian grabs Naomi by her left wrist.

She raises her right arm high in the air, making a fist, then lets out a yell as she hammers the fist down toward my brother's hand. She stops less than an inch before making contact, gives him a cheeky grin, then very slowly moves it the rest of the way to demonstrate where she'd want her punch to land.

"Very good," Kimba cheers. "If you were really trying to get away, you'd hit as hard as you could right at the depression at the base of the thumb. This is sometimes called the snuffbox. Bones, nerves, tendons, and other things meet here so you can really do damage, which is why we don't go all out during practice. No one needs a broken bone or worse."

"But if it's really a bad guy, hit him hard, right?" Naomi asks.

"Right. I want you to each do this escape ten times on each hand, then switch and let your partners try. Rey and I will come around for questions while you're working. And yell. You should sound intimidating when you're defending yourself."

Nicole doesn't waste any time grabbing my wrist. I do a way less dramatic move than little Naomi did and make zero noise. There's definitely nothing intimidating about me.

"Use your voice, Sadie," Nicole encourages. "If nothing else, you can shock them and let the rest of us know you need help. And take your arm all the way over your head before you bring it down. Get the power you need to break those little bones."

I do a couple more, none really any better than the first and most without yells, or as Kimba sometimes calls them kihaps. About halfway through, Kimba stops me and adjusts my hand.

"You'll break your thumb with it inside your fist," she says. "Now let me see your best effort, and let me hear you yell."

I take a deep breath. Giving a big, exaggerated move with my arm, I let out a yelp on the way down.

"Very good!" Kimba gushes. "You're really doing well, Sadie."

Pride washes over me. I hide the smile that wants to escape. Kimba moves to the next person, and we finish out our set. When I grab Nicole's wrist, the yell she lets out scares me and I let go.

She laughs. "See?"

After we've all done the snuffbox punch, we move to a different escape for the same hold. For this one, we step into the attacker while making a fist of the hand with the wrist being held. Then we quickly step back, opening our hand and pulling the wrist away.

Nicole escapes first this time, making this look easy too. When it's my turn to escape, Kimba comes around and makes a few adjustments to my move. The first time I get out of Nicole's grip, I lose my balance and almost fall on the ground.

"Wow!" Nicole cheers. "You did it perfectly. There wasn't anything I could do to hold on to your wrist."

"I almost fell."

"You can work on keeping your balance. Now that you're learning the moves, the rest will fall into place."

"Did you do this stuff before?"

"Before? Oh, before the apocalypse? Some, but not like we do now. I took taekwondo for a year or so when I was around Naomi's age. But it was too hard to remember everything, so I didn't stick with it. Mom and Dad taught us about stranger danger—you know, since we lived in the city. But it wasn't like it is now. My dad was gone a lot for work, so there wasn't time for practicing together."

"Spy work?"

She lets out a laugh. "No. They both stopped that before I was born. And even though everyone calls them spies, it wasn't exactly what they did. Mom was . . . "

Her voice drops to a whisper. "She was an undercover operative. She had a, um, knack, I guess would be the right word, for convincing people she was someone different than who she said she was. Dad was more behind the scenes. They met on some overseas thing. Mom quit shortly afterward. Dad quit about a year later when they decided to get married. They started a consulting business, and that's what they've done since before I was born. That's why we lived in Denver. It was a good location for flying places."

"Did you fly?"

"Sure. Have you been on an airplane?"

I shake my head. "Sometimes Sebastian and I would go with Mom for her work things, but only when it was within driving distance."

"Okay, everyone." Kimba claps her hands. "Bear hug escapes. Rey, let's remind them how this is done."

Rey grabs Kimba from behind, pinning her arms to her side. Kimba talks through what she does to escape and then shows how, once she's loose, she punches him in the sternum.

Rey fakes an *oomph* noise.

"And again, the elbow goes into his gut. Then I turn and heel-palm strike him to the nose. Now he's hurting. I've put a little distance between us, too, so I can either make my getaway or pull out my handgun and . . . " Kimba lets her voice fade away as she lifts the palms of her hands. "Remember, we keep going until the threat is eliminated. That means you can either get safely away, help has arrived, or he's down and not getting back up."

Nicole and I practice the bear hug a few times each, then Kimba has us switch partners so someone larger than us can do the bear hug and we can try and escape. I partner with Sebastian while he tries to get away from me. Then I'm partnered with Asher to try and escape. I'm surprised when it actually works.

"Wow, Sadie." Asher offers his hand in a high-five.

I connect my palm with his and shrug.

"You did great getting your body low and throwing your arms up. You can really do this one."

Rey announces we'll move on to handgun drills. Everyone except Sebastian, Naomi, Nate, and me wear a gun on their hips. Some wear more than one gun, having backups on their ankles or somewhere else. Kimba even wears a tank top that has a holster under her armpit with a super small gun she carries there.

"Nate? Sadie? Let's have you work with us for a bit." Rey glances at my mom, who gives him a slight nod of agreement. "You're with me, Nate. Sadie will work with Kimba."

49

Kimba motions toward me as she instructs everyone to empty their weapons and put their magazines and ammo in their bags. "Asher, I want you to check everyone."

She waits until I'm with her before she shows me how to remove the magazine and makes sure there isn't a bullet—she calls them cartridges—in the barrel.

"We practice with empty weapons," she says. "At least at first. Do you know how to load and unload a semi-automatic pistol?"

I give a slight shake of my head. Kimba smiles at me before taking me through the process. I'm sure the blank look on my face did little to instill confidence. Sometimes, I regret my dad not having guns or Ben and Mom not teaching me how to use them last winter.

I glance over at Nicole. She looks so confident. Will I ever look like that?

"What do you think, Sadie? Want to squeeze the trigger?"

"It's the same as the rifle?"

"Pretty much, yes. Even though we know this gun is unloaded, we're going to treat it like it's got a round in it—not just a single round but a full magazine. We'll follow all the rules of safe gun handling. Your target is the tree." She points to a tree a dozen feet away.

"All right, everyone," Kimba calls out to the group. "Holster your weapons. The range is hot, and Sadie is on the firing line."

I feel the color creep up my neck as everyone looks at me.

Kimba spends several minutes helping me with my stance and showing me how to look through the sights and where my finger will go on the trigger. "You want your finger in the proper location, otherwise your accuracy will be affected."

Once she's happy with my stance and my trigger-finger placement, along with how I'm holding the gun and securing it with my non-shooting hand, she says, "You look good. Nice, strong stance. I've already closed the slide for you, so it's ready to fire."

I look down the sight and gently pull back on the trigger. The slight click causes me to jump.

"Not bad, but it jerked a bit. Dry firing is a great way to learn to be smooth. When I was training for accuracy, I must have dry fired guns thousands and thousands of times. It helps. And we'll have you do it much more."

She shows me how to reset the trigger by pulling back on the slide. "Don't ride the slide," she cautions. "Just pull it back and keep your hand going toward your shoulder."

We spend only a few more minutes practicing before Rey declares it's time for the drills.

"You did well, Sadie." Kimba smiles. "We'll keep at it, and you'll be comfortable in no time. Go join your brother and Naomi. You can watch us drill."

Nate makes a face as he plods next to me, less than happy about not being able to do anything further than learning how to ensure the gun is unloaded.

"That wasn't much of a lesson," he mutters.

Personally, I thought it was enough. I'll never remember the little bit Kimba showed me tonight. I'm glad she didn't add anything more to it.

Chapter 9

"Only two days and we'll reach Roundup, right? That's what Rey said?"

"Yeah, almost there." I tweak my brother's nose.

He flicks my hand away. "Will it be a nice town?"

"I hope so."

"Are you going to help with the scavenger hunt? I'm going to the garage with the A Team to see what's left behind. I have a feeling there will be some good stuff at this house."

"Why's that?"

"Because . . . you know."

I put my hand on Sebastian's shoulder and meet his sad eyes. "Yeah, I do."

Because it's a death house.

We only caught a glimpse of this house, set far off the road, when we were cresting a hill at least a mile back. At first, we weren't exactly sure what it was, just a glint of metal caught by the setting sun.

Atticus pulled out his binoculars and said he thought it might be some sort of metal sculpture. It was Donnie, perched on his horse and scoping with his binos, who decided it was a weathervane on top of a roof.

The set-back location provided a perfect place to spend the night, but from the road, we had no way of knowing if it was vacant. Rey and Kimba decided it was worth checking out, especially when Atticus pointed out the brewing rainstorm and said he thought it may be a big one. So now, here we are.

And it really is the perfect place to spend the night . . . except for the not long dead family in the living room. We've set up our tents in the large barn.

With the threat of weather, we stopped early. We would've liked to put in a few more miles and get closer to Roundup, Montana. A shorter day today will mean a shorter day tomorrow too.

We'll often camp a few miles out so it's full daylight when we arrive at a town—no use risking not being properly seen. From Roundup, it's only like seventy-five miles to Lewistown. About a week and a half and our journey will be over.

"So, you gonna?" Sebastian pokes me in the arm.

"Gonna what?"

"Help with the search. Rey said he and Kimba will do the main house, but we can help with the garage, barn, and other buildings. Jennifer says she's going foraging. You doing that instead?"

"Maybe. What's Mom doing?" I ask.

"She's going to help Rey with the main house, I think. You know it doesn't bother her much. Not after . . . before."

"Yeah," I agree with a nod.

Before. When we were walking to Wyoming, she checked lots of houses, some with people who hadn't been dead very long and some with people who'd almost turned into mummies after dying in the heat of summer. Then they'd freeze in the winter.

Mom would go in anyway, trying to find us things we needed to survive another day. We do the same things now, checking the vacant houses and buildings.

"I guess I'll forage. Maybe we'll find something good."

"I wish chocolate grew around here."

"You and me both! At least there's a lot of water and everything's green. I was tired of being in the desert."

"The desert was green, too, because of all the rain." My little brother looks at me like I'm daft.

"Um, yeah, I know. I just meant . . . never mind."

It's only a few minutes later when Rey and Kimba show up and hand out work assignments. We'll salvage and forage, then have dinner followed by training if the salvaging is done. If there's more to do, which Rey thinks might be the case based on the quick look he got of the buildings, we'll skip training and see what else we can find.

"Better hurry with any outside stuff," Atticus says. "This storm's going to be a doozy."

Jennifer, Nicole, and I are sent off to forage. Donnie and Jameson will keep watch while everyone else goes through the dead people's things.

The three of us head farther up a lush hillside. "I'm pretty sure there's a creek over there," Jennifer says, pointing to a line of brush. "Might be a good place to start."

"Anything special we should be looking for?" Nicole asks.

"The usual. Dandelion, lamb's-quarter, wild onion and chives, salsify. I'm hoping we'll find some cattail along the water. We'll split up, but if you aren't sure of something, leave it. We can look at it together. And never take more than a third of the crop. We want to leave enough for it to continue growing."

We only started foraging about a month ago. Until then, there was so much snow on the ground, we couldn't find anything growing. Everyone said this winter was worse than any they'd remembered.

Normally, they'd get a good snow that would last a few days, then it'd warm up and melt off. It'd get cold again, snow again, and then warm up, repeating the cycle until spring.

This winter, the cold started in September and the snow in October. It never did warm up enough to melt. There were several feet of snow on the ground until almost the end of April.

As the snow began to melt, we had several days of mud. Walking on the main road wasn't awful, but getting off the road to camp was nuts. With the rain, the mud and wet continues.

Even though it isn't raining at the moment, the tall grass is still wet from the earlier drizzle. My jeans are soon damp to my knees. Making a point of dodging the worst of the mud and deep puddles, our movements are slow and cautious as I trudge behind Jennifer and Nicole, like a little duckling.

We each carry a canvas bag to put our treasures in. Fresh food is something I've missed. Even if it seems like we're eating weeds, it's definitely a treat. Not quite the treat of the chocolate from my birthday—I still have six of those left—but it's still a thrill.

We find a spot with dandelions and harvest a small amount, leaving the proper amount for propagating.

I find it funny we don't take all of them. My Grandpa Martin would spend his entire summer trying to wipe out the dandelions in his lawn. Sprays were his first choice, but when that didn't get them all, he'd get out his pocketknife and dig them up, trying to get the entire root.

Jennifer lets out a little squeal when she sees a brown blob poking out in the marshy area ahead: the cattails she was hoping to find.

"These are perfect! Archer—he was my husband—was always complaining about the cattails growing in the marshy area we had near the river. His mom had transplanted them years before. She insisted they were important to grow after reading some obscure report out of

54

Germany in World War II. She said they discovered carbohydrates from a single acre of cattails could feed ten thousand people."

"Is that true?" Nicole asks.

"I don't know, but she thought so. Unfortunately, after she died, Archer dozed the cattail farm. We had a few stragglers but not near the amount as when she was alive."

As we move closer to this little cattail farm, Jennifer says, "We're definitely feasting tonight, maybe for several days. Let's fill up our sacks and then empty the cattails out, then we'll continue with more foraging."

"We have a few more bags," Nicole says. "Maybe one of us should run back for them now while the other two work? Sadie? You could go."

"Good idea." Jennifer turns toward me. "You mind making the trek again?"

"I'll do it," I answer. What's another half mile of walking on top of the six or so I've put in today? As I say this, there's an ache in my big toe, something I noticed when we stopped for lunch but hasn't really bothered me since. I'll have to check it tonight.

I hand off my bag to them with a promise to be right back.

Walking back isn't bad; it's a gradual downhill. I'm within two hundred yards of the house when Jameson steps out from behind a tree, causing me to gasp and jump back.

"What's your problem, fraidy cat?" he asks.

I shake my head and step around him.

"Hey, I'm talking to you." He moves in front of me.

"I need to get something."

"No, what you need is to show some respect, you little brat. When your elders—or those who are better than you—talk to you, you need to acknowledge them."

Why is he always such a snot? With my heart pounding and tears threatening, I move to the right.

Stepping with me, he curls his lip in a sneer. "Did you hear me? Respect. Now."

My voice is barely a whisper. "Just . . . just let me by. They're waiting for me."

"Nope. First you'll— " He lets out a harsh laugh. "Are you crying? Wook at the wittle baby, crying her eyes out. Boo-hoo-hoo."

I move fast to rush past him. He grabs me by the arm and spins me around.

"I told you!" he shouts. "An ugly little twit like you doesn't get to walk away from me. You *will* show me the respect I deserve!" As he yells, his hand slides down my arm and locks on to my wrist.

Hot, angry tears stream down my face. I take a deep breath and adjust my posture. One leg to the front, the other behind in a slightly wide stance. I bend my knees, just a smidge. Then I make a fist on the arm he's holding.

"Eek," I cry out, barely above a whisper, as I open my hand and pull it toward where his thumb and fingers connect. His eyes go wide as I slip out of his grasp.

I'm free! As soon as I realize it, I also realize my balance is gone. I flail my arms, trying to regain my footing. Failing, I find myself flat on my bottom in the muddy, wet grass.

Jameson howls with laughter. "What an idiot you are! Trying to use those kung fu moves on me. All the training, and you're still nothing but a loser. You might as well just give up."

"Jameson!" Donnie calls as he's jogging toward us. "What's going on here?"

"Ask her." He curls his lip at me. "She thought she could show off and . . . look at her!" He looks back at me. "Loser."

"Sadie, are you hurt?"

I try and stand, slipping again in the mud. This time, instead of landing on my bottom, I fall forward.

"She's not hurt," Jameson says, "just as clumsy as a— "

"Enough!" Donnie roars. "Sadie? Are you okay?"

I nod as I, again, try to get my feet under me. The slippery ground refuses to yield.

Donnie puts his hands around my biceps and lifts me out of the slop and onto a patch of grass.

"You're a mess." Jameson laughs. "But I think the mud covering your face is an improvement."

"Shut your trap," Donnie snarls between clenched teeth. "Get your sorry excuse of a . . . just go!" He motions Jameson away.

Jameson points at me. "She did this to herself, thought she could do some of the fancy moves and get out of my grasp. It's not my fault she's like a pig covered in mud."

"Get out of your grasp?"

Jameson's eyes go wide as he realizes his mistake. "It was . . . just a joke. She . . . she took it wrong."

"I'm not telling you again." Donnie's voice is low, barely controlled. "Get out of my sight."

Jameson shoots me a dirty look before spinning to leave. He catches the edge of the mud hole, momentarily losing his balance. Unlike me, he recovers. With a smirk over his shoulder, he walks away, head held high like he's the king of the forest.

Chapter 10

With his eyes narrowed and a scowl on his face, Donnie watches until Jameson is halfway back to the house. "What really happened? Did he hurt you?"

Swallowing hard, I open my mouth to answer. There's a lump in my throat, and a wave of anger overtakes me—not anger so much at Jameson but at myself. What a loser I am. My shoulders shake as I swivel my head back and forth in response.

"I'll kill him," Donnie whispers. "If he hurt you, so help me."

"I . . . I'm not hurt. Just . . . embarrassed. And mad." I wipe my eyes with the back of my hand, managing to displace the mud and swirl it around. I can't even imagine how bad I look.

"Donnie?" Rey calls from the house. "Everything okay?"

Donnie lifts a hand. "We're okay."

"Don't tell him," I beg.

"Oh, I'm telling him all right. Jameson's going to be held accountable for this. I saw enough to know he was harassing you, and we won't stand for that. We can't. There're too many threats in this world. We can't be in fear of our own people, even if it is a little punk. Let's have your mom help you get cleaned up."

"They're waiting for me—Jennifer and Nicole. I'm supposed to take a couple more bags to them."

"I'll send someone. You're sure you're not hurt? You can walk?"

With a nod, I take a tentative step toward the house. I'm not hurt, but the slick mud still has me feeling wobbly and unsure of my footing. And my toe throbs.

Rey's still standing at the edge of the house, watching us.

Donnie raises his hand again.

Rey responds with a nod but stays in place. A second later, Kimba's by his side.

We're close to the house when my mom comes around the corner. "What happened?" Her voice carries on a slight breeze.

"Not sure," Kimba answers. "Sadie fell . . . or was pushed."

"Pushed? Who pushed her?" Mom takes off toward me, her stride brisk and determined. "Are you okay?"

"Fine, Mom. Just . . . I'm fine."

"Did Jameson do this to you?"

I tilt my head to the side in response while Donnie snarls. "Sure did, that rat."

"I heard him telling his mom you attacked him. That can't be right."

"*I* attacked *him*?" A laugh of disbelief escapes me. Not even. Not only did I not attack him, but I also couldn't defend myself—not properly anyway.

He's right. All the training I've done, and I'm still a loser. Maybe his mom is right too. I'll never be able to stand up for myself and will need a man to watch over me, but as ugly as I am . . .

"Donnie, did you see it?" Mom asks, her voice several pitches too high.

"I just caught the end. Saw he had her by the wrist and she did one of those fancy getaways, then she lost her footing in the mud and *splat.*"

I cringe at the way he says splat. Embarrassment washes over me again as I remember the way Jameson laughed at me, the way he called me a pig and taunted me.

Then I remember how he said I needed to treat him with respect because he was my elder—he's not—and better than me. Does that even matter anymore? In the world we live in, is there even such a thing as elites? He may have been from a rich family before and had everything handed to him, but now he's fatherless and homeless, no different than me.

"Nicole and Jennifer are waiting on more bags," I say. "We found cattails, lots of them."

We're close enough to Kimba and Rey that they hear me. "I'll go," Kimba offers. "Leanne, once you get Sadie put right, we'll get to the bottom of this. Things like this can't happen."

"You're right, it can't." Donnie crosses his arms. "Little twerp needs an attitude adjustment."

"If he touches my daughter again, he'll get more than that." Mom's tone leaves no doubt she means it.

"We'll make sure it doesn't happen again." Rey's usual light-British accent is more pronounced with his agitation.

"Mom?" Sebastian calls out as he runs over, Naomi by his side. "Oh! Sadie, what happened?"

"She's fine," Mom answers. "We'll get her cleaned up. Stay with Naomi."

Mom nudges me toward the barn. "We'll go in the tack room, get you a little privacy. You want me to take the time to warm up some water?"

"I just want the mud off. It's starting to itch."

"You know, I've heard women used to pay big bucks for mud baths." She scrunches her nose.

"Pass. Mom, I— " Tears threaten again.

"Shh. Let's just get you cleaned up. Then we'll . . . we'll sort it out."

She grabs my pack, muttering about how Jameson's going to learn to treat people right, even if she has to beat the kindness into him.

I cover my laugh with a cough. My mom can be a little fiery. Even before the world fell apart, she'd present this calm, Godly exterior. But in private, she'd sometimes be riled up.

One day, not long after my dad died, we were in the grocery store. Sebastian was with our grandma, so it was just Mom and me. A lady she'd known from high school was in town visiting her parents.

Unlike me, Mom was popular in school. She wasn't too short and too skinny with a big nose and ears sticking out. She was petite, but in a good way. And instead of being painfully shy, she was a cheerleader. Her size meant she was usually at the top of the pyramids—they called her a flyer. The lady from the store was also on the cheer squad, but they weren't friends.

I don't know exactly why they didn't like each other, but whatever happened in high school was still an issue all those years later. Mom saw the lady—her name was Suzy—and their eyes met. Mom gave a cordial smile and a nod. She muttered to me to keep moving. But Suzy called out to her.

"Oh, Leanne Randolf, so interesting to run into you here."

"Yes, hello, Suzy, nice to see you."

"It's Suzanne now, of course. I had a small break in my schedule and stopped by to visit my mom."

"That's good," Mom said. "I hope you have a nice visit." We started moving again.

"So, you're still living here? You didn't do anything to get out of this backwater town?"

60

With a shrug, Mom said, "I like it here. It's a nice place to raise children."

"Is this your son?" she asked, gesturing toward me.

"My daughter, Sadie."

"Daughter? Oh, you should let your hair grow out a little, sweetie. It might help."

"Nice to see you again, Suzy." Mom had a clip to her voice.

"Suzanne."

"Have a nice visit."

"We should get together, catch up on all we've been doing since high school. My life has been nothing short of amazing. I'm so glad I left here and started to really live."

"My dad just died," I blurted out. To this day I have no idea why I said it. Even when I was young, I was quiet and reserved in public. With my mom and dad, or grandma and grandpa, I had no trouble talking and laughing. But with others, I always felt awkward.

"Oh, you poor thing," Suzy said. "That must have been so terrible. We really must get together, Leanne. We'll get a couple of drinks and help you get over the death of your husband."

"No, Suzy, we're not going to get together. I didn't like you in high school, and these few minutes with you here have been more than enough time catching up. Let's go, Sadie."

As Mom moved us quickly down the aisle, Suzy yelled out, "You're still the same nothing you were in high school. You'll always be a nothing. And so will your kid!"

Tears ran down my face as Mom hustled me along.

"Don't listen to her, Sadie. Her opinion never mattered to me before, and it doesn't matter now. And it shouldn't matter to you either. She doesn't know you. She doesn't know how amazing you are. Don't let people like her get to you. You are God's handiwork, made in his image."

"She thought . . . she said I was a boy."

"Humph. I knew Suzy in grade school. Believe me when I tell you that she probably gets up plenty early in the morning to look the way she does today. But it doesn't matter how much makeup she puts on or how good she might think she looks. It's what's inside that counts. And she's not that pretty on the inside. She needs our prayers. She needs God in her life because she can't ever be pretty on the inside without His saving grace."

61

I learned a lot about my mom that day. Her fiery temper was abundant when one of her children, or anyone really, was being wronged. Her dedication to me and Sebastian hasn't changed. The things we've been through since the attacks started have made her even more fierce. Even though she turned her back on God, she's still the same in most ways.

Inside the tack room, Mom turns on her small flashlight. She runs it over me and frowns. "You're a bit of a mess, baby girl. Did you find a pond or anything?"

"A stream and kind of a boggy area."

"Maybe we should take you there? I'm not sure a washcloth is going to do it."

"Can we at least get the mud off my face?"

After wiping down my face and feeling somewhat human again without the caked-on mud, Mom says we'll go to the creek.

As we step out of the barn, Victoria sees us. She throws back her shoulders and stomps toward us. "Sadie! You need to be careful. You could've hurt Jameson and you both doing that combat stuff improperly."

"I . . . I did it correctly," I whisper.

"Jameson should've kept his hands off her." My mom points at Victoria. "You need to step up and take your parenting seriously, start teaching him right from wrong. Grabbing on to Sadie like he did was wrong."

"I know, I know." Victoria puts her hands up. "I've talked to him, and there will be, um, punishment—not only from me but from the group as well."

She puts her hand down and moves it toward her waist. She's wearing a holster—two of them in fact, one on each side. In the holsters are axes, or something like an axe. They're smaller than the kind my grandpa used for chopping branches off trees.

This is new. I want to ask where she found them, but I'm more interested in getting the itchy mud off.

"We'll discuss this later," Mom says. "Right now, I'm taking Sadie to get cleaned up."

Cleaning up in the creek isn't easy. It's really not much more than a ditch and is plenty muddy on its own. I go in fully clothed, using soap and my washcloth to clean my clothes first. Mom holds up a towel to shield me from any prying eyes as I get out of my wet clothes,

62

clean my body, and get into dry things. By the time I'm done, my teeth are chattering.

After dinner—a feast of cattail corn on the cob, which are boiled cattails sprinkled with some of our precious salt; boiled cattail stalks, which tasted a little like asparagus; and chucker stew, compliments of Nate Hoffmann and his slingshot—Rey says, "It's time to address the elephant in the room."

"Hey, I told you," Jameson says in a rush, "I didn't push her. Sadie fell on her own. It's not my fault she's clumsy."

I drop my gaze. Focusing on my breathing, I will the threatening tears away.

"You put your hands on her." Donnie narrows his eyes while pointing at Jameson. "This isn't the first time we've had trouble with you doing this. None of us have forgotten when you slapped your mama and pushed Rochelle down."

Jameson drops his gaze. At least he has the decency to look ashamed. I want to glare at him, let him know what he did was wrong. I also want to tell him that he may think he's better than me, but he's not older than me. He's the brat, not me.

"It can't happen again," Rey says. "We're a team, and we work together. We don't work against each other. If you have a problem with someone, we discuss it. You've asked before to be treated as an adult. But so far, you haven't acted like one."

"What was this about?" Kimba asks. "Did Sadie do something to upset you?"

My eyes go wide as I vigorously shake my head.

"*Noooo.* Not exactly," Jameson answers. "I just . . . I saw her walking and thought it'd be fun to scare her. When she jumped, I guess . . . " He lets out a loud breath. "I started off only teasing and then . . . " He shakes his head and then whispers, "Then I turned mean."

His entire body seems to shrink as his ears turn red and pain washes over his face. He gives a slow shake of his head. "I'm sorry. I shouldn't . . . I was . . . " He lifts his hands up.

The entire room is quiet for several seconds as his brother, Brett, moves toward him. He rests a hand on Jameson's shoulder. "This, admitting you were wrong, is the closest you've come to being a man."

Chapter 11

The storm Atticus predicted hit in the middle of the night. The thunder was so loud the barn shook. None of us slept much, especially after a flash of lightning lit up the space like it was daylight, and the boom following was almost instant.

That had everyone up and looking for sparks. The last thing we need is a fire. Of course, as wet as it is, the green grass is unlikely to start. The thunder and lightning eased off after a short while, with the rain continuing through the night and into the morning.

There was so much water in such a short time, new streams were created by the runoff. We ended up taking a rest day instead of walking through the muck to get back to the main road.

This property is an anomaly. Even though we're not terribly far from the town of Roundup, it still holds many treasures. Mom says it's probably because it was occupied until recently; the family hasn't been dead long—marauders, she thinks. They took what was easy to take and left the rest. The barn, tack room, and paddocks suggest they had several horses.

Donnie said he's surprised the small family lasted as long as they did. Defending a place with only two adults would be a fool's errand. They should've packed up everything and moved into town. Safety in numbers.

We found several amazing treasures while searching the place, things we can certainly use. One great find was a heavy-duty wheelbarrow. Wheelbarrow probably isn't even the right description for it. The size is more like a small dumpster, and it has four wheels. Two of them are the kind I'd expect on a wheelbarrow, but the other two are small little casters. And it doesn't have wheelbarrow handles, but rather a small red bar.

Donnie said it's some kind of specialty item used when doing construction. The workers would fill it up inside the house, then haul it out to a big, rented dumpster. With a few of the other things we've found, it seems the homeowner may have been a builder or carpenter of some sort.

We moved everything from the utility cart we'd been using—which was starting to deteriorate after the miles its traveled, definitely not what it was designed for—and loaded up the wheelbarrow. The wagon we used for carrying Robyn Sorensen will hopefully hold up until we can find a replacement for it.

Scrounging around, we added in many useful things, including a couple of new tents and bedding. Brett even found a new pair of shoes—a matching pair that fit him perfectly.

The axes I saw Victoria wearing are matching hatchets, each with a leather sheath designed to attach to a belt. Brett found them on an upper shelf in the garage. As soon as he saw them, he said he knew they'd be perfect for his mom. They're probably not designed to be worn as a pair, but if it makes Victoria happy, then whatever.

I believe there's a tie between our two best discoveries: an unopened fifty-pound bag of animal salt, and a toiletries bag full of bathroom travel goods. The salt is larger chunks, similar in size to wheat kernels, and a light reddish color. It might be packaged and labeled for livestock use, but we're commandeering it for ourselves.

When we left the ski lodge, we were given a good supply of salt, which has since dwindled. We use the salt not only for seasoning but also for preserving the meat. For my little family, it's even been a dietary supplement.

We were directed by the nurses at the ski lodge to make sure we kept up on our salt intake. They worried our already stressed hearts may suffer more if our electrolytes were off. Calcium, magnesium, potassium, and a few other things were also of concern.

As part of our rations, we were given multivitamins along with a few specialty foods—items others in our traveling group weren't given—to help us recover from the stress our bodies had already endured. The vitamins ran out weeks ago, as did the foods. I think those things, along with the high-fat geese we feasted on in the spring, really made a difference.

I feel good—almost back to normal, the way I did before the attacks and EMP.

But everyone has been talking about how low our salt was getting, especially with summer and the warmer weather. We'll need the salt in our diets. The more we sweat, the more we'll lose and the sicker we could become. No one seems at all concerned about using the salt marketed for animals.

And even better, the package says it contains other trace minerals, including magnesium, calcium, and potassium. The ski lodge nurses would be happy about this.

The toiletries bag not only has soap, shampoo, lotion, and toothpaste, but four toothbrushes—looking only slightly used—two razors, a bottle of over-the-counter pain reliever, and several other miscellaneous items. The kitchen and bathroom cabinets had been stripped clean of all usable goods, easy pickings for the killers, but this hidden gem was overlooked.

During lunch, Brett shares a little about his mom and why the hatchets are perfect for her. Before everything fell apart, when they were living in Bakerville and his dad was a lawyer in nearby Prospect, Victoria lived a comfortable life. They all did.

She didn't work, but instead volunteered and spent time with her friends. She and her friends would often go away for long "girls' weekends" to different, sometimes exotic locations. And occasionally, they'd take shorter overnight trips closer to home.

One of their favorite overnight excursions was to Cody, Wyoming, just south of Prospect. On one of their trips, they decided to try axe throwing. Victoria loved it, so much she convinced her husband and children they needed to try it too. While they all thought it was fun, it became a passion for her.

Before her family moved to Bakerville, when they were still living in Prospect, she'd travel to Cody regularly—with or without her friends—to spend an hour or so on the lane. After they built their home in Bakerville, she convinced her husband she needed an at-home setup.

There's a soft smile on Victoria's face and extra color to her cheeks. "I really enjoyed it. It was a great way to blow off steam."

"She was wicked with it too." Brett smiles at his mom.

Jameson has been uncharacteristically quiet since the incident the day before. *Incident. Ha.* Funny that's how I think of it. It was an attack. Maybe attack isn't the right word either. Maybe he really was just messing with me and it got out of hand.

Either way, he's said little since it happened but does chime in to add that his mom tried to teach him how to throw, too, but he isn't a natural like her.

A shy, yet proud, look crosses Victoria's face as she lifts a shoulder. "It's nice to be good at something."

For the first time, I feel like I'm seeing the real Victoria. And she's a lot like me: timid and afraid.

Mom thinks Victoria was abused. She said she saw similar things in the work she did. Many of the women that came to her clinic for help were either physically or mentally mistreated.

And most likely Brett and Jameson were also victimized, which helps explain Jameson's behavior. The likely culprit is their dad.

Mom did quickly add how she wasn't excusing Jameson's actions, but said that if he didn't have a good model for proper conduct, and was often bullied himself, he might not realize how wrong he was.

Watching the three of them as they talk about things they enjoy and smile at each other, looking almost like a loving family, allows some of my anger toward Jameson to fade. But the anger I feel toward myself is still there.

As hard as I've been training and trying to learn the things Rey and Kimba teach us, I still failed. If Jameson had truly intended to harm me, he would've succeeded.

I may have escaped the wrist hold, but by landing on my butt in the mud and then being unable to get myself out of the sloppy, mucky mess . . . it would've been awful. Deadly. Worse maybe.

In the evening, after the ground's dried up a bit, Victoria gives a demonstration in axe throwing. Brett wasn't kidding about her being wicked with them. After her demo, we have a lesson and she gives us all pointers. We all try it, but not even Kimba—who throws knives— is as good as Victoria.

When we're finished, I find a spot away from everyone to practice my combat skills. I run through blocks, kicks, and punches. Then I pretend I'm being grabbed and practice my escapes. I'm hot and sweaty when I move on to leg reaps and sweeps.

I'm just about to quit when Nicole joins me. "You look good. Want to spar with me a bit?"

"Um . . . I guess."

"Free spar, no contact." We stand several feet apart, facing each other. "We should bow, like we did when we practiced at the ski lodge. It's a sign of respect."

She bows to me, and I do the same to her. Then she puts her right leg back into fighting stance as she kihaps. I do the same, minus the yell. She gives me a smile and then makes a motion with her hand, the same motion Rey and Kimba use when they want us to move—to go.

I cock an eyebrow at her. "Ready?"

She does the motion again. I take a tentative step forward and throw a weak punch. She counters with a front kick followed by a roundhouse. I turn slightly for a side kick.

"There you go!" she encourages. "Keep it up."

I'm breathing hard but having a great time when I accidentally land a back kick to her hip. It's barely a brush, but I immediately apologize.

"That was awesome, Sadie! You did great. You want to rest for a few minutes and then go again?"

We end up doing three rounds, resting and sipping water between. Then she asks if I want to work on the leg sweeps and grappling.

Grappling, or ground fighting, isn't easy, especially with my size. I don't have much hope of escape. "Seems dry enough. I, uh, guess we could try."

We start with leg reaps, a way to put someone on the ground when you're in close range. She takes me down first, then moves me into a submission hold. I tap the ground after only a few seconds, letting her know I've had enough. We continue the reaps for many minutes, alternating back and forth and attempting different ground moves and escapes.

After that, we move on to the leg sweeps—both judo style, where we're holding on to each other, and a different type where we're farther apart, called a tiger tail sweep. I'm much better at the tiger tail and am able to take Nicole to the ground in a smooth motion.

I'm exhausted by the time we're done. Exhausted, yet happy.

Chapter 12

We stayed a second night in the barn of the death house. Yesterday was a short, easy walk. When an increased number of houses started coming into view, we left the highway and set up camp for the night so we could approach the town of Roundup in full light.

As we start the final stretch into town, my toe begins to ache again. With all that happened with Jameson the other day, I forgot about it hurting. Our rest day, followed by a short walk yesterday, didn't bother it much, just a slight ache near the end of the miles.

I took a look at the toe last night, noticing the toenail looked bruised and maybe the edges a little swollen. This morning, it started hurting almost immediately. I gasp when the next step feels like someone jabs a hot poker in my toe.

"Sadie?" Mom asks.

I shake my head in response. No use saying anything. We're so close to Roundup, stopping wouldn't make sense. Besides, it'd probably just give Jameson something new to be mad at me over.

By the time it's apparent we'll be entering town anytime, based on the increase in houses and street signs, my toe throbs. I'm doing my best not to limp, but I'm failing miserably.

Rey's put us all on alert, telling us to "look alive." He reminds us to keep space between us instead of clumping up. Sebastian and Naomi are directly in front of me. If things go badly, they know to get in the ditch. I know I'm in charge of staying with them.

"What's going on?" Mom asks in my ear.

"Nothing, I'm okay. Just— "

"Just what?"

"My toe hurts."

She furrows her brow. "Since when?"

"Not long. It's fine. When we stop, I'll take a look."

"You can't risk an injury. You should've said something sooner, before we reached the populated area."

"I know, but it wasn't too bad then. We need to stay spread out, Mom."

She gives me a look—a glare really—followed by a curt nod before dropping back. She's right. I should've stopped and checked it out when it first started hurting. Any injury, even minor, can be life threatening.

"Roadblock ahead," someone in our group says in a low voice, having heard it from a person ahead of them. I hear Mom say the same thing so those behind her will also know it's time.

My heart is pounding, my toe throbbing in time with it. Approaching a town is scary.

Sebastian looks over his shoulder and gives me a smile. "They're going to be friendly."

"Shh," Mom cautions.

The *clomp, clomp* of Donnie's horse's hooves on the pavement, along with a slight rattle from the wagon and wheelbarrow carts, is the only sound as we approach Roundup. That and my pounding heart. I take a deep breath, willing myself to calm down.

I glance over at Donnie. He often rides Gordie off the pavement, in the soft grass alongside, but this close to town, he's dismounted and walking alongside the horse. Donnie and the horse make us targets. We saw what people will do for horses at the last house. They'll kill entire families.

Kimba, at the front of our group, motions us to stop when we're within yelling distance of the roadblock. The roadblock is no surprise; this is what we expect to see as we approach towns straddling a main road. Kimba gives a quick look to Rey, who responds with a nod.

I watch as she visibly straightens before calling out, "Hello! We're traveling through."

After a few minutes, we're all near the barricade and being told the rules for passage through the town, which are surprisingly lax and almost inviting.

"Are you going through straight away?" The lady at the roadblock gives a sweeping motion with her arm. "We have lodging set up if you need an overnight stay."

Kimba and Rey share a look before Kimba steps forward. "It's still early in the day. But it looks like we might get more rain."

Kimba turns to Atticus, who gives a nod. "It'd be good to get set up before it hits."

Turning back to the woman at the roadblock, Kimba smiles. "We'd be much obliged."

"All right, we'll have someone escort you." The lady turns to the man next to her, whispering something before he steps away.

He puts a radio to his mouth. With the distance between us, I don't hear his conversation.

It's not long until someone shows up, several people actually, to guide us to the camping area. They've set the roadblock up before a bridge and still a couple of miles from the actual town. Each step I take is more painful than the one before. By the time we get to what's obviously the downtown and main street, I'm sweating profusely and feel sick to my stomach.

"We're almost there now." One of the escorts, a boy only slightly older than me, motions ahead. "Just a few more blocks."

There are many townspeople walking around, and several businesses appear open, almost like a town would've been before the apocalypse.

"You have trade set up?" Rey asks.

"Some, yeah. We have people who travel between the towns hauling goods. Drayers."

"Drayers?" Kimba asks.

"Yeah, you know, like a drayage service? One of the women who runs it said it sounds better than freight haulers. You'll probably meet them while you're here."

After we've gone two blocks, I start looking for a park where we'll be able to set up our tents. We're still in town, but the businesses here are closed. Some have boards over the windows, but most are just sad and vacant.

"Here we are." The boy motions to a motel sign.

Mom lets out a small noise. I'm filled with visions of comfortable beds and hot showers. The hot shower might be unrealistic, unless they have a generator or solar system powering the place, but maybe we'll have a comfortable bed.

Since the weather has warmed up, even when we find a vacant house to stay in, we don't sleep in the beds. We learned that lesson quickly when we saw a bug-infested bed at one of the abandoned homes. I thought it was bedbugs, but Rey said it was lice. I itch just thinking about it.

"Let me get Alex. She'll get your rooms for you."

"*Rooms?*" my mom whispers, her wide eyes.

71

We're given three rooms. The Hoffmanns share one. Mom, Sebastian, and I share a room with Jennifer and Victoria. Donnie, the A Boys, and the Dawson brothers share the last.

There are flowers and vegetables growing in wooden boxes set up on the walkways between the rooms. Alex points at the small gardens. "We're trying to use our space the best we can. There're community gardens also. These smaller ones are mainly for fresh eating, but the community ones are what we'll preserve for winter . . . if all goes well."

She turns an old-fashioned key in the door lock. "I'll tell you, we're sure glad we never switched over to electronic locks."

She grins at us before pushing open the door. "Each of the rooms will be pretty much the same, two queen beds and a twin. We can get a cot for you gentlemen since there'll be six of you in your room. It's a little tighter than when we were a regular hotel, but we keep 'em clean."

It's more than clean. The room is bright and cheery, not like any hotel I've ever seen. The floors look like wood, and the wall behind the queen bed headboards has some sort of large leaf wallpaper.

Alex is right about it being a little tight with the addition of a twin bed at the foot of the queens and up against the wall, probably where a large cabinet would've held a television when there was still electricity. But it's been decorated to look like a couch with extra pillows. A round table and two chairs, along with a bookshelf, complete the furniture. The overall feel of the room is very warm and inviting.

"It's lovely." My mom's voice is full of awe.

"Thank you. We were in the process of a remodel and rebranding when everything fell apart. We still have some of the second-floor rooms in the original style."

"You're just letting people stay here?" Sebastian asks.

"We're doing what we can to help people who are displaced or in need. People usually only stay for a night or two, but we also have work-stay options or trade options for extended lodging." She gives Sebastian a smile. "There're books on the shelf, coloring books too. Make yourselves comfortable. We have a grill set up outside so you can cook. Do you have supplies?"

"We have some," Rey answers.

72

"Good. There's a covered space too. It isn't terribly large, but it'll help if the storm hits." Alex spends a few minutes showing us the room and delivering instructions before taking the others to their rooms.

Chapter 13

As soon as the rest of our group leaves our comfortable motel room, I hobble toward the bookshelf.

Mom touches my arm. "Take off your shoe, baby girl. Let me see your foot."

I cringe at Mom calling me *baby girl* when others can hear. The nickname's something I outgrew long ago.

"What's wrong?" Jennifer asks.

"I'm fine," I say.

Mom shakes her head. "She's limping and says her toe hurts."

I give my mom a look. It's not like her to let anyone know when something's wrong. Even removing my shoe hurts. As I begin to peel off my sock, the fabric sticks to my toe. I let out a yelp of pain.

"Don't yank it," Mom cautions. "Let's get some water on it so it'll loosen up."

I limp to the bathroom.

This area is decorated as nicely as the rest of the room. The sink area, which doesn't have running water since that and the city sewer stopped working months ago, has a large countertop and closet space open to the beds. It's been painted green, which coordinates well with the leaves in the wallpaper behind the headboards. There're already filled jugs on the countertop next to the sink.

The tub and toilet are in a separate room. This room has also been redone, with stone floors and green shower tiles. The toilet now holds a garbage bag filled with sawdust. When we use it, we've been instructed to sprinkle more sawdust over the top.

There's a plastic bin in the tub we can use for sponge baths and washing up; the water is to be dumped outside the door on the flowers. Mom has me sit on the edge of the tub while she pours water over my crusted sock.

"Let it set for a second," she instructs. "Then gently move the fabric away before trying to pull it off."

"I know, Mom."

She gives me a look. "This could be serious, Sadie. You should've . . . never mind. We need to deal with this."

When I finally get my sock off, my aching big toe is oozing and swollen to twice its normal size. The toenail is darker than when I looked at it last night, and the nail bed around it is red and angry. It's all much worse. My stomach sinks as I realize I should've done more, should've told Mom about it before it got to this point.

"Oh, no," Mom whispers.

"How's it look?" Jennifer asks from the other side of the bathroom door.

I meet Mom's eyes. They're filled with tears. "You should've said something when it first started hurting," she says in a harsh whisper. Raising her voice, she responds to Jennifer, "It's not good. Go ahead and open the door."

I watch Jennifer's face as she takes in the sight of my foot. She scrunches her nose. "Looks like it really hurts. An ingrown toenail maybe, combined with bruising? Let me get the first aid kit out of my bag."

After Jennifer leaves, Mom puts a hand on my forehead. "I don't think you're running a fever."

In hushed voices, Jennifer and Victoria discuss what would be best for my toe from the meager first aid kit. Sebastian asks if I'm okay. Jennifer tells him I'm fine, just have a puffy and sore toe.

"I have a few alcohol pads," Jennifer says, returning to the room. "And maybe we should use a needle from my sewing kit to pierce the edge, see if we can release the infection?"

"It's already coming out," Mom says. "At least on one side of the nail."

"Did you hit it on something?" Victoria asks, peering around Jennifer.

"I don't think so. Maybe my shoe's a little tight?"

"Could be." Jennifer nods. "I've heard about long-distance hikers losing their toenails. I think we should clean it up as best we can and bandage it. Keep off it until it's time to go again. If we keep it clean, we might stop the infection from progressing. Maybe put her in a larger shoe so it doesn't irritate it further. How's the other one feel? Is it too tight?"

I lift my shoulder in a shrug. "Sometimes, by the end of the day, my shoes feel too small. The winter boots are especially tight, even when I first put them on. But the tennis shoes aren't as bad."

"You've been wearing those boots when we walk in the rain, right?"

"They help keep my feet dry."

"How about I boil a little water?" Victoria asks. "We can clean it and then use the alcohol. Or maybe dissolve some salt in the water and flush it out? I think I've read somewhere a saline wash can help prevent infection."

Fifteen minutes later, both my feet are soaking in a basin of hot saltwater. The swollen toe throbs from the heat and the salt stings. When Victoria went outside to heat the water on one of our small camp stoves, she must have told Kimba because she came back with her, carrying a bag of medical supplies.

"Just a few more minutes. Draw out the infection. Then we'll have you soap both feet really well. After that," Kimba says with a smile, "I'll pour this over the problem toe." She holds up a small bottle of Vodka, something we'd found in one of the houses we pilfered. It's only half full, the other half was poured into another glass bottle and willow bark shavings were added to make a pain-relieving tincture.

"Then we'll wrap it in gauze and go from there," Kimba says. "I think you'll be fine."

"You think that'll be enough?" Mom asks.

Kimba answers with a shrug. "We'll do what we can. Are you in much pain? Do you want one of the pain relievers?"

I lift a shoulder. "It only hurts a little."

Mom gives me a long look. "Let's give her a couple, just to take the edge off it."

Kimba rifles through her bag. "Say, did you know there's an outdoor area set up for doing laundry? There's a couple of nice big pots, which will make things much easier than we're used to. Rey's getting the fire going if you all want to bring your things. Let's see if we can get it washed and rinsed before the rain arrives." She hands me two of the pills while Mom gives me my water bottle.

"In the courtyard space Alex pointed out?" Jennifer asks.

"Yep. There're chairs and a firepit, too, along with the covered space. If the rain's light enough, which Atticus insists it will be, we should be able to cook and eat there," Kimba says with her hand on the doorknob. "I'll see you all shortly?"

After she's gone, Mom says, "Sebastian, get the shorts and T-shirt you sleep in. Change into them in the bathroom. I want the rest of

76

your clothes put in a pile for washing. You too, Sadie. Put your yoga pants on."

Washing clothes is truly a treat. While we rinse out our undergarments and socks on a regular basis, our pants and shirts are rarely cleaned. Our pajamas are the cleanest clothes we own—and they're still filthy.

I'm changed into my lounge clothes, with my foot clean and bandaged, and socks on as extra protection. Jennifer offers me a pair of too-large shower sandals so I don't have to put my shoes back on.

Like Mom, Sebastian, and me, Jennifer and Victoria also put on their pajamas. Everything else is put in a large garbage bag to get washed.

I stifle a laugh when Victoria straps her belt on top of her yoga pants so she can carry her hatchets. Then, when Mom and Jennifer put on their belts so they can carry their guns, I lean into Mom and ask if I should carry my knife.

"I think you're okay without it," she replies. "Besides, everyone else is obviously armed."

I limp my way to the courtyard, being extremely careful to keep weight off the sore toe. It already feels a little better, either from the cleaning or being out of my shoe. Jennifer says she'll take our laundry bag to where she sees Kimba by a firepit with a large pot.

"I'll be right there," Mom assures her as she leads Sebastian and me to chairs. There're several others staying at the motel, and the atmosphere is almost festive.

"You doing okay?" Atticus asks as Mom helps me into my chair.

I respond with a nod.

"My mom says Sadie will be fine," Sebastian says. "She just needs to stay off her foot."

"I heard you have an infected toenail," a trim lady sitting next to a burly looking man says. "Those hurt like the dickens."

"Walking every day is hard on the feet," the man adds. "Been a few others through here with similar issues."

"Do you live in Roundup?" Victoria asks.

"Dewey and Marie run one of the drayage services the young man was telling us about earlier," Rey says.

"Yep," Dewey, the burly man, states. "We stay here on our turn around now."

"Are you from here?" Victoria motions with her arms. "From Roundup?"

"We've lived here a few years, in the trailer park outside of town," Marie answers. "It burned down last fall. We were on one of the runs to Lewistown when it happened. We kept the runs up until the weather became too terrible, but now we're back at it. Soon, we'll start having crops to take between the towns, bartering and trading for what each community needs."

"Has the military been up here?" Jennifer asks, stepping into the circle of chairs. "What a blessing they are."

"Not yet. The other team that goes to Billings sees them. They should've been back by now. We were talking with your friends before you came out. They said you saw a wagon a few days ago."

"Yours?" Mom asks.

"Not sure. The timing doesn't sound right."

"Hello!" a light cheery voice calls out. A woman with long black hair, wearing a flowing blue dress, steps into the courtyard. "I heard we have new visitors."

Dewey shakes his head, as Marie quietly cautions, "Be nice," before raising her voice. "Hi, Becky. Where's your brother?"

"Oh, here and there." The woman in the dress keeps walking toward us. She stops abruptly and points to Sebastian. "Where have you been, young man? I've been looking everywhere for you."

Sebastian looks to Mom, then me, before lifting a finger and pointing at his chest. "Are you talking to me?"

"Don't you sass me. Who else would I be talking to, Taylor Dean Robidoux?"

Mom reaches over and puts a hand on Sebastian's arm.

Dewey, the guy we just met, lets out a noisy sigh. "That's not your kid, Becky. Your kid— "

"Let's go find Greg." Marie lifts herself out of the chair.

"Come along, Taylor." The lady holds her hand out to Sebastian.

"No, Becky." Marie rests a hand on the woman's forearm. "He needs to stay here. We'll find your brother first, then we can come back, okay? Dewey and these nice people will watch him."

"Taylor, you mind him well. I'll be right back with your Uncle Greg and then we'll get you home. You need a bath. Your hair's a greasy mess." Becky narrows her eyes at Dewey. "You'd better keep a close eye on him. The boy is always slipping away from me."

"That's not all that's slipping away from you," Dewey mutters under his breath.

Marie shoots him a look and makes a shushing noise.

As soon as the two women leave the courtyard, my mom turns to the man. "What was that about?"

"Becky's cheese has done slid off her cracker. Taylor—that was her son—died last summer. There's a few other kids in town she gets confused about too."

"Confused about?" Mom asks. "Like she thinks they're her son?"

"Right. But I will say, your boy does look a little like Taylor. The others, not so much. She was always slightly off. Her husband left her a few years ago. Then everything went to pot, Taylor got sick, and . . . well, she just can't hold it together. Her brother, Greg, he helps her quite a bit."

"Is she dangerous?" Kimba asks.

"To herself. She's had a couple of close calls. Threw herself in the river after the boy died. But she's been better lately."

"Praise the Lord for that," Jennifer says. "Mental health issues at a time like this . . . " She shakes her head.

Dewey gives her a strange look. "Not sure there's much to be praising about where Becky's concerned. A guy showed up in town, and she took a liking to him. It seems to have helped with her suicidal tendencies, but . . . well, he's a bit of a derelict. Her brother tolerates him dating his sister, but just barely. There's some concern he may have been involved in some thefts. Can't prove it—yet. But let's just say he's in town on borrowed time."

There are several minutes of discussion about Becky. It seems to be wrapping up when Marie returns.

"You get her sorted out?" Dewey asks.

"She's with Greg. He said he'll keep an eye on her and won't let her bother these folks while they're here."

After more visiting, Kimba says we should start some dinner.

"Can I go get the coloring books and use them out here?" Sebastian asks Mom.

"That's fine. I'll go with you. It looks like it's about our turn to use the laundry basin." Mom looks toward the darkening sky. "We might even get the wash done in time."

"Let me go, Mom," I offer.

"I don't want you putting weight on your toe."

"Don't worry, I won't. My hip is hurting from walking funny. I think the exercise will do me good."

"You can walk with us," Mom replies. "As long as you're careful."

The first few steps are painful. And it's not just my toe. As I told my mom, my hip hurts too. In the hotel room, I decide I'll grab a book to read. There're several choices. Mom points at the cover of one showing a man without a shirt. "Not that one. How about this one?" She points at *To Kill a Mockingbird*.

"I've read it."

"Might as well read it again."

"I suppose," I mutter.

Mom grabs a book for herself, though I doubt she'll read it. We'll get back out there, and she'll start the laundry and then help with dinner or whatever else they do. She wants to make sure she's useful. Things haven't been easy or comfortable on this trip. Mom's personality often clashes with the others.

It seems like everyone annoys her: Jennifer and her incessant cheeriness, Victoria with her wishy-washiness, Victoria's children—especially Jameson, but he annoys everyone. Even Donnie, who she's in some sort of relationship with, annoys her. Oh, she won't come out and admit they're having *a thing*, but I'm not stupid. I see the long gazes and lingering touches.

Even though Mom may butt heads with people, she makes sure she does her fair share of work and then some. I've overheard Kimba tell Rey what a hard worker Mom is. I'll admit, hearing it gave me a surge of pride. In today's world, being nice doesn't really get you too far, but working hard keeps you alive.

"Ready to head back to the courtyard?" Mom asks, motioning to my foot.

"I have crayons and two coloring books," Sebastian says. "I'm bringing the second one so Naomi can color too."

"Good idea." I ruffle his hair. The crazy lady was right about it needing to be washed.

As I follow Sebastian out the door, Mom warns, "Remember not to put your weight on that foot."

As I turn to tell her I know, I'm shoved hard, pushing me into the doorframe and then pinballing me into Mom. We both let out a yelp as we go down.

80

Sebastian screams, as a gravelly voice says, "Here! Grab him. Put your hand over his mouth. I'll get the girl."

I try and scramble off Mom as a feminine voice says, "We don't need the girl."

"Let go of my son!" Mom yells.

I move off Mom and am against the door frame when a man drops to his knee and punches my mom in the face. She instantly goes limp. I let out a guttural yell and lift my uninjured foot, kicking him hard in the leg.

"You little— "

"Leave her! We have Taylor. Let's go," the woman says.

"I'm taking the girl," the ragged-looking man growls. "I told you that was the deal."

I kick him again; this time he grabs my foot. I watch as he pulls back his arm. I instinctively lift my own arm in a block, which prevents the punch from landing on my face but sends a shockwave through my entire body.

He grabs me by the hair.

I open my mouth to scream, but he puts his disgusting, sweaty hand over my mouth and nose and then yanks me up with his other arm. Without much effort, he's holding me against his chest, my legs dangling several feet above the ground.

I look to my mom; she's starting to stir. I turn my head hard to the left, searching for Sebastian, when the disgusting man snarls, "Let's go. We need to move now."

"C'mon, Taylor," the woman from earlier, Becky, says. "We'll get you home and everything will be fine. Just fine. You'll see."

The woman's holding Sebastian in an almost identical manner to the way I'm being held.

I kick my legs, trying to connect with my captor. I feel one of the shower sandals—the one on my uninjured foot—barely holding on to my socked foot. I let it drop off. We're moving, running away from the hotel.

"Sadie! Sebastian!" Mom screams at the top of her lungs.

Chapter 14

"You stop that right now, Taylor!" The woman's words come in gasps as my brother fights against her. "You stop your squirming or your mama's going to put you in the corner for a week."

"I say beat the brat." The man holding on to me tightens his grip. "It's smart of you to keep still, girl. At least you know what's good for you."

When it was apparent my kicks and thrashing were doing nothing to get me lose, I made my body limp. Although his right arm is wrapped securely around me, at least his stinky left hand is no longer covering my nose and smothering me. But it's still over my mouth, preventing me from screaming.

Maybe, if I hold still, he'll let his guard down. I'll be able to yell—and yell I will, louder than I've ever yelled in my life—then someone will find us.

We've gone several blocks to the north and are now on the edge of the little town. My mom will find us. It's not like Roundup is terribly big. And the people in the courtyard know this lady—Becky. They'll know where to find her. That's my hope anyway.

I try and keep track of where we are, watching for any type of landmark. A two-story gray house is on the corner when we turn east on a street—no street sign. As soon as we turn the corner, I let the second shower sandal fall to the ground. Maybe Mom will see it. It'll give her a clue how to find us.

"Right here, Becky," the man says as a large rain drop hits me on the nose. "This will be a good place until it gets dark, then we'll move to the other location."

"What about the rain, Jamesy? I don't want Taylor to catch a cold."

"We'll go between cloud bursts. A few days staying out of sight, then we'll head north. Couple of weeks, we'll be in Canada."

The man ushers us toward a burned-out house. Half the roof is caved in on itself; the other half looks like it could go at any time.

"We should've taken the time to put gags on them." The man presses harder against my mouth. "I feel like I need a third hand to make this work."

Anticipating my chance to scream at the top of my lungs is approaching, I take several deep breaths through my nose. His sweaty, disgusting hand fills my nostrils with an odor that makes me want to barf.

"Don't get any ideas, little girl," he orders as we step into the ramshackle house. There's no need to stop and open the front door since there isn't one.

As soon as we're inside the darkened structure, he flings me against the wall. It happens so quickly, all I can do is gasp. I hit the wall with a thump. As I take in a breath to let out a yell, his fist slams into my head. Everything goes dark.

~~~~~~

My head is pounding. My toe is throbbing. My shoulders are pulled tight, uncomfortable. I cautiously open my eyes.

Sebastian's green eyes, wild and scared, stare back at me. A red bandanna is tied around his mouth, giving the appearance of a weird looking smile. He mumbles something around the cloth, which may be, "You're okay."

I nod my head, instantly regretting the motion as the pounding pain ratchets up several notches. Taking stock of my body, I realize I have the same style of gag around my mouth. My shoulders are tight because my hands are tied behind me.

"Oh, little girl, I'm glad you're awake. James thought maybe he hit you a little too hard and it might be a while," Becky coos from a nearby chair. "It's not right my own son has to be tied up, but James says it's better like this until we can get you both out of here. Taylor, you were so naughty to put up a fight like you did. You need to treat your mama with respect. I just don't know what's gotten into you." She shakes her head.

"But don't you worry, we'll make a nice little family again. James will be your daddy, and this skinny girl will be your sister. We'll all live together happy and sound—where my stupid brother and his friends can't bother us, putting awful thoughts in my head, trying to convince me . . . oh, I can't even bear to tell you what they've been saying, Taylor-pooh. It was so awful. I just don't know why your Uncle Greg would even say those things."

I watch as she rocks back and forth in the chair, her knitting needles clicking together. She starts humming a song. I can't make it out at first, but after a few bars, I recognize it as *Twinkle, Twinkle, Little Star.*

While she hums, I move my hands, testing to see what I'm tied with. It doesn't feel like rope; it's smooth and thin. My addled brain takes a couple of seconds to realize it must be tape of some sort. It's thin and tight, cutting into my wrists.

Becky abruptly stops humming and bounces from her chair, tossing her knitting on the seat.

I move my head to follow her motion as she goes to what was once a window and is now a gaping hole.

She stands to the side of it, just enough to peer out. She's on alert and looks concerned. Then she lets out a sigh and drops her shoulders before she moves out of my view.

From a different room, the man's voice sounds—James. She called him James. "Little brat kicked off her shoe," he says. "Good thing I found it before someone else did."

I close my eyes. When the first sandal fell, it was an accident. But as soon as it did, I realized it could be a sign, a way for my mom to find us. Dropping the second one was on purpose. Now there's no indication of which way we went.

"Just the one?" Becky asks.

"She lost the other near the hotel. That's not a concern."

"The way she was thrashing about, it's no wonder her shoes fell off. Did you see my brother?"

"Not specifically. The whole town's out looking for us. Wouldn't think they'd care so much about kids passing through."

I smile behind my gag and give Sebastian a nod at the news. They're looking for us. They'll find us.

"Taylor isn't *passing through.* He's born and raised here," Becky says. "I just don't understand why Greg thought it was okay for him to be with those people. He acted like I was plumb nuts, tried telling me again how Taylor was gone. He wouldn't even listen to reason when I told him he was wrong. Why, he wouldn't even go with me to see him, to talk to his own nephew."

"Right, Becky. That's what I meant. Taylor is yours, of course. But the girl, I guess it's her they're looking for."

"You were smart to want to bring her. It'll be good for Taylor to have an older sister. I always wished Greg would've been a girl. I would've loved an older sister. Oh, and she's awake now."

"She's awake? You shouldn't have left them in there alone."

As footsteps clomp across the floor, I give Sebastian a nod before closing my eyes. I don't want to give the crazy guy a reason to hit me again. I hurt so bad. I need to just rest and recover.

I must have gone back to sleep. The next thing I know, I'm being lifted to my feet in the complete darkness.

"This time, you're going to walk and behave," James growls. "Wear the slipper you kicked off. Go ahead. Slip your foot in it."

"Are you sure we should move them?" It's so dark, Becky's voice only floats on the night. "Taylor's just a little boy and needs his sleep."

"We're not going far. I told ya that already. We're just moving them to the building on the edge of town. We'll lie low until they stop searching. Then we'll get moving and be a happy little family, just like we've discussed. You'll have your little Taylor, and I'll have my— what's your name, darlin'?" He pauses a moment as if awaiting my answer.

Maybe he's forgotten I have a gag in my mouth?

"Don't matter. Becky, what should we name this girl of ours?"

Becky lets out a small laugh. "I'm sure, at her age, she already has a name, you silly."

"Sure, sure. But now she's part of our new family, so we can call her whatever we want. In fact, you know what I was thinking?" James asks in a low voice as he marches me out the door.

I stumble on the step, my sock-covered foot slipping. At least my foot with the sore toe is the one with the sandal, which is at least providing some protection.

James lets out a few cuss words before mumbling, "Are you always so clumsy?"

"What'd you say, Jamesy? Oh, Taylor, watch your step here, sweetie. Mama doesn't want you to fall."

We walk in silence for a bit. The wet ground from the earlier rain soon has my socked foot soaking wet. The chill in the night air causes me to shiver. Though it's late in May and warm during the day— when it's not pouring rain—nights are still cold enough for a jacket, which I'm not wearing. Neither is Sebastian. I hope he's okay.

My feet manage to keep me upright. My toe hurts even more than it did earlier today, but at least my headache has lessened. Sebastian's walking, too, though Becky seems much more concerned about preventing him from stumbling than James does me.

When I lose my footing again, he pokes me hard in the back before yanking on my arm.

After we've walked for many minutes, James asks Becky, "You ever see that TV series *Big Love*?"

"*Big Love*? Maybe. It sounds kind of familiar."

"This guy has three wives and lots of children. They live a great life together."

"Oh, was that hottie Bill Paxton in it? I was so sad when he died. You know, after he died, he came to me in a dream and told me he wasn't really dead, that he just had to leave Hollywood because of all the bad things there. He called it Hollyweird. I wonder what he thinks about all this? Do you think Hollywood has the power back?"

"I think they got bombed. A nuke probably blew them all to smithereens. But, yeah, that's the show, the one with Bill Paxton. Maybe we should do the same thing. You could have sister wives."

"Sister wives," Becky repeats.

"They'd help you run the house, and we'd all be one big, happy family. I met a guy west of here doing the same thing. He's got amazing plans. He's working on building his family too."

I have no idea what show he's talking about, but I know there was some sort of reality show about a man married to more than one person. I never watched it but heard people in school talking about it and making fun of it. Reality TV was a big deal . . . when there was still TV.

Even though I don't know exactly what he's talking about, I don't like the sound of it. What kind of weirdo would want to have several wives and a boatload of children, especially with the way things are now? I can't imagine wanting to have a baby during the apocalypse.

Sebastian and I need to get away from these two. James sounds about as nutty as Becky. And meaner too.

We stumble through the dark for many minutes before James says, "It's just ahead. This'll be a good spot to lay low for a few days till their people move on. Then we'll take off and build our new lives. It'll be great, Becky."

"You hear that, Taylor? Just a few days and then we'll be okay, away from your Uncle Greg who insists on keeping us apart."

Through the darkness, the outline of a large building begins to take shape.

"S'pose we'd better let these two do their business before going in," James says.

"Should we untie them?" Becky asks.

"No way. Can't trust them. 'Specially the girl."

"How can they . . . with their hands tied?"

"You'll help them. Take the girl first, just around the corner." He grabs my shoulders and stares into my eyes.

Even in the darkness, I can see the evil there.

His voice is low, menacing. "I'll kill the boy if you so much as think of trying to escape. Got it?" He pulls a gun out of the back of his pants, carelessly waving it in Sebastian's direction. Noises escape from both me and my brother. He'd do it. He'd kill him.

Swallowing hard, I give a nod.

Becky helps me shimmy my pants down so I can go to the bathroom. I'm embarrassed and angry—scared too—but after James's threat, I do what I need to do.

She then helps Sebastian while James presses me against the side of the building with one hand, the gun in the other. He's not exactly pointing it at me, but I certainly understand the implication.

After we're finished, we move toward the front door.

"You were so smart to find this place for us," Becky gushes. "I'd forgotten all about it. When I was a little girl, they held dances here. But, goodness, it's been a long time since it was used for anything."

"I thought you said it was a schoolhouse?" James asks as he opens a door. It lets out a groan of protest.

"First it was a one-room schoolhouse, then after they closed it down, they used it for community parties and dances. Oh, we'd have such fun."

"Over here," James orders, marching me across the wooden floor.

Becky lets out a little squeal of delight. "Oh look, Taylor! Your new daddy made a perfect little nest for you."

She gently helps Sebastian onto a large mattress covered in a sheet and piled high with pillows—some used for sleeping, others are fancy decorator pillows with sayings embroidered on them, fringe, tassels, or other items. It's quite the collection.

James shoves me on to the same mattress. "Yeah, well, your brother and those others better not try anything, or else we'll show them."

"You said that would only be a last resort. I don't . . . you promised no one would get hurt. Greg isn't a bad man. He just doesn't understand how much I need to be with my son. I don't know why he's been keeping Taylor from me, but I'm sure he has his reasons. You can't hurt him."

"I'm not going to hurt him. We talked about this. I'll create a diversion so we can get away. They'll be so focused on what's happening, they'll never even know we slipped out the back."

I glance to Sebastian. His eyes are drooping as he fights to stay awake. Does he understand what's going on?

In the almost year since the planes were shot out of the sky, he's managed to partially maintain his little boy innocence, thanks to our mom. Even when things were terrible, with death all around us, she did her best to protect him. Me too. It wasn't completely possible to shield us from everything, but we were truly spared from the worst of it.

But now we're held captive by a couple of crazies. This could get bad.

Becky is clearly—what'd that guy in the courtyard say about her? Something about cheese and a cracker. And James, he's his own brand of crazy, talking about sister wives and now this plan for a diversion.

As the two continue their conversation of being followed and hiding out, the subject suddenly changes. Becky declares she needs a new dress and more clothes for Sebastian.

Then she even mentions me. "If we're going to have a daughter, too, she and I could get matching outfits. I always thought it was so cute when mothers and daughters dressed alike."

"It's not like there's a mall to go and buy those now," James scoffs. "I suppose maybe I could find jeans and the same-colored T-shirts for you."

"I don't wear jeans, silly. You know I'm a dresses-only kind of gal. Beautiful, flowing, feminine dresses. They're what I like. And that's what our new daughter—what'd we decide to name her?"

"Didn't come up with anything yet. We could just ask her what her name is. It might be a fine name she has already."

Becky looks over to me. Even in the darkness, I can see the smile she gives me. It's kind, almost loving. "Is that right, sweetie?" she asks me. "Do you have a perfectly fine name?"

I make a mumbling sound through my gag, the movement of the cloth in my mouth causing my gag reflex to react.

"Don't you dare puke!" James rushes toward me. "I can't handle that nasty stuff."

With my eyes watering, I take several deep breaths through my nose. As I start to calm and the urge to vomit leaves, James clenches his fist, lifting it in my direction. "You'd best be glad you got that under control."

"Maybe we should take it out of her mouth and let her breathe normally for a bit. Taylor too. And we should get them some water. They must be so thirsty."

James shakes his head. "Can't risk it. We need them quiet in case the searchers head out this way. We'll let them settle in and get them a drink in a bit."

"I know you're right. I just hate seeing them uncomfortable. Look at my poor Taylor. He's ready to fall asleep but just isn't comfortable."

"He's on a nest of pillows! He'll be fine. Both of them will be."

Becky moves toward us, slipping out of her shoes. She plops on the mattress and positions herself between Sebastian and me. "There now, Mommy's here." She reaches out a hand to pat my head. "You can both relax and go back to sleep."

I don't know how long I slept, but it's still completely dark when Becky shakes me awake. In a whisper, she says, "I'm going to push your bandanna down and give you a drink of water. You can't make a sound or James will hear and . . . well, that wouldn't be good. Not good at all."

She moves the bandanna and holds a glass to my lips. I drink greedily. When she takes the glass away, my voice is hoarse as I say, "Seb—I mean, *Taylor*, did he get water?"

"Shh. Of course my little Taylor-pooh did." She moves slightly so I can see Sebastian.

He gives me a nod as Becky moves my bandanna back into place.

"Now both of you get a good night's sleep. We'll rest here a few days, then we're going to Canada. It's going to be so great. I heard they even have electricity and running cars there. We'll be a happy family."

Chapter 15

I wake to humming, not *Twinkle, Twinkle* this time but some sort of other children's song. Daylight fills the room. I look to the other side of the mattress.

Sebastian is sitting up, leaning against the wall. He still has the gag in place—so do I—but his hands are no longer secured behind his back. They're now taped in front. Unlike me, with my numb arms awkwardly behind my back, he looks a lot more comfortable.

Glancing around the space, I take in the sparse room. There're boxes piled in a far corner and a couple of chairs near us. Becky's again in a rocker, possibly the same one as before, as she hums and knits. Her needles are clicking away, out of tune with the song.

I adjust my position. The movement causes my bladder to scream out in need of relief. A growl from my stomach reminds me how long it's been since we've eaten.

Looking up, she gives me a smile. "Good morning, Daisy."

Daisy? Goodness, no. That's as old fashioned as Sadie.

Becky furrows her brow and makes a face. "No, that's not right. When I say it out loud, it just doesn't fit. You're not a Daisy." She moves her mouth around, making her upper lip touch her nose. "How about Amanda?"

I raise my eyebrows at her.

She lets out a soft laugh. "Nope, guess not. You know, I think, if we pull up your hair to show off those amazing cheekbones, a new name will reveal itself. It's like finding a crystal. The right one will reveal its name to you. Have you ever had a crystal tell you its name?"

I give a shake of my head, not entirely sure what she's talking about.

"You poor dear. You must be so uncomfortable. I wanted to untie you and Taylor completely, but James said it's just too risky. He thinks you might try and run away. I know my little Taylor-pooh won't go anywhere. He's just happy to be with his mama now, after being kept away from me for so long. With you being new to our family . . . well, maybe Jamesy is right. But . . . "

She screws up her face again. "I could loosen your arms so you can move them around a little, then we'll move them to the front. Would that help?"

Anticipation courses through me as I give a vigorous nod. If she loosens my hands, maybe, just maybe, I can use them to attack. If I can get her on the ground, it could give us enough time to get away. I close my eyes and take a deep breath. I need a plan.

Being in this position for so long, my arms are like spaghetti—numb and useless. Hopefully my legs are still strong.

We've practiced a lot of kicks, but most from standing. A few times, we've done forward rolls—something like a somersault—followed by a side kick from the ground. A side kick might just work.

I close my eyes as I remember how I kicked James as he was grabbing for me. That kick barely even slowed him down.

I can do better. I'll put all my strength in it, flipping to my side and kicking with the leg off the mattress. My kicking leg needs to be the one with my good toe. Today, the hurt one is not only throbbing but feels like it's on fire. It's about a hundred times worse than yesterday.

Taking a deep breath, I make my plan.

As soon as my hands are loose, I'll roll to the right side and kick hard with my left foot. Then we'll . . .

We'll what?

Getting off the mattress might be hard with all these stupid pillows everywhere. And I need to grab Sebastian too—with my useless spaghetti arms—then limp out of here without putting weight on my aching toe.

And where's James? He's not here. Is he outside? Or gone? If he's gone, maybe, just maybe, we can get away.

I look over at Sebastian. He opens his eyes wide and gives me a slight nod as he lifts his hands a few inches above his lap. The tape is loose, barely hanging there. He's been working it.

I attempt a smile around my gag. Whatever I do, Sebastian will be ready.

He's had most of the same combat training as I have. While there're a few things Kimba and Rey don't let him and Naomi do, because they're smaller and younger, he still watches and knows the things I know. In fact, he may be better at some of it than I am.

My heart falls as I remember the day Jameson grabbed me and how I flubbed my getaway, landing smack in the mud. For a moment, it strikes me as funny that my two nemeses' have such similar names.

I close my eyes. Even though Jameson is often a pain, and he did land me in the mud, I don't think he truly wished to harm me. James, on the other hand, may put up a show for Becky, but he'd hurt me— and Sebastian too—without hesitation. I can see it in his eyes. He's evil through and through.

"Just let me finish this row, then we'll untie you for a minute and let you stretch your arms. After that, I'll put them in front of you, just like I did for Taylor." A look of concern crosses Becky's face. "You wouldn't . . . I can trust you, right?"

I bob my head up and down, smiling at her around my gag.

Sure, Becky. You can trust me all right. Trust me to do whatever it takes to get Sebastian away from you.

"That's good, dear. Taylor needs an older sister who can look out for him. Jamesy was right about you being an asset. You'll be able to help us with not just Taylor-pooh but all the other children too. See this?" She lifts the knitting she's working on.

"It's a baby blanket. I don't think it'll be long before we have a little brother or sister for you. It's going to be so wonderful. I always wanted a big family. But when the doctor said— " Becky lets out a sigh. "It doesn't matter now. James loves children and wants to fill up a house with the pitter patter of little feet. Isn't that cute?" Becky giggles.

Her last row of knitting seems to take forever. She's humming again, a new song I don't recognize. I force myself to remain calm. Envisioning the plan in my head helps. I think about each move, about how my foot needs to be flat and my toes pulled back. A solid kick can get me the time we'll need to escape the fluffy mattress.

When she reaches the end of the row, she turns the project to start a new one.

Did she forget about me? I make a noise in my throat.

Becky looks up with a start. "Oh, dear. I got so wrapped up in my baby blanket."

She puts her knitting in a bag on the floor next to her chair, poking the single loose needle into the ball of yarn, before heaving herself up. She's not a heavy person, hardly anyone is these days, but she seems weary as she makes her way to her feet.

I wonder how much sleep she got last night. Can her tiredness be an advantage to us as we attempt our escape?

Not attempt. We *will* escape. We must.

Becky takes a step toward the mattress before stopping and cocking her head to one side. "What do you think of Crystal? Does that sound like a name you might like?"

Crystal isn't bad. I give a slight lift of my shoulders, which results in pain running through my body.

"No, maybe not. Hmm. We'll keep working on it. Don't you worry none. We'll find the perfect name for you." She gives me a smile, one that's sweet and kind.

A pang of guilt runs through me as I think about what I'm about to do. It's obvious Becky is mentally ill. I don't want to hurt her. But I may have to in order for us to get away.

When she reaches the edge of the mattress, I'm shaking with nervousness.

"Now turn a little so I can get to your arms."

I gasp at the sound of a knife—a switchblade—opening.

"Don't be scared. I need to cut the tape. It'll be easier. Try not to move. I don't want to nick you." There's a new tone to her voice—not the light, playful, almost childlike tone she usually has. Something harder, sinister maybe.

A stab of pain shoots through my wrist, causing me to jump.

"I told you to hold still," Becky says, her voice gruff and angry. "Now you're bleeding like a stuck pig. I'll have to get something to bandage it. There. You're loose."

My arms sag to my side.

"Don't just let those arms hang. Put some pressure on your cut while I find a towel or something."

After so many hours in the same position, even trying to bring my hands together in front of me is a challenge. The cut, on the thumb side of my left wrist, is bleeding freely. It doesn't really hurt, not beyond the first shock of pain anyway.

I struggle to force my right hand toward my left, then press my thumb against it. The pressure isn't much, since everything feels far away.

I look for Becky. She's rummaging through one of the boxes. Sitting on the floor, next to the mattress, is the knife she used.

With an old piece of clothing in hand, Becky strides back to the mattress. "Did you get the bleeding stopped?"

I lift a shoulder in response.

"Let me see," she demands.

With my thumb still pressed over the cut, I feebly lift my arms in her direction. A tingly burn runs from my fingertips up my wrists. I rotate my shoulders.

Becky presses an orange shirt against the cut. "It doesn't look too bad. It's almost stopped bleeding." She gives me a smile.

I bob my head once. No matter how nice she may seem at the moment, I'm doing what I must to get Sebastian out of here. There's definitely a dark side to her, as evidenced by the cut on my wrist. I can't help but think that, from the way she was acting, the wound was on purpose.

She fusses with me for several minutes, making sure the bleeding has stopped, then takes her knife and cuts a strip of material from the bottom of the shirt. "We'll tie this around it like a bandage. Is the feeling coming back now?"

I flex my fingers and rotate my shoulders. I'm better.

"Yes?" she asks. "If so, we'd better get you secured again. Can't have James coming back and seeing you undone. He wouldn't like that. Not at all. He told me before he left, 'Becky, you don't let those kids loose, not until we're safely away from here.' But I knew how uncomfortable you were. Once I reworked Taylor's arms, he felt much better. Didn't you, Taylor?"

She looks over at Sebastian; he answers with a shrug.

I look at him and raise my eyebrows, trying to send a signal—a signal to be ready.

My dry mouth begs for another drink of water. I lift my hands to the gag and yank it down. "Water?" I croak.

"Oh, dear me. Of course. Taylor, honey, do you need another drink too? You just hold on a minute, let me get your arms put back and we'll get you a drink." She motions to a jug sitting beside her knitting bag.

As much as I want the water, I know now it's time to make my move, not let her tie me up again, get the water, and then attack. *Now.* I move my mouth around, flexing the muscles and relishing in being free. I consider screaming but assume there's no point.

94

She grabs a roll of tape, then moves toward me. "Now we need to get you put back together before Jamesy returns. He won't be happy about you being loose. I'm so glad you're being such a good little girl and not causing me trouble. Such a wonderful child you are." She gives me a huge smile.

"When we get to Canada and find our nice, new home, we're going to be such a happy family. I already know you're going to be a big help to me with your little brothers and sisters." She motions for me to move my arms to the front.

I give her a nod, putting my wrists together and keeping my arms pulled tight at my sides. My hands rest on my belly button.

Her brow furrows as she moves closer.

When she's at the edge of the mattress, I drop to my right side. Giving a loud grunt, I kick her in the hip with my left foot.

She lets out a gasp.

As she bends over, I kick her again, this time catching her shoulder and sending her sailing several feet.

She lets out a cry of pain as she hits the ground—hard.

I jump up, hitting the floor. The pain in my toe soars through my body.

Sebastian is by my side; Becky's curled in a ball, crying.

Sebastian motions to my single shower sandal. His hands are undone, and he yanks down his gag.

I slide into my shoe and grab his hand, yanking him toward the front door.

"Wait," he says, running toward the water jug.

Seeing the knitting needle, poked into the yarn ball but not attached to the work, I tell him, "Grab the needle too."

He looks where I'm pointing and gives me a nod. "Where's her knife?"

"By the mattress," I say as I run back for it.

"Don't!" Becky cries around her tears. "Please don't do this. Don't take my Taylor away from me again."

"I'm not Taylor." My brother puffs up his chest. "My name is Sebastian. And she's my sister, Sadie—my *real* sister. I don't know you. I'm sorry . . . sorry you don't have your son with you. But I'm not him."

"Let's go." I shove the knife in my pocket. "We have to get out of here."

"No, please!" Becky wails. "Stay. Please stay. We'll be so happy. So happy together, a real family."

Sebastian puts his hands on his hips. "I'm not your son. I'm sorry."

Chapter 16

Becky's cries grow louder as we run to the front door. She pleads with us to stay. I urge Sebastian out the door, the brightness of the day nearly blinding us.

"Where do we go?" Sebastian asks. "Do you know where town is?"

"Not really. Let's get away from here. Stay hidden in case that crazy James comes back." I motion to a line of trees a hundred yards away. "Give me the jug."

"Your arm's bleeding again." He hands me the water.

I give a nod. "Let's go. I'll fix it when we get there." I carry the water with my cut arm and hold on to the bandage with the other hand, trying to keep from dripping blood on the ground. My one-shoed gait is awkward.

I glance down at Sebastian's feet; he's still wearing his tennis shoes and is moving without issue.

When we reach the tree line, which is bordering a narrow creek or ditch, Sebastian asks which way we should go.

"I think they said we're north of town, so . . . " I point to the right. "That should be the way toward town." I reposition the cloth around my wrist, turning it so a clean spot captures the blood, tightening it enough to hold it in place.

"Should be? Don't you know?"

"Take a drink of water, then we have to go."

"You first. I had some while you were asleep."

I give a nod before tilting the jug up. The plastic gallon container is just under half full. As the cool, clear water fills my mouth and dribbles down my chin, I hope it's been purified and isn't straight from this stream we're walking next to. The last thing we need is to get sick from dirty water. As soon as I'm done drinking, I pass it to Sebastian.

He gulps some down before handing it back. "Do you think she's okay? Did you hurt her?" he asks.

"She's fine, now let's move." I grab his arm.

He stops moving, digging in his feet. "Are you sure? There's something wrong in her head. But she was nice to us."

"We have to go." I pull his arm. "And kidnapping and tying us up isn't being nice."

He gives me a nod and starts to move. "I know. She's just . . . there's something really wrong with her. I don't think she meant to hurt us. But James—he'll hurt us. He has mean eyes."

I give a slight nod. He's looney tunes also, but Sebastian's right. Where Becky thought Sebastian was her son, and she showed him love—me too, but to a lesser degree—James is just plain mean.

We've gone about two hundred yards when a booming voice yells, "Where are you little brats? Get yourselves back here right now and apologize to your mama!"

Sebastian makes a whimpering sound.

"Shh." I motion for him to bend down.

He stares at me with wide eyes, gesturing in the direction of James's voice.

I keep my voice low. "We have to keep moving, but try not to make any sound or move the trees and brush." I'm limping and moving as quickly as I can on my sore toe. Even with the pain, I pick up the pace. James can't catch us. If he does . . .

"Where is he?" Sebastian whispers.

"Don't whisper, just talk low but normal. Remember?" Last winter, while making our way to Wyoming, Mom and Ben taught us how to move quietly and talk so we wouldn't be heard.

Sebastian nods and lifts his hands.

"We need to keep going," I command.

We move fast but carefully. As the stream makes a bend, a house comes into view.

"Should we go there?" Sebastian asks.

"No, keep moving."

More yelling from James, including a string of profanities, causes my heart rate to increase. James is closer now—too close. And from the way his voice is carrying, he's not in the trees but next to them, making better time than we are.

Another house appears on the opposite side of the small stream. "There. Cross over the creek."

Making a big jump, Sebastian lands easily on the other side. I step over and plop my foot in the mud, which sucks at my sandal. I pull hard to release it, and the plastic strap across the top breaks off.

A crashing through the brush causes me to turn and look. I catch a glimpse of James, still behind us but moving fast. He's now along the water.

"You!" he yells.

"C'mon," Sebastian cries, yanking on my arm.

We take off running, me in stocking feet, Sebastian by my side.

"Go around the house." I motion with my arm.

"Knock on the door? See if someone can help us?"

Several windows have been broken out. "No one's here. Keep running. There's another house up ahead."

"More than one!" Sebastian says. "It's the town. We found the town!"

As we reach the next house, the dirt to my right puffs up, followed by a large bang.

"What's that?" Sebastian asks, turning to look at me. "Did he— "

"Keep going! Run in front of the building." I push him around the corner of the house as another shot hits the ground.

"He's shooting at us?" My brother's eyes are wide.

"We need t-to keep something between us and h-him." I pant out my words. "Keep going to the next house. Over there."

The distance between the houses is decreasing, but the roads are still gravel instead of pavement. We may be in a more populated area, but we're still not in town.

We've reached the next house when James fires two more times, one right after the other. Unlike before, there isn't a cloud of dirt or any indication where the shot hit.

"Where do we go?" Sebastian asks, breathing hard.

"This one's abandoned too. Go to the next houses. We have to keep moving."

"I don't know . . . if I can. I'm having . . . a hard . . . time," Sebastian pants.

"We must!" I say through my own ragged breath. My toe throbs, and the heel of the other foot aches where I came down hard on a piece of gravel. I want to stop, too, but if we do, there's no telling what James will do to us.

Sebastian gives me a weary nod.

"Run fast." I give him a slight push. "We need distance between him and us."

Pulling on an unknown strength, Sebastian digs in, sprinting to the next house. I'm right behind him.

"The barn there, let's find a place to hide." I point to a barn hidden by the house.

"Is it safe?" he asks as we continue our run.

I come down hard on my messed-up toe, letting out a small yelp.

"Sadie!" Sebastian hisses. "Are you okay?"

"Keep going."

He gives me a nod. When we reach the large barn door, he shakes his head. "How does it open?"

"Find a smaller door, something easier." We rush around the side of the barn.

"There!" Sebastian points to a regular walk-in door at the far end of the building.

"Good job!" We hustle to the door.

Sebastian turns the knob. "I can't get it."

"Scootch." I bump him with my hip, then turn the knob hard to the left. It moves, but the latch stays engaged.

Please don't let it be locked.

I turn it the other way, then wiggle it back and forth, giving a hard yank. The door blows open, knocking me back.

"Inside," I say needlessly.

Sebastian's already moving into the building. "Can you lock it?"

"I don't know," I answer as I shut the door. I fumble with the door a moment until I notice a simple push-button lock. It isn't much, but it's something.

"Will he find us? Did we leave footprints?"

"The gravel should help," I answer. "I hope so at least. I don't know how easy, or hard, it'll be for him to track us, but . . . we need to hide."

"Over there?" He points to a tractor parked on the far side. "Or there?" His finger moves to a stall of some sort.

"Yep, there."

The stall is closer to the door but might give us a better chance to get back out of the barn if James comes in. The tractor is too far away, and I'm afraid we'll end up trapped.

As soon as we're situated and our breathing has returned to normal, Sebastian asks, "Is your foot okay?"

"Which one?" I give a small laugh.

"Did you hurt the other one?"

"Bruised my heel or something from running barefoot. I'm fine. Here, have some water."

He takes several noisy gulps before passing it back to me. "We need to pray."

I narrow my eyes at my little brother. "Go ahead. But keep quiet about it."

He grabs for my hand, the one with the strip of material around the wrist. It's not actively bleeding, though the blood-crusted cloth looks pretty terrible.

Sebastian drops his head and closes his eyes. His lips move, but no sound comes out for several seconds. Then his eyes pop open and he lifts his head. "We're going to be okay. But we need . . . we need to be ready. And you need to pray too."

I start to shake my head but stop midmotion, switching it to a nod. I give his hand a squeeze and bob my head. Sebastian increases the pressure on my hand.

In a quiet, completely calm voice, which sounds many years older than his age of eight, my brother says, "Lord, we ask you fill us with Your Holy Presence. Let us feel Your protection. Keep us safe and hidden under Your wings. Cover that man's eyes so he can't see us, his ears so he can't hear us. Please just . . . please, God. Help us."

He squeezes my hand. From our days of round-robin praying with my mom and grandma, I know he's suggesting it's my turn.

I let out a breath. Sebastian was so earnest, so fervent in his prayer. And I know he truly believes there's a God and He'll step in and save us, even with everything we've been through.

When Mom did the things she did to keep us safe—when Uncle Wes was killed, when we found our grandparents dead, and all the terrible things we knew were happening as we made our way from Oregon to Washington, through Idaho and Montana, and then into Wyoming—Sebastian has always been faithful.

He always believed God would keep us safe.

But not me. When I examine my heart, there's no "religion" there. There's no belief there's someone, some omnipresent figure, able or willing to help us. When it comes down to it, I lack any belief in God. And not just because of the bad things that happened. I never believed before.

We'd go to church, pray, and read our Bible during family time. I did it all, but not because I believed, only because it was expected of me. I didn't think Mom and Sebastian believing was wrong or unreasonable. It was just never something I accepted. *God* was not something I accepted.

I'll admit, when Mom turned her back on God, part of me was happy. She and I could have this in common. She'd always been so ardent before, and I went along with it. I never told her or anyone else how I really felt, that it was fine for them but not for me. I didn't feel the same way as her about God. I didn't believe He was my Lord and Savior.

I'd made a profession of faith and was baptized, but it was all fake. Phony. I might know the words to say, but that's as far as it went. But even after Mom walked away from God, from Jesus, I couldn't bear to tell her the truth—I'd always been a faker.

I shake my head. "Okay, God. If You're there, we need Your help. Like, really need Your help."

"Amen." Sebastian squeezes my hand.

We sit quietly, my ears straining for any sounds that might indicate James has found us. The water I gulped down sloshes slightly in my empty stomach. We haven't eaten since yesterday. Sitting in the quiet, dark barn, the hunger rushes over me like a wave. My stomach lets out a loud rumble.

Sebastian flares his eyes at me and juts out his chin, then his stomach makes the same noise, as if answering mine. Or commiserating.

Twenty-four hours without food isn't much. We've done that before—many times, in fact. Going days without food, holed up waiting out a storm, with Ben going out any time it was clear enough to see so he could check the snares—which were almost always empty—was much more difficult than this. At least it should've been.

Maybe eating regularly for the past several months has made my system miss it more. My body's no longer used to being starved half to death. And judging by the sounds coming from Sebastian, he's in the same boat.

"I need to go to the bathroom." His voice is low, like it should be.

"Number one or number two?"

"Just one."

I give him a nod. "Step over there. I'll go after you're done."

After relieving ourselves, we move back to our hiding spot. It feels like hours as we hide in the darkened barn. The small cut on my arm is no longer a problem, and even my feet have stopped hurting. The toe doesn't throb, and the heel doesn't hurt. Other than being hungry, I don't feel too bad.

We've finished the water when Sebastian says, "Maybe he gave up?"

I shake my head. "I don't know. I wouldn't think he would, but . . . maybe. Maybe he thinks we got away and made it back to town."

"And they took off? So they don't get in trouble?"

I tilt my head to the side. Could it be?

A look crosses my brother's face before he shakes his head. "I don't think so. They didn't give up. We should go, leave this barn and find somewhere else to hide."

"Why?"

"I don't know. I just . . . we need to go."

Searching his face in the dim light, I ask, "What's wrong?"

He shakes his head. "My stomach hurts. I want to get out of here and keep moving. I want to find Mom."

"Mine hurts too. I'm starving."

"No, that's not the problem."

"Are you scared? It's okay to be scared."

"It's not that. We need to go." He stands up, clutching the knitting needle like it's a knife and he's some kind of maniac psycho ready to commit murder. "You need the knife. And we should bring the jug so we can refill it." A grimace crosses his face as he wearily bends and picks up the empty plastic container.

"Are you okay?" I put a hand on his arm.

"We need to go." He takes several intentional steps toward the door.

I grip his arm. "Wait. Let me check outside and make sure it's safe." My heart is pounding again. Like Sebastian, I now feel an urgency to leave.

"The knife, Sadie." He wags his finger at me.

"Fine, *Dad.*" I stick my tongue out at him.

He returns the gesture. The moment of frivolity lessens the knot in my stomach.

I slide the knife out of my pocket and click the button to extend the blade. Once open, the size is comparable to the knife Kimba gave me for my birthday. The weight of it feels similar, too, maybe a little heavier than mine but not substantially.

Left hand on the doorknob, right hand holding the knife and at the ready, I turn to Sebastian and mouth, "You ready?"

He makes a shooing motion with his hands. "We need to go." There's a tremor in his voice. Fear?

My instincts say to ease the door open, peek out and make sure no one is there. But both Kimba and Rey have told us over and over to open the door and go out ready. That's part of the firearms training, though. Is it the same when we're carrying a knife and a knitting needle?

"We're going to go fast," I say. "We're running straight for the next house down the road."

"Your feet are okay to run?"

"Don't worry about me. You run. Get to the house and move behind it. Then we'll keep going."

As soon as I tell Sebastian to go, he's out of the barn like a shot. I'm right behind him.

He makes it to the house in what's probably world-record speed. If things ever return to normal, I'm going to tell our mom to start training Sebastian for the Olympics. He could beat every sprinter there.

When I round the house, I skid to a stop.

Sebastian is standing stock still, staring at Becky. She's been crying, her eyes red and her face dirty with smudges.

"Why'd you do it, Taylor?" she asks, her voice full of sadness. "Why'd you leave your mama?"

"I'm not Taylor." My brother's voice is quiet. "I know you miss your little boy, but I'm not him. My mom is Leanne. She's had a hard time, too, and I need to get back to her. I think . . . she might not be okay if my sister and I don't go back. Some of the things . . . "

Becky blinks several times. "The things that happened, they've been bad." She shakes her head and then squints her eyes. "You're not Taylor."

"I'm not Taylor," Sebastian confirms.

"I can see that now. You don't even really look much like him. I've made a mistake."

104

"Please," Sebastian begs. "We need to go. I'm sorry about your little boy, but we need to go."

He turns toward me. His eyes go wide. "Sa— "

Strong arms go around me and crush my arms to my side. I let out a yell, louder than any noise I've made in my life.

Sebastian joins me, screaming at the top of his lungs. "Let my sister go! We're not staying here!"

James's stinky hand comes over my mouth. "Shut that kid up," he orders Becky.

"He's not Taylor." Tears stream down her face. "I don't know what I was thinking. He's not my son."

Sebastian's yelling so loud I can barely hear Becky.

James lets out a roar. "It doesn't matter! We're taking these brats and starting our family."

I bite James's hand, catching enough skin he lets out a yelp and moves it. With my mouth free, I yell, "Run, Sebastian!"

"Mom! Help us! Find us! Mom!" Sebastian yells.

James's hand finds my mouth again. "Shut up, boy, or I'll kill her." He adjusts his grip on me. Other than covering my mouth and holding my head still, I'm almost loose. I start to move when something hard presses against my shoulder. I move my eyes to the side, turning my head slightly. He's jabbed his handgun against me.

Sebastian's mouth slams shut as his eyes puddle with tears. He gives a slight nod.

"Step over by your mama," James says, using the gun as a pointer.

"He's not Taylor." Becky lets out a sigh. "I was wrong, James. I don't know what I was thinking. We need to keep looking for my little boy."

"Of course he isn't Taylor! Your kid is dead."

Becky gasps.

"But that don't matter none. The boy will make a fine replacement. You'll love him just like your own son. And we'll start our little family, adding more children as we go. This girl here— " He jabs the gun in my arm again. "She might not be much to look at, but she'll be a help to us, taking care of the little ones and . . . and maybe more."

"No, James." Becky shakes her head. "I don't want to take this boy from his own mama. Didn't you hear him? She's been through too much. And I know you're lying to me about my Taylor. You just want me to go with you to Canada, but I can't. I have to stay here. I must stay and find my Taylor. Just like this little boy misses his mama, my Taylor is missing me."

"You're nuttier than a fruitcake, lady," James growls. "Your kid is dead. If you want to have a family, the only way is by starting with these two. Heck, you can't even have any more kids, so we need this girl to get us babies. Don't you understand that?"

I close my eyes. Becky's not the only one who's nuttier than a fruitcake. James is not only nuts, but also an absolute predator. I clench my hand around the grip of the knife. Lifting my wrist slightly, I stare at Sebastian, trying to get his attention. His eyes are focused on James. I make a noise deep in my throat.

"Shut up," James orders.

Sebastian looks at me. I lift my wrist again and open my eyes wide. He's still gripping the knitting needle in his hand. I lift my chin and raise my eyebrows. Sebastian responds by lifting his chin and moving the hand holding the knitting needle.

I take a deep breath and let it out slowly. Then another. This time, as I'm letting it out, I stop and hold it. With a quick motion, I jab the knife backward, aiming for James's leg.

It connects. He lets out a howl.

As he instinctively bends forward, I ram my head back, connecting with his chin, or maybe his nose—something hard and bony that hurts both me and him. He releases his grip on me as I jam my elbow into his sternum.

Sebastian is by my side. Letting out a war cry, he plunges the sharp knitting needle into James's arm—the arm that was holding the pistol.

James screams as the gun drops to the ground. With a knife in his leg and a wooden needle sticking out of his arm, I turn and raise my sock-clad foot with the injured toe, kicking him solid in the gut and sending him backward. He lands hard on his butt.

With James on the ground, I bend over and pick up the gun.

"Run!" I yell to Sebastian.

Not only does he take off, once again sprinting like an Olympian, but so does Becky.

"Becky! Don't you do this!" James's voice booms through the air.

"Keep going," Becky calls. "I'll make sure he doesn't hurt you!"

"Don't stop, Sebastian," I order when he looks back at Becky and me.

I feel her fall back. I turn to look over my shoulder. She's still near us, running, but dropping back several yards.

James is limping toward us. His angry words move with him, promising we're all *going to get it* as soon as he catches us. I dig in, speeding up to run side by side with my brother.

Sebastian reaches out his hand. "C'mon, Sadie. We can't let him catch us."

A lady steps out in front of us, blocking our path.

"Sebastian!" I cry as I yank on his arm.

"It's okay!" the woman yells. "I'm Marie. We met before. Keep running. I'll help you!"

"Marie!" Becky yells. "James has gone nuts. He thinks . . . you have to find my brother. We need help."

"This isn't over!" James yells as Sebastian and I move past Marie. I glance over my shoulder. James is wagging his finger at us as he turns around and begins limping in the other direction.

"He's probably . . . going after . . . the rifle," Becky gasps as she catches up to us. "She grabbed the gun."

I look down at my hand, wrapped around the grip of the gun. At least my finger isn't anywhere near the trigger. I don't even consciously remember holding it while I was running. "Here." I say, keeping the muzzle down while I hand it to Marie.

A small smile crosses my face when Marie opens the wheel of the revolver to check if it's loaded. "Let's go." She nods. "Let's get you to town."

"How'd you find us?" Sebastian asks, narrowing his eyes.

"We've been looking for you. I heard the yelling. I was with a friend, but she went for help."

Marie takes us past another house and turns down a road. We've barely made the corner when she says, "See? There's your mom and some of your people."

"Mom!" Sebastian yells, sprinting once again.

I follow his lead, not only running but calling out for my mom.

"They found you! You're okay?" Mom asks as she runs toward us. Within seconds, she's crushing us in a hug. As skinny as my mom is, she's still plenty strong. "My babies! I was hoping . . . *praying* . . . we'd find you, that you'd be okay." She kisses my cheek, my hair, then does the same to Sebastian.

"We're okay," I say. "Okay . . . " My breathing comes in short gasps. Everything begins to spin, then turns gray.

Chapter 17

"Good morning, baby girl! Time to get ready for school."

I turn over, pushing the pillow over my head.

"C'mon Sadie, your alarm went off fifteen minutes ago. You need to get up or you won't have time for breakfast."

I open one eye and peer at Mom. She's already dressed for work, hair nicely done, understated but perfect makeup, and a smile on her face—a kind and engaging smile. "I made pancakes. Sebastian's already eating."

"Pancakes," I repeat as my stomach rumbles. "You only make pancakes on Saturday."

She lifts a shoulder. "And special occasions. Your first day of high school counts, don't you think?"

"I do love pancakes." I stretch my arms over my head. Something pulls slightly as I do, giving me a twinge of pain. I furrow my brow.

"Sadie? Did you say something?"

"Hmm?" I mutter as I shift slightly, trying to get comfortable.

"Oh, baby girl! You're waking up!"

"Mom?" I stare at the white ceiling. One of my arms feels heavy. There's tape on it and a tube coming out. My eyes follow the tube to a hook on the cheery wallpapered wall. I glance to my side, where I heard Mom's voice. She's there, next to me.

My mom.

But not wearing work clothes or makeup. Not even wearing a smile—not a real one anyway. Her hair hangs limp around her shoulders, her face drawn. And she's too skinny. Tears stream down her face as she gives me a nod.

"Hey, sleeping beauty." A grimace crosses her face. "I was . . ." She shakes her head. "It's been a rough few days." She reaches out to gently brush a strand of hair away from my face. "But you're okay. And Sebastian's okay. Everything will be fine."

"Did you make pancakes?" I ask.

She gives a slight shake of her head. "We have stew. Do you feel well enough to sit up and eat, have more than you're getting from the bag of saline?"

"I must have been dreaming. You made pancakes. We were . . . we were back home." I look around the hotel room as memories of the previous months since the attacks come rushing back. The memories overwhelm me. I bury my face in the pillow and bawl.

Mom rubs my back while making soothing sounds. It's several minutes before my crying settles and turns in to hiccups.

Mom lets out a small laugh. "There you go, it's passing now. You've been so brave all these months. I don't . . . I can't even remember you crying before now."

I shake my head. Not like this. Definitely not. Hot, angry tears will often sting my eyes, tears filled with frustration. And there have been a few weepy tears when things were bad, when my mom was taken away and I thought I'd never see her again. Even then, I tried to be brave, to keep it together so Sebastian didn't know how scared I was.

And maybe I had a small cry once when it had been a few days since we'd eaten and I thought we might starve to death. That was hard. I was so scared then. Scared Mom and Sebastian would die first and I'd be all alone. Then Ben came back with food and . . . well, here we are, still alive and in Roundup, Montana. We're almost to Lewistown, where Mom's aunt lives and where we'll hopefully find safety.

"You're okay, baby girl. He didn't . . . he didn't hurt you, right?"

"I'm fine. Who did this?" I ask, lifting my arm with the IV.

"There's a doctor in town. The wagon that was late getting back . . . do you remember that discussion?"

"Yeah. The lady who found us, she was talking about it when we met them in the courtyard. She asked us if we'd seen them."

"Right. Well, they arrived shortly after you and Sebastian went missing."

"Where's Sebastian?"

"He's with Kimba. He's fine."

"And Becky?"

My mom narrows her eyes. She drops her head for a moment, and I watch as her lips move. When she lifts her head back up, she says, "Her brother's taking care of her."

"She isn't well. She thought Sebastian was her dead son. She kept calling him Taylor."

"I know. She was mostly lucid and knew she'd done wrong when we found you. But, well, she slips back to being confused. Her brother's keeping her locked up."

"And James? The man who was with her?"

Mom shakes her head. "They went after him—Rey, Kimba, the townsfolk. He's dead. There was an explosion."

His diversion. "Was anyone else hurt?"

Mom's face drops and her eyes fill with tears. "Asher." Her voice cracks as she says his name.

I gasp. "Will he be okay?"

"He . . . we lost him."

My hand goes to my mouth. "No, Mom. That can't . . . that can't be true. Not Asher." The tears return full force. Mom comforts me until I pull myself together enough to ask how Atticus and the rest of the family are doing.

"As well as can be expected. Jennifer says they're leaning on the Lord. At least she has that comfort."

I snort out a response, which takes me back to a crying fit.

Mom motions me to scoot over, sliding next to me in the queen-size bed. She holds me until I fall asleep.

When I wake up, she's still there. She offers me a wobbly smile.

"How?" I croak out the single word.

"That man, he set up some kind of bomb. There was no warning, it just exploded. Killed himself and two others instantly. Asher held on a few minutes. Atticus was with him when he . . . " Mom's voice fades away. "He was such a kind boy, a kind man. Always so pleasant with a ready smile."

"I can't even imagine how Atticus is feeling, losing not just a brother but his twin. Will there be a funeral?"

"It was this morning, for him and the other two."

"Did you go?"

"I stayed with you. Sebastian went. He said it was nice, a funeral for a hero."

"What will we do? Stay here while we— " I lift a hand, trying to find the words.

"Grieve? A few days, yes. It'll give you time to get well too. The doctor . . . do you remember me mentioning her? She put in the IV. The wagon that came from Billings had medical supplies provided by the military. The doctor said it was a miracle. And she's a real doctor,

111

not an herbalist, nurse, veterinarian, or pharmacist, but a real doctor. Can you believe it?"

"She couldn't help Asher."

"His injuries were too severe."

"Then she might as well have been an herbalist. At least the one who operated on Ben's foot saved him. And when we lived at the ski lodge, those nurses and the veterinarian helped lots of people. And remember, Mom? A pharmacist saved your life, cured your pneumonia. What good is a doctor if our friend is dead?" I turn my head from her.

"Anger is normal. I was angry too. While you were sleeping, I was very angry. I've been praying— "

"You've been *what*?"

"I know. It surprised me too. But when you and Sebastian were missing, I called out to Him. I begged, pleaded, prayed fervently. And He heard me."

"Maybe you should've prayed for no one to die."

"Yes, perhaps. Here's the thing, though, I knew God was there, that He's been there, been with me, no matter what happened. I knew He heard my prayers, and even before you were found, I was . . . comforted. I still didn't know you'd be found safe, but I knew He'd be with me either way. Just like He's with Jennifer now."

"I thought you said God doesn't care about us? And if He does, why'd He let Asher die? Not just Asher, but millions of others."

"I don't know the answer. No one really does, and we won't until God explains it."

"Humph. And when does that happen?"

"Asher's death reminded me of something important, something I need to remind you of. We need to be prepared to meet God."

My eyes dart to her as I shake my head.

One side of her mouth lifts slightly. "Have you ever heard the phrase, 'There are no atheists in foxholes'?"

I glare at her.

"It's a cliché, something people say to convince others in times of stress, or war, that everyone needs to turn to God. But for me, well, you know my experience has been the opposite. But the truth is, God wants us to just believe, to have faith, to trust. Not only in times of crisis, but always. It was wrong of me to turn to God when I was desperate, but I did."

112

Mom's smile is sad but real, the first real one since last summer before the attacks, since before we were captured and Uncle Wes was killed.

"Things have changed for me. In my desperation, I called out to God and begged Him to bring you and Sebastian back to me. I bargained, promised, said whatever I thought I should say to persuade God to bring you back. But somewhere along the way . . . " Her eyes light up as they rim with tears.

In a choked voice, Mom says, "Somewhere along the way, I found Him. I felt God's love wrap around me. He comforted me while I grieved."

"You're a Christian again?"

She releases a contented sigh. "Maybe for the first time. I don't know. Was I really a Christian before? I mean, I knew all the . . . " She drops her eyes.

Her voice grows thick. Quiet. "I knew all the stuff, all the verses and the words to say. When I was Sebastian's age, I started memorizing verses. My mom expected it. Everyone expected it of me. I was smart like you and could remember long sections. Everyone was so impressed, and I loved showing off my skills. But I was never like Sebastian, never had the passion, the belief he does. I didn't pray, or even care to understand what I was reading. I just memorized and recited, like a robot. I was . . . well, Sadie, I was more like you."

My eyes go wide.

"I just went through the motions because it was expected of me." She gives me a nod. "Of course, I've known you weren't really a Believer. I didn't care, though, because . . . " She shrugs again. "Why should I force you to believe in something I wasn't convinced of myself?"

"But all the church things we did, the stuff you were involved in, the pregnancy center, Mom . . . it was a *Christian* center."

"Oh, I know. Believe me, I know. And sometimes I felt bad about it. I was raised in the church, you know. Grandma Jackie and Aunt Karla, they were true Christians. And I loved the church. I loved being involved and wanted, needed even. I loved . . . " She lets out a sigh.

"I loved how people thought of me, the things they said about me. Especially when they found out I worked at the pregnancy center. I was saving the lives of the unborn. I was doing good work." She shakes her head. "If they only knew the truth."

113

"That you were faking it?"

"That . . . and more."

"What more?"

"Later, Sadie. I can only handle bearing so much of my soul at one time."

I respond with a nod. "What's different now? How do you know you're not faking it again?"

"Before, deep down, I knew I was a fraud. Yes, saving babies was important to me. That part was real. But I wasn't doing it out of a Biblical command. It, too, was for my own selfish reasons. I was running a racket of sorts. 'You'll know them by their fruit.' My fruit was rotten.

"It wasn't like I did terrible things, but I still . . . anyway, what's different now? I've received God's true gift. The gift of His Son, Jesus. I've asked Him to live in me, to make me more like Him. All that mumbo jumbo Jennifer and Kimba are always talking about— " she gives a light laugh " —the Bible reading, the praying, it's been working on me. Little by little, I've listened and . . . I've started to wonder.

"When you and Sebastian were taken, everything changed. We looked everywhere for you, until it was too dark to see. I stumbled and fell in a hole. While I was on the ground, on my knees, that's when I begged—begged God to find you. That's when I realized just how I'd used my status before. Oh, I knew I was a fake, but for some reason lying on the dusty ground, aching to find you and your brother, everything came rushing over me.

"All the lies. The sin. How I pretended to be faithful. My piousness at the women who I deemed less than me, the ones who didn't do all I did for the church, for our community, to save babies. Right then and there, I realized what I'd missed, how it was so easy for me to turn away from God. I was never His. He never had a hold of me, not a true hold."

I bite my lip as I consider what she's saying. "And now you're the real deal?"

"I— " She lets out a small laugh. "I'm almost scared to say it out loud. But God tells us we should not only believe in our heart but confess with our mouth." She looks at me, raising her eyebrows.

I motion for her to go on.

114

"Yes, baby girl—Sadie. I believe. I believe Jesus died for my sins. *Mine*. Leanne Monroe's sins, of which there are numerous. And I believe, even had you been lost to me, even if you and Sebastian were taken from me, God would help me through it. Before . . . "

Mom lets out a breath. "Before, it was me. Just me. When your dad died, I pulled myself up by my bootstraps. I'd spent the months your dad was sick secretly cursing God, throwing my anger at Him. Your dad knew how I felt and would try and help me—isn't that rich? He was the one dying, and he spent his time trying to keep his wife from losing it, from going off on a tangent."

"I never knew," I say. "When Dad was alive, you seemed so . . . faithful. You and he were always going to church. We did Bible readings all the time, prayed all the time."

She tilts her head. "It was your dad. He was the real deal—an actual Christian. I was angry, even then. Not outwardly angry like I've been the last few months, since the EMP and everything went so terribly wrong, but still angry.

"I was angry God took my husband away from me, from you and Sebastian. But I put on a good front, just like always. I pretended to be all pious and said things like, 'God needed another angel.' But really, I was seething inside.

"When the pregnancy center offered me full-time work, I used it as a diversion and started doing more with the church. Not because I thought it was the right thing to do or to honor God. Nope. Because it showed people how awesome I was. Do you understand, Sadie? Do you understand I was *playing* at being a Christian?"

I lift a shoulder. "And now?"

With her eyes still moist, she smiles—the beautiful, brilliant smile she used to have, not the awful fake smile of the past few months. This smile, there's something different about it. This smile's filled with peace. "Now who am I going to impress? I'm truly and faithfully calling on the name of God and asking Him to be Lord of my life."

I want to be happy for her, to congratulate her on finding God. But I'm angry. Fuming. And hurting. Asher is dead. "I don't know how you can smile at a time like this."

"Do you think I'm not mourning Asher? I am. We all are. His mom and brothers will miss him terribly, but they know they'll see him again. And they know he's celebrating in heaven."

"Oh, great. They can just get over their sadness since he's in heaven. Perfect, Mom."

"That's not what I said. They'll be sad for a long time. They'll miss him. Their lives will never be the same. Jennifer lost her husband last year. She knows the pain of loss. I still miss your dad. Like Asher, he's in heaven too. Now I have the promise, like your brother does, that I'll see him again. I didn't have that promise before."

"So that's it? You're telling me this to convince me to . . . to what? To turn to God?"

"I'm not trying to convince you of anything. That won't work. You must realize your need for God, for Jesus, on your own."

"Asher," I whisper as the tears overcome me again.

After many minutes of Mom trying to comfort me again, she says, "Let's get you something to eat. Then I'll tell the doc you're awake."

"How long has it been?"

"Since you got away? Yesterday, so not long. You had a good night's sleep is all."

"Why?" I ask as she rises from the bed. "I passed out, right?"

"The doctor thinks it was from not eating and being a little dehydrated, combined with the stress of all of it and maybe the infection in your toe."

"Is it bad? The infection?"

"She said you'll lose the toenail, but the infection isn't going to spread. It's minor. And thanks to the military and the wagon that came back from Billings, she had antibiotics for you. The little cut on your wrist, it's fine too."

"The IV?"

"It'll help with dehydration." Mom moves to the bathroom counter. "Alex—do you remember her? She owns the hotel. She brought this thermos of stew for you. Many people in town feel responsible. They knew Becky was . . . "

"Unhinged?" I offer.

"They knew she wasn't well, but they didn't think she'd go to the extreme of kidnapping. James—they knew he was trouble but not a . . . a murderer." She chokes on her words.

"Anyway, someone has been making sure we always have food. They've really been helping us as we grieve. They've even been praying for you, praying you'll heal quickly. When we leave, which won't be until the doctor says you're able to travel and Jennifer and

116

her boys feel ready, we'll be riding with Marie and Dewey when they take their wagon to Lewistown."

"We're riding?"

"We won't all fit in the wagon, but they're bringing a couple of horses too. They originally planned to pony them to the wagon, but a couple of us will ride instead."

"I don't want to ride a horse."

"I'll ride. Atticus and Axel will too, maybe Jennifer. And Brett knows how to ride. Jameson . . . maybe. They're trading the horses for milking goats, so we just need to get them there."

I close my eyes. Not walking will be nice. We were in a wagon the first few weeks of this journey, and while I'd sometimes be stiff from sitting too long, it's sure easier than walking all day. At least our group realizes we aren't professional hikers and that we have young children, so they limit our travel to something manageable. Even so, it isn't easy.

Mom sits in the chair, a bowl balanced in one hand and a spoon in the other. "Want to sit up a bit and I'll help you eat?"

"Really, Mom?"

"Indulge me. Let me dote on you. I know . . . I know I haven't really been there for you these last few months. You've been expected to do more than you should."

"You've kept us alive."

"I've been cruel."

"Not to me. And not to Sebastian."

She tilts her head. "There have been many times I've snapped at you, talked to you in ways I shouldn't have. I hope you'll forgive me, Sadie."

"You were just upset. I understand."

"Lean in a little." She teeters the spoon over the bowl.

I move in, accepting the spoonful of warm soup. It's mostly broth, but it's still delicious.

"Good, huh? Upset or not, I was hurtful way too many times. I've apologized to your brother, too, and . . . " She lets out a sigh. "I apologized to those we're traveling with. I know I've treated them poorly."

I raise my eyebrows at her.

Mom lets out a slight laugh. "Okay, that's an understatement. They were truly gracious about it, though, most of them anyway."

"Let me guess, not Victoria or Jameson."

117

"Jameson said, and I quote, 'Whatever, dude.' Victoria was nice enough and said she accepted my apology, but there was something in her eyes. You know she has her own struggles. I'm even more convinced than ever she's had plenty of bad things happen to her, too, but not just since the lights went out. She and her boys have dropped enough hints to make me think they were probably living in a state of terror long before then."

"You mean the abuse?"

"We know about her husband, about what he did to the people on the mountain. My guess is he'd been abusing them for years. Maybe not physically, but certainly psychologically."

"You've mentioned that before, said you've seen the signs from your work at the pregnancy center. But how do you know?"

"Oh, I don't know for sure. But I've seen enough to recognize survivors of domestic violence. Those boys and Victoria show all the signs."

"What about Donnie?"

She furrows her brow. "What about him?"

"What does he think about this new Leanne?"

"He's, uh . . . he's a little confused. He knows I've been struggling. Christianity isn't important to him, so he doesn't really get the magnitude of my . . . commitment."

"He said he used to go to church."

"Sure, yeah. He went with his brother sometimes and did some men's group stuff with him and PJ Cameron. But he's not . . . he doesn't even pretend to be a Christian, a Believer."

"What about you and him?"

She drops her gaze. "What do you mean?"

"Really, Mom?"

"How long have you— "

"Weeks. When he was shot in the hand and you were fretting over him, then when he was shot in the head, you were almost . . . tender."

"I told him he'd better stop getting in the way of bullets. He's like a pin cushion."

"Is that why you like him? Because you feel sorry for him?"

"*Noooo.* He's . . . I'm not sure what will happen between us. He's asked if he can stay with us for a while once we get to Aunt Karla's so we can get to know each other better and decide— " Mom gives an exaggerated shrug.

"I don't know. Right now, I'm just thinking of you and Sebastian, about how happy I am you're okay. And I'm sad about Asher. Donnie is too. He got along well with him."

I close my eyes as memories of Asher wash over me. His smile. His kindness. The way he and his brothers were always so helpful. He never wanted the leadership role his twin Atticus has, but he was a valuable part of our group. More than valuable.

A sob escapes me.

"I know, baby girl. Let it out. You cry as much as you need, as much as you want. When you're ready, we'll go on to Lewistown and settle in at Aunt Karla's place. Once we're safely there, then we'll talk about other things and begin our healing journey."

Chapter 18

"Whoa there." Dewey brings the wagon to a stop. "This is our camping spot for tonight."

Riding in the wagon truly is a luxury. I glance over at my mom. She's on one of the horses being taken for trade, a beautiful blue roan.

I don't know anything about horses, but Dewey explained a roan is a horse with a gene that produces a color pattern of white over a dark base color. This horse would be black, but the white on top gives a silvery look known as a blue roan. The coloring truly is impressive.

Atticus is riding the other trade horse, a brown one Dewey called a chestnut. He's not as pretty and seems a little ornery.

Other than Donnie, who's on his own horse, the rest of us are walking or are in the wagon, piled on top of and in between the cargo. Naomi and Sebastian often take turns riding on the seat with Dewey and Marie. Sebastian loves that, especially when Dewey lets him hold the reins to drive the team.

We only stayed one day past the morning I woke up in the hotel room. After Mom fed me the bowl of soup, she got the doctor. Following a quick exam, she unhooked the IV and instructed me to rest.

I napped and ate the day away, with Mom and Sebastian keeping me company when I was awake. The next day, I was allowed up and spent time in the courtyard while everyone else helped with preparations to leave.

Being with everyone as we continued to mourn Asher was hard, yet also good. There are still tears, many tears, but I love how we talk about him and the memories we share. I already miss him so much—his smile, the way he saw good in almost everything, how he'd go out of his way to share an encouraging word.

As Mom said, Jennifer, Atticus, and Axel are holding up okay. I can see they take solace in knowing Asher's in heaven and they'll see him again. Seeing them and how convinced they are, along with how my mom is now sure God is real and loving, makes me wonder if they may be right. Am I the one who doesn't know the truth? They believe heaven is real.

While I didn't see Becky again, her brother dropped by and offered his apologies. He said he'd make sure nothing like that ever happened again. As he crumpled his ballcap in his hands and rocked back and forth on his well-worn boots, I knew he was sincere. And embarrassed.

Jennifer went to him, pulling him into an embrace. He kept saying over and over how sorry he was for the death of her son. Leaving Roundup yesterday at dawn, he was one of many to wish us safe travels.

With the team and wagon, we're making better time than on foot. Marie and Dewey, who've made this trip dozens of times, say we'll reach Lewistown mid to late afternoon in six days. Some stretches will go faster than others, but the uphill areas slow us down. And some of the hills are so steep, we all get out and walk to lighten the load.

We've already had a few of those, but short walks, even uphill, aren't terrible. Because of the wagon and being able to rest while we ride, we're traveling a few miles past our usual ten-mile daily limit.

My toe doesn't ache and throb like it did before, and I'm even wearing shoes again—a new pair that are a size and a half larger. The doctor said my tight shoes and boots were likely the main reason for my toenail issue.

These, donated by someone from town, are a little too big. The doctor found a heel pad to add to them to keep them from slipping, but she wanted the extra room in the toes for when my feet swell if I'm on them too long.

They also found me a pair of heavy soled, midcalf cowboy boots to keep my feet dry in the weather. Even though I'm mostly healed and feel okay, I'm still in the wagon most of the time.

I even got a few new books in Roundup, allowing me the luxury of reading as we travel.

Being around my mom now is super weird. While part of me likes how nice and calm she is, the rest of me isn't sure this is a good idea. When she was nice before, things didn't turn out well. Those men took her and . . . whatever happened, I don't even want to think about that. But how she acted, all scary and mean, was probably part of the reason we've survived.

Now that she's found God again—or, according to her, for the first time—I'm worried she'll let her guard down and actually believe He'll take care of us. Thinking like that will get us killed.

After we get camp set up in a spot Dewey and Marie use each time they stop here, Atticus walks to where I'm standing with my mom. "I was wondering if you feel up to hunting with me?"

"Me?" I ask, pointing at my chest.

"Yeah, if it's okay with your mom. Mrs. Monroe?"

Mom responds with an awkward, yet genuine, smile. "Fine by me. Sadie?"

I chew on my upper lip, remembering the last time I went hunting with Atticus and how I couldn't shoot the rabbit. "Okay, yeah."

"Good. Dewey said they often see deer through here."

"Let me get my pack. I need a minute to unload the extra things."

The large backpack I've been hauling around since we left the ski lodge is looking pretty tattered. There's little room in our small tent for anything other than the three of us, so we keep the packs outside on a section of plastic tarp.

That's fine when the weather's nice, like today, but during the snowy months and rainy days, we had a terrible time wrapping the plastic around our bags to keep them dry. That's probably part of the reason my bag not only looks awful but also stinks like mildew.

As I'm pulling things out that I won't need for a short hunting excursion, my hands fall on the wooden plaque Asher made me for my birthday. As I caress the smooth wood, tears fill my eyes. I blink rapidly to try and shoo them away. The words Asher added come into focus: *He will make your paths straight. Proverbs 3:6.*

After he gave me this gift, Sebastian begged Asher to teach him how to do the pokerwork. Asher gave my brother a few lessons, but not enough for him to really know the process. And now . . . I let out a long breath.

"Ready?" Atticus asks, standing near my tent. I look up at him with the plaque still in my hands. His gaze goes to it, and he blinks several times. "Asher really did a nice job on that. He— " Atticus clears his throat. "He hoped it'd be meaningful to you."

"I love it," I whisper.

"People say it'll get easier, that the hurt will lessen. I know it's true, to a point. My dad's been gone almost a year now, died a couple of days after the EMP. I still miss him." Atticus lets out a sigh. "But the pain is less sharp. At least we know he and Asher are together."

"Your dad was a Christian?"

"He was."

"My dad too."

"How old were you when he died?"

"Ten."

"Oh? I thought . . . Sebastian said he was just a baby."

"Um, are you ready? Should we go?"

Atticus gives me a strange look. "I'm ready."

As I stand, a loud thump comes from the edge of camp. We turn our heads quickly to see Victoria and Jameson moving a log. "What are they up to?" I motion at them with my chin.

"Looks like axe throwing practice. She's really wicked with those things. Jameson seems to be getting the hang of it too."

"Okay, that's good," I say, wondering if it really is. Jameson is so volatile at times, the idea of him with an axe causes me to shudder. Of course, he already carries a knife and a gun, so . . .

"I agree." Atticus hefts his backpack of essentials into place. "It might help him release some of his pent-up frustrations, take them out on the target instead of people." He gives me a nod, indicating he remembers how Jameson acted toward me. "Nate's been practicing too. You should try it. You might like it."

"Maybe."

As we walk past Victoria and Jameson, the boy gives me a slight wave. "Looks like you're getting around pretty good." He motions to my foot. "Not even much of a limp."

"Thanks." I drop my gaze.

Even though he seems nice enough, I don't trust him—not after how he's been. Mom may believe Victoria and he act the way they do because of past abuse, but I don't care. Jameson's older brother isn't like that. He's kind and goes out of his way to help people. He's not a jerk like Jameson, or cruel like Victoria.

The sting of remembering how Victoria talked about me after my birthday celebration rushes over me. Unwanted tears sting my eyes as I remember her vile words.

I straighten my shoulders, willing the emotions away. Maybe I am ugly and no man will ever want me. That doesn't matter. I can take care of myself. I proved it by getting away from Becky and James. Sebastian and I escaped. We were a great team.

"We'll head over there." Atticus points off in the distance. "Dewey says there's a draw that he's killed a couple of deer in before. Remember, we're only looking for bucks. It's birthing season for the does, so we'll leave them be. Don't want to risk killing one getting ready to fawn or with a fawn hidden in the brush we can't see."

We walk a little farther before Atticus asks, "You want to carry the big rifle? Take the shot?"

I close my eyes for a moment. *Do I?* Not really, but . . . "I'll do it."

We swap rifles. I hand him the .22, while he passes me the .243. I check to make sure the safety is on, then hoist it on my back by the sling.

We've gone about a hundred yards from camp when Atticus points to a fluff of fur on the ground. "Let's check this out."

Walking near it, it's obvious it's a dead rabbit.

"Coyote?" I ask.

"No, look at its face."

I take a few steps closer and see a smear of blood covering its nose and mouth. I furrow my brow.

"They were talking about this in Roundup," Atticus says. "There's a disease going around that's killing the rabbits."

I take several steps back. "Is it contagious?"

"Not to humans. But it's very contagious to other rabbits, both wild and domestic. They're pretty concerned about it and are afraid they might lose their meat rabbits."

"What is it?"

He lifts a shoulder. "Some kind of hemorrhagic disease. It damages the blood vessels and causes internal bleeding."

I give a nod. I've read about diseases like that. "And that's why they have the blood on their nose?"

"Right."

I shake my head. A disease like this could greatly impact the food supply, especially if it affects both wild and caged rabbits. I understand why the townspeople are worried.

"Ready to go on?" Atticus asks.

"Will we need to stop hunting rabbits? I mean, once the cold snap returns and the bugs are gone off them?"

"Even with the bugs, if we needed the food . . . " He lifts his hands. "I don't know, though. We're definitely not seeing them like we were. I didn't think much about it until I heard about the disease. I thought maybe it was just the area or the season. But now, I'm sure there are less rabbits than there should be."

124

We start walking again, going at least a half mile from our camp, when Atticus touches my arm. "Okay, see up ahead where the terrain changes? We're close enough to slow our walk and keep quiet. When we get to the edge of the draw, we'll walk crouched over and make our silhouettes small in case there're deer down there. We want to sneak up on them. Got it?"

I indicate I understand.

"Why don't you go first? That way you can be ready."

It takes only a few minutes before we reach the ravine. I stoop over and slow my pace. I glance over my shoulder to make sure I'm doing it right.

Atticus gives me a thumbs up.

As we reach the edge, I start looking. Is there a deer in there? Part of me hopes there isn't. But I know we need the meat. I can do this. I can help provide for our group.

I must do this.

With the warmer daytime temps, we'll be in a rush to get the meat processed. At least the nights are cold enough we'll be able to field dress and skin it, letting the meat cool overnight.

In the morning, before we start traveling, we'll need to make sure it's wrapped up and put in a cool spot of the wagon. Then we'll need to completely cook and dry it when we stop tomorrow.

Dewey made a point of saying the days of being able to hunt big game while traveling this route are likely coming to an end until fall. If the days get too much warmer, the meat will spoil before it can be cooked or dried.

We still have enough dried food to get us to Lewistown, but Atticus and the rest of them will be continuing on past Great Falls, over a hundred miles farther. The pressure of knowing people rely on me for food makes my heart pound even harder.

I'm still creeping forward when I feel a hand on my shoulder. I stop moving and look at Atticus.

He motions with his finger, pointing to the right and down. There're several deer standing there, munching clumps of grass.

I let out a slow breath. They're close and are on this side of the ravine. I can do this. I give Atticus a nod as I get down on one knee.

We've practiced several different positions for shooting. While Rey and Kimba insist prone is the most accurate, lying flat on our stomach and using a backpack as a rest, it's the hardest for me. I like kneeling

125

on one knee or sitting flat on my bottom. Kneeling seems smart for here.

One of the deer stops eating, lifts her head, and flattens her ears. The buck standing next to her keeps eating, but I know if she spooks, he'll run too. I need to be quick. As I move the rifle off my back, I finger the safety, thinking it'll save me a few seconds of getting set.

I have the rifle halfway up when a loud bang shatters the quiet. I drop the gun as the deer run off. I'm panting. Breathing hard. *What just happened?*

"You okay?" Atticus asks.

"I don't . . . I didn't mean for it to go off."

"I know. Accidental discharge. Or as my dad would say, negligent discharge."

My ears are ringing, and I feel sick to my stomach. "Is the gun broken?"

"From when you dropped it?" He picks it up, blowing some dirt from the scope, then looks it over.

"No! Why'd it go off? It must . . . it must be broken."

He crinkles his forehead. "You pulled the trigger somehow. I was watching the deer and not you, but somehow you pulled the trigger. Did you take the safety off?"

I close my eyes. "I . . . yes. I thought I'd save a step. I was worried they'd spook. I know I'm supposed to wait, make sure I have the scope on the target and then take the safety off. I did it wrong. But I don't think I squeezed the trigger."

"Well . . . " He shrugs.

"Why would your dad call it a negligent discharge? It was an accident. I don't know how it happened, but it was definitely an accident."

"Let's sit for a minute and get a little more comfortable." He motions to the ground.

I move from my kneeling position to sitting on my bottom. I still don't feel great with the ringing in my ears. I'm even a little dizzy.

"Should we go after the deer?" I ask.

"They're long gone."

"Sorry," I whisper. "I don't know what happened."

"You remember the four rules of gun safety? I know you do. My dad was adamant you could break one rule and maybe—*just maybe*—no one would be hurt or killed. But more than one . . . all bets were

126

off. He was also adamant there are no accidents around firearms, just negligence.

"He drilled them into us, those gun-safety rules. Fortunately, you were aware enough to keep the muzzle pointed in a safe direction, so when the trigger was pulled, it wasn't a catastrophic event. We'll go back to camp empty handed, but we're uninjured."

"I don't know what happened. I took the safety off too soon, but I just don't remember even having my finger anywhere near the trigger. I didn't even realize it was my gun that went off—not at first. I'm . . . I'm so sorry."

"We're both okay. God was watching out for us. We have neighbors back in Simms—I've told you about them. They push the gun rules all the time. More than once, my dad talked to them about their carelessness. One of these days . . . say, you feeling okay? You look a little pale."

"Not so great," I answer as my stomach drops. My eyes go wide, and I turn my head just as the vomit spews out. I bend over, heaving on the grass. After what feels like forever, it finally stops. My face is hot with embarrassment. "Sorry."

"It happens. My mom used to get sick after shooting. She said if her ears started ringing, she'd get tinnitus and then it was all downhill from there. Are your ears ringing?"

"They were. Not so bad now."

"You ready to head back to camp?"

"I'm really sorry I messed up the hunt."

As we walk back, my head hangs low. I'd been feeling pretty good before, like this was something I could do. I kept Sebastian and me safe, fighting off our kidnappers. I thought maybe I wasn't a huge loser. *Wrong again.* I'm never going to be able to survive in this world if I can't even kill food. I let out a breath.

And now, with Mom and her newfound trust in God, I have new concerns. At least before I knew no one would mess with her. She looked like a wildcat with the way she scowled at everyone. Now she has this calm, serene look about her. And she acts the same way.

One of us needs to be tough if we're going to make it. Otherwise, our only hope is Aunt Karla will be able to care for us and keep us safe. Being an ugly loser, with a mom who's suddenly gone soft, doesn't give me much hope for survival.

127

Back at camp, Mom takes one look at me and immediately asks, "Are you all right?"

"She had an accidental discharge," Atticus says.

Even though he calls it accidental instead of negligent, I still want the ground to swallow me up.

"No injuries?" Kimba looks us over.

"We're fine."

"Which rule did you break?" Her eyes drill into me.

"I took the safety off too soon."

"And?"

"I must have had my finger on the trigger before it was time. But I don't remember doing it."

Kimba spends many minutes going over the safety rules again and pretty much repeats everything Atticus already told me about how breaking the gun-safety rules can result in death.

"Okay, then," Kimba says. "Let's not beat this horse any longer. Grab the .22. We're going shooting." She takes the larger rifle from Atticus, the one I just accidentally fired, and slings it on her back.

"What? No." I lift my hands.

"Right now, you're feeling bad, scared and overwhelmed and maybe—from the look of it—you're a little sick. Let's go shoot this rifle and get you a little confidence back. If we don't do it now, you'll make guns into a big boogie man. And we can't have that."

"She's right," Mom says. "You need to be comfortable shooting. This world we live in . . . " She shakes her head.

Maybe she doesn't have complete trust God will protect us. Maybe a little of my old mom is still there.

Kimba makes me shoot the .22 twice. "You've done fine. Now the .243."

"No."

She gives me a smile. "One shot with it and then we're done."

With my face hot, I carefully take the rifle.

"It's empty, so you'll need to load it." She gives me a single cartridge. "I know you're scared. I had an unintentional discharge when I was training once. As in your case, no one was injured, but I couldn't stop thinking *what if.* Your mind's a powerful weapon. Don't let it get the best of you."

She talks me through everything—positioning, breathing, all of it. I take the shot and hit the target.

"See?" Kimba cheers. "That wasn't so bad. You think you're good? We can take another couple of shots if you need to."

I've already wasted too much ammo today, and we have nothing to show for it. I shake my head.

Back at camp, Mom greets me with a smile. "You look better. I take it things went well?"

"Fine." I point to the kettle cooking over one of the multi-fuel camp stoves. "What's cooking?"

"While you were with Kimba, Nate got a grouse with his slingshot."

I roll my eyes. *Of course he did.* Nate's always managing to put food on the table, or the stick. Whatever. I'm glad about it but jeez.

The one thing I can say about Nate is, other than he's good at feeding us, he's quiet about it. He's never one to boast or make a big deal about his successes. For a thirteen-year-old boy, he's surprisingly mature. Just as the thought goes through my head, he makes a face at his little sister. Okay, maybe not that mature. Or maybe all boys are dweebs where sisters are concerned.

After dinner, Dewey says, "You know, I never asked about your folks in Lewistown. I wonder if I know them."

"Just Leanne and her kids will be staying there," Kimba answers. "The rest of us are heading on to the Dosens' ranch, west of Great Falls."

"Yup. I remember you saying that. 'Cept Donnie. He's staying with Leanne, right?"

"We'll see," Mom says, while Donnie answers, "I'll make sure they're settled before I even think of leaving." There're a few beats of silence as their eyes meet.

"Your family?" Dewey asks.

"My aunt," Mom says. "Karla Belvedere. Do you know her?"

He looks to Marie, who shakes her head. "Can't say I do. She's not part of that crazy cult, right?"

Mom shakes her head. "Of course not."

Many people in our group give each other questioning looks.

"What cult?" Kimba asks.

"Don't rightly know if they have a name. I think they sprung up after the events. Strange ones, they are."

"Working together isn't so strange," Marie says. "Dewey just thinks they have some weird rules. He and several others call them a cult, but we don't really know that's what they are."

"What kind of rules?" Jameson asks.

"They don't let people in or out of their community," Dewey answers. "Only a few of them have privileges to come into town and trade. Sounds like a cult to me."

"Not letting people in sounds smart—safe." Kimba smiles. "And maybe the controlled exit is also a safety feature?"

"The ones who come in are always spouting weird stuff."

"Like 'praise the Lord'?" Jennifer asks, a smile playing across her face.

Marie gives a hearty laugh.

"No . . . " Dewey shakes his head. "Other stuff. You'd have to be there and hear not just what they say but how they say it. I'm telling you, it's a cult."

Chapter 19

The rest of our days traveling by wagon passed without any major events. Each night when we stopped, we'd work on our self-defense stuff. Dewey even showed us some things he learned when he was a Marine, including more ways to defend against knives and other blades.

Nicole and I have continued our sparring practice, with Mom insisting we take it easy so I didn't reinjure my toe. We go at half speed, and even so, I'm surprised by how much better I'm getting.

We're all still missing Asher, of course, which hangs over us.

We're on the final day of our journey and just a few miles outside of Lewistown when we see a small herd of antelope a few hundred yards away.

"Is it okay to go after those?" Rey asks Dewey and Marie.

"Might as well," Dewey answers. "I'm surprised to see them this close to town. We don't usually. Probably best to only take one, and make sure it's a buck."

Once we reach a dip in the road, low enough to conceal the horses, Atticus, Donnie, and Brett take off after the antelope. Rey and a few others stay behind with the horses while the rest of us start moving again.

I watch as they begin stalking the antelope, keeping a hillside between them and the herd. Staying hidden might allow them to get close enough for a shot.

The wagon travels a little farther, cresting a small hill before beginning our descent, when Dewey says in a low voice, "We'll wait at the bottom and make sure those speed goats can't see us." A few minutes more and Dewey brings the team to a stop. "Antelope don't have the best hearing, but we should stay quiet anyway."

Mom pulls her horse up alongside the wagon before getting off. She does a few stretches and then ties the horse's lead rope to a metal ring on the wagon. The rest of us get out of the wagon to move around. Even though riding is better than walking, it's good to stretch.

I keep looking over to see what the guys are doing. Within a few minutes, I lose sight of Atticus and Donnie.

My mom opens her mouth to say something when a loud percussion carries across the land.

"I hope they got it." Victoria gives me a pointed look. "We need the meat."

"I think they did," Jennifer says. "Even from here, it sounded like a solid hit."

Victoria lets out a soft laugh. "You can't be serious."

"She is." Kimba nods. "There's a different sound when the bullet hits something solid. A dirt bank or flesh sounds different than hitting a rock."

"You don't even hunt," Victoria scoffs.

"I didn't say animal flesh."

"Well, I, for one, wouldn't know. I'm not a murderer."

"We'll know soon enough if they got the antelope," Jennifer says, attempting to change the subject.

The way Victoria says murderer reminds me of her husband and what he did to the ski lodge community before we moved there.

My eyes travel to my mom. She gives me a slight nod. Even with the small gesture, I can almost read her mind: Victoria is hurting. She was likely abused by her husband during her marriage but is still grieving his death, which makes little sense to me.

But Mom's nod says even more. She's not just thinking about Victoria hurting in this world, but for all eternity.

Victoria, Jameson, and Brett Dawson are *lost*. They don't have God in their lives. Now that Mom has found Jesus, she's ultra-focused on everyone else's salvation.

In the days since Sebastian and I escaped from James and Asher was killed, Mom's been annoyingly preachy. I almost miss the old grumpy mom. I definitely miss the fake Christian mom from before the EMP. At least then I didn't feel like she was judging me. Now, I can almost see it in her eyes that she finds me lacking. She's concerned about *my* salvation.

I can definitely see times when it almost felt like something supernatural helped us get through things. Times when Sebastian would tell us—*promise us*—God would help us and things seemed to work out, like in the barn when Sebastian insisted we needed to leave. After I woke up in the hotel room, while Mom went to get the doctor, I started wondering why my brother was so frantic about us getting out of the barn.

Leaving the barn was when we ran into Becky and James. If we'd stayed hidden, they might not have found us. But I later found out, from Marie who heard it from Becky, James *knew* we were in there. He was skirting around the buildings and planned to light a fire on one side of the barn to flush us out. Why he thought that was a good idea, I'll never know.

But if we wouldn't have left when we did . . . a shiver runs through me as I think of how it could've ended. Sebastian and I could've been trapped in the old building and unable to escape. So, yeah, maybe there is something to this God thing and listening to His urgings, like Sebastian does. Or maybe Sebastian just knows things—the way Atticus can predict the weather. I don't know.

What I do know is I'm already sick of my mom and her judgmental looks. And I'm way tired of her mentioning what a comfort Jennifer has knowing that her son and husband are in heaven and she'll see them again one day.

As if she knows I'm thinking of her, she taps my arm and smiles. "Only a few more miles. I can't wait for Aunt Karla to see you again. You were still so young last time. She's going to be so amazed at the beautiful girl you've become."

Beautiful? Yeah, right.

"Brave too." Sebastian beams at me. "When Becky had us, Sadie made sure we got away."

"You're very blessed to have such an amazing big sister." Jennifer ruffles Sebastian's hair. "And I heard Sadie thought you were pretty amazing too."

He lifts a shoulder while grinning.

"You were both so brave." Mom drops her gaze as she bites her lip. "There's something I need to tell everyone, something I've been keeping from you."

All eyes are on my mom. She gives a shy smile before adding, "Sadie and Sebastian have also, at my insistence, been conspiring with me to keep this secret."

My eyes go wide. "Mom?" I whisper.

"It's time, Sadie." She smiles. "For the longest time, I've done what I thought was best to keep you safe, to protect you. And maybe it worked. But now . . . *Go forth and sin no more.* God wants us to have victory over sin. He wants us to be perfect, to be like Him. I've got . . . " She lets out a laugh. "Boy, do I have a long way to go!"

"Amen." Kimba gives her own chuckle.

Jennifer raises her hands, like she's pumping them in the air, something she does when she agrees and is giving glory to God.

Victoria rolls her eyes.

I force myself not to join Victoria's eye rolling. Here Mom goes, getting all preachy again. But even worse, she's going to say something that will change everything. Not just for her, but for me too.

Mom rests a hand on my shoulder. "I think you all know things weren't always easy for my children and me. We encountered many difficulties on our journey. When we were trying to get to our home, we were kidnapped. During our escape, my brother was killed." Mom's eyes go to Jennifer.

They share a sad smile before Jennifer gives a single bob of her head. "We've lost too many."

"We have," Mom agrees. "Way too many."

"Please." Jennifer motions with her hand. "Continue your story."

Mom looks first to me, then to Sebastian. "Thankfully, we weren't alone. Ben Ferguson, who we'd been traveling with and was also kidnapped, helped us get away. But not before some terrible things happened while we were captured. Terrible things happened to me. I didn't . . . I was afraid the same things might happen to Sadie. It was my hope, if our captors thought she was only a child, they'd leave her be." Mom glances at the others.

Marie shakes her head. "I'm so sorry, Leanne. I've heard so many stories about . . . " She clears her throat, knowing the younger children with us don't need details.

Personally, I don't think Mom needs to be talking about this at all.

"Isn't Sadie a child?" Victoria looks me up and down. "Or does she have some weird disease that makes her look young when she's really an adult?"

I let out a snort of laughter. Leave it to Victoria.

"Oh, no weird disease," Mom says. "But she's not as young as I've told you she is. The other day, when we celebrated her birthday, it was really her sixteenth, not her thirteenth."

A series of *ohs* and other noises carry through the wagon.

"That explains several things," Kimba says, giving me a smile. "I've always thought you were mature beyond your years."

Nicole gives me a smile. "So, we're almost the same age?"

I lift a shoulder in response.

"Cool," she says. "I'm with my mom. I thought you acted a lot older than my brother."

"Hey!" Nate makes a face at her.

Nicole sticks her tongue out at him. "It's true."

"That's enough. Leave your brother be," Kimba says, then turns to my mom. "I can see why you'd use the ruse. Anything to keep your child safe. And while I appreciate you coming clean with us, I must wonder if it's not a good idea to keep it up. Sadie's small in stature and can definitely pass for thirteen, so . . . "

"It's dishonest," Mom says.

"Yeah." Kimba nods. "But keeping our children safe should be a priority. What do you think, Victoria?"

Victoria looks surprised to be asked. "I . . . well, I can see both sides of it. I'd like to think I'd do whatever I need to do to keep my boys safe." She quickly looks to Jennifer, her cheeks coloring slightly before she averts her gaze. "But the truth is, I'm not sure I would, or that I could. We know . . . we know how things can happen."

Kimba slips an arm around Jennifer's shoulder. "We do know."

"I don't seem to be as strong as the rest of you." Victoria stares off into the distance, her voice sounding faraway, toneless. "Most of the time, it's Brett keeping Jameson and me out of harm's way. I'm . . . I guess I don't have a good view on this."

"I think your view is just fine." Jennifer wipes her eyes. "We all have struggles. I've allowed Atticus to take the lead in our family. He feels some responsibility for the death of his brother. Oh, he knows it's not his fault, but he still feels responsible to a point."

Jennifer smiles at Victoria. "Brett's becoming a fine man, so it makes sense you'd let him lead you and Jameson. That doesn't mean you aren't still the mom and willing to do what's needed. The past few days, you and Jameson seem to really be bonding over your axe throwing. Whatever happened in the past, you can change it in the present and future."

There're several quiet moments as Jennifer gives Victoria a chance to say something.

When she doesn't respond, Jennifer continues, "While I agree you shouldn't be deceitful, Leanne, I can see Kimba's point of doing what's needed to keep Sadie safe. Will continuing the ruse of her age help? It may. Can you keep it going and still feel you're on the path God wants you to be on? I don't know."

"Of course she can!" Kimba declares. "Our job is to protect our children. God gave them to us and gave us this duty."

Jennifer taps her index finger to her chin. "We're also to raise them in the way of the Lord. This time we're living in is dangerous and complicated. God promises to be with us during times like this, to hide us under the shadow of His wing."

"And maybe that's what He's doing," Kimba says, leaning forward. "He's providing a way to keep Sadie safe. He made her how she is, tiny and young looking. How do we know it isn't His plan for Leanne to pass her off as younger than she is?"

"I don't think God would want me to lie," Mom says, her words coming out in a rush. "I've spent most of my life being someone I wasn't, fabricating my . . . my everything, just to try and look pious."

"No one really wants to *look* pious, do they?" Victoria asks.

"Maybe that's not the right word," Mom agrees. "But I pretended to be someone I wasn't. And I've asked Sadie to do the same thing, to pretend she isn't who she really is. I just don't think either of us should live a lie."

"Well, I appreciate your passion," Kimba says. "And it's wonderful to experience this transformation with you. Truly, Leanne, you answering God's call has been a blessing to me."

"To me also," Jennifer adds. "We've been praying for you, praying the troubles you've experienced would be taken off your heart and replaced with God's love. And— " Jennifer's eyes fill with tears as her voice turns thick. "And He answered our prayers."

"Praise the Lord," Marie says.

I glance at her in time to see Dewey shoot her a look. Is she mocking Dewey? Mocking my mom?

"It was a surprise to me," Mom says. "When I was at my lowest, the last thing I expected was to find God there. All those years . . . anyway, thank you for praying for me. I know being around me wasn't always pleasant." She lets out a laugh, causing the other women and even the children to laugh too.

Nicole shoots me a wink.

For the first time in a long time, I feel like I belong. I haven't felt this way since things were normal, since I was in school and had my friends. But then, someone like Nicole wouldn't have winked at me. The pretty, popular girls didn't know I existed. That was fine, at least they didn't pick on me like they did a few of the others.

If Nicole and I had met then, before the world changed, would she have been as friendly and kind? Would she have sent me conspiratorial winks?

Sure, she was nice to me before, nice enough anyway. But I never felt included like I do today. Now that she knows the truth about me, it's almost like she sees more than just a little kid the same age as her younger brother.

My breath catches as I think of Asher. What would he think? I close my eyes to keep the tears at bay. I wish he knew. I wish I would've told him.

"Look!" Nate points at the hill we came down a short while ago. The men are returning, walking the horses. Flung across Donnie's saddle is the carcass of an antelope.

Chapter 20

We're only a few miles from the outskirts of Lewistown where Dewey and Marie meet up to empty the goods. Originally, before Mom's big conversion to Christianity, she'd insisted the group drop us off in Lewistown and continue on their way, then we'd walk the final few miles out of town to Aunt Karla's lodge.

But the last few days, she's said it'd be great if they could join us at Aunt Karla's and rest a couple of days before traveling on. And now, with the antelope and needing to process and dry the meat, it's more reason for them to stay.

"Karla has a beautiful firepit by a gazebo. It's the perfect place to smoke the meat. And since she lives on the edge of a forest, maybe you can harvest a deer or elk while you're there and build up your food stores a little more," Mom says as we finish packing the meat into the wagon.

"We're not seeing many deer 'round," Dewey declares. "But there were some decent elk herds in the mountains, some rugged area to go after them."

"Thanks so much for the offer, Leanne. The chance for an elk would be good." Rey hefts the final bag filled with antelope into the wagon.

"The chances would be slim." Dewey shakes his head.

"Understood." Rey nods. "Does everyone agree we should take Leanne up on staying? Even if we can't harvest an elk?"

"I'll be staying to make sure she's settled, no matter what you all decide." Donnie pats his horse on the neck.

Mom gives him a smile. "I'm sure you'll be welcome to stay as long as you wish." Their eyes meet and their gazes hold for several beats before Mom finally glances at her horse.

The group agrees staying at least long enough to take care of the meat is a good idea. Jameson asks if Mom's sure Aunt Karla will welcome them.

"Of course I'm sure. Karla's one of the kindest people I've ever known, always willing to help everyone."

No one mentions there's a chance Aunt Karla, like her sister—my Grandma Jackie—may not have survived in the time since the attacks.

Worry courses through me. What if Aunt Karla really is dead and our plans to live with her in the safety of the lodge come crashing down? We know just how fleeting life is, here now and gone too soon.

Mom's really been pinning her hopes on reaching Aunt Karla's lodge. Even when Mom was so bitter over everything, she'd talk longingly about the lodge she worked at during the summers of her high school and college years. From her stories, it was hard work—cleaning rooms, serving meals, helping with reservations, checking people in, and even doing the yard work—but she loved it.

She loved working with Aunt Karla and her late husband, Uncle Ralph. After my mom and dad were married, we visited them a few times. I was only six or seven the last time I came here; that was a year or so before Uncle Ralph died.

I still remember him and how he had this weird mustache that curved down the sides of his mouth all the way to his chin. And he wore a giant cowboy hat. My dad said it was a ten-gallon hat.

Uncle Ralph let me try it on once, and the thing covered my entire face. The next year, he was killed in a car accident. Mom and Dad went to the funeral with my grandma and grandpa, while I stayed with friends of my mom's.

Mom visited Aunt Karla another time, without me and Dad. She was already pregnant with Sebastian, and Dad was already sick. Then Dad died. Aunt Karla was sick with the flu and couldn't come back for Dad's funeral. Mom talked to her on the phone sometimes, but we hadn't visited. Aunt Karla hasn't even met Sebastian.

A brick sign announcing *Lewistown* sends my heart racing.

"We're almost there," Marie announces. "Just ahead is the roadblock." Other than Mom, Atticus, and Donnie on their horses, the rest of us are piled in the wagon and ready to finish this trip.

"Grab ahold of something," Dewey, who's also ready to be done, calls out. "We're putting the speed on." He makes a clucking sound with his mouth. The horses move from their sedate walk to a much faster pace, not exactly a trot but something quick. Mom and the others on horseback keep pace.

Soon, we're on the edge of town, with people waving and hollering greetings. After a super quick stop at the roadblock, Dewey directs the team into the parking lot of an old shopping center.

An older man, with his own team and wagon, raises a hand and says, "I was beginning to wonder if you'd make it today. Didn't expect you to bring passengers."

"Yup." Dewey climbs off the bench. "Stopped so they could whack an antelope. There's a herd a few miles out of town."

"Out of *our* town?" someone says. "And you let— "

"You should send a hunting party out," Marie quickly says. "It's a good-sized herd, several young bucks."

A few rough words are muttered as plans are made to send out a hunting party.

"I didn't expect people to ride my horses here," the man with the wagon says as my mom climbs down from the roan. "Thought you'd pony them."

"These folks had a spell of trouble in Roundup. Seemed neighborly to help them get here."

"We've all had a spell of trouble," the man scoffs. "No matter. Let's get this taken care of. We're already late."

While Dewey and Marie move a few things from their wagon to the man's wagon, Mom and Atticus unsaddle the horses. While the horses were part of a trade, the saddles belong to someone from Roundup and will go back on Dewey and Marie's return trip.

The rest of us begin unloading our meager belongings from the wagon. Because of the wagon ride, we left the wheelbarrow and homemade wagon behind. Those going on to Great Falls pared down their belongings to only carry what they can in their backpacks.

Everyone agreed the ride was worth losing the carts and a few things. While in Lewistown, we'll even be able to trade some of our excess for things we need.

Once the grumpy man is taken care of and tells Dewey he'll be back in three days with the goats being traded for the horses, other townspeople move in to get whatever goods Dewey brought for them. The entire process takes only about twenty minutes.

When the wagon's empty, we begin our goodbyes.

"You know where you're going from here?" Dewey asks.

"I do," Mom says. "It's about six miles out of town. I'm not sure if we can reach it before dark, but it shouldn't be a problem to camp and get there in the morning. What about you? You'll get the goats in three days?"

140

"We'll rest in the meantime," Marie answers. "We have a place we stay at here, just like in Roundup. We could give you a ride."

Even though she offers, the look on her face makes me wonder if she means it. And the look Dewey shoots her tells me he's done for the day and is ready to get to wherever it is they stay.

"We're fine." Kimba waves a hand, understanding their silent communication. "Stretching our legs sounds good. And you've already been more than generous."

"We wanted to give you this." Atticus hands Dewey one of the bags with an antelope quarter in it. "Thanks for the ride."

"Appreciate it." Dewey tips his hat. "You're able to handle the rest of the meat okay?"

"Yep, no problem," Atticus says, showing how he's tied a bag at the bottom of his pack. Rey has done something similar, while Donnie has the final bag on his horse.

"Which way is it to your aunt's place?" Marie asks.

"North." Mom points in the general direction.

"North?" Dewey's eyes go wide. "Thought you said she wasn't part of the cult."

"I'm . . . I'm sure she's not," Mom answers.

"Well, as far as I know, they've got their setup just outside of town, to the north."

"There's lots of land in that direction." Marie pats Dewey's arm. "I'm sure they'll be fine." She gives Mom a smile. "Like Dewey said, we'll be here a few days. We stay at the Calvert. If you need . . . well, we'll be there a few days."

"We'll be fine," Mom says. "Aunt Karla's place will be okay. She'll be happy to see us. Knowing her, I wouldn't be surprised if she's filled up the lodge with people."

"The lodge?" Dewey asks.

"She owns Fergus Peak Lodge."

Dewey shakes his head. "She's right in the thick of it. That lodge houses the cultists."

With Dewey's declaration of Aunt Karla's lodge being home to the cult, Rey and Kimba spend many minutes quizzing him and Marie for information. Unsatisfied with what they know, Rey asks if there's someone else around who can give better details. Dewey motions to a man with an unruly gray beard.

141

"What's up, Dew?" the man asks, his two missing front teeth causing a slight whistle when he speaks.

"These people are going to Fergus Peak Lodge."

He creases his forehead. "Why'd you want to do that?"

"We have family there," Rey answers.

"Humph. You related to Karla?"

Mom smiles and begins to respond, but Kimba rests a hand on her shoulder before saying, "Do you know Karla?"

"Used to. Haven't seen her in forever."

"Is she still at the lodge?"

"Couldn't tell ya. I'd like to think so. But them people pretty much keep to themselves. Didn't you tell them, Dewey?"

"I tried to tell them, but . . . " He lifts his hands.

Rey leans slightly toward the gray-bearded man. "We were looking for a little more information."

"Like I said, don't know what to tell ya. They keep to themselves. Come into town 'bout once a month and try to time it to meet the wagon. They'll bring veggies or meat to trade. Today wasn't their day, so none are around."

"Anything else?"

He shakes his head. "Sorry, folks. Us mere mortals aren't allowed 'round there. What you'll find is anyone's guess."

"Meaning?" Kimba asks.

"Meanin', I hope Karla's okay. She's a nice lady. But I wouldn't count on it."

"But you don't know." My mom steps forward.

"Nope."

Kimba and Rey share a look before thanking the man for the information. After another round of goodbyes, we watch as Dewey and Marie ride away.

"What should we do?" Donnie asks.

"I'm going to Karla's," Mom says. "I have to know."

Kimba looks toward the west. "It's getting late in the day. Let's start in that direction, and then camp tonight and continue in the morning. We'll make a plan after we have camp set up."

Chapter 21

It's only a few blocks walk to the turnoff Mom says will get us to Aunt Karla's. We don't talk, but there are plenty of concerned looks. What if Dewey's right and Aunt Karla's lodge has been overtaken?

It's not until we reach what's now an overgrown golf course, the grass deep green but too high, when Donnie, who's leading his horse instead of riding, asks, "Are we going to discuss the possibility Leanne's aunt is part of a cult?"

"Let's focus on getting out of this bottom land." Rey motions to the steep incline ahead of us. "As Kimba said, we'll set up camp and make a plan."

"Places like this always give me the creeps," Kimba says. "Give me the high ground any day."

Almost as if on instinct, everyone starts walking faster. By the time we reach the top of the hill, I'm panting and out of breath.

"This is better," Kimba declares.

"Is it?" Rey motions farther ahead with his chin, where there's an obvious roadblock.

My mom furrows her brow. "I don't understand. Karla's house is still miles away, and on another road."

"Dewey did tell us they have the area north of town," Rey says. "Might as well find out what's happening."

Mom grabs Sebastian's hand and then reaches for mine. "We're going to be fine," she whispers. "God's with us. We'll be fine."

Sebastian bobs his head enthusiastically. I force myself not to roll my eyes. The two of them may believe God is with us, but I'm not convinced. Besides, will it even matter if Aunt Karla has been forced from her home by the cult? We've been counting on her being there and being able to take us in.

We've encountered dozens of roadblocks before, including the one we just passed entering Lewistown. But somehow this one feels different, like it doesn't belong.

"Do you want me to take the lead?" My mom directs her question toward Rey and Kimba.

"You recognize anyone?" Kimba asks.

Mom squints her eyes. "We're not close enough. I only knew a few people around here. My aunt, of course, and there were a few neighbors who worked at the lodge, and . . . " Mom's voice fades away as she nibbles on her lip.

"And?" Donnie asks, walking beside her.

"Jack Mosher."

"Who's that?" Sebastian asks as we tromp along.

I'm searching my memory for his name. Was he someone she worked with? She used to talk a lot about how much fun it was working at the lodge. I'll admit, making beds and doing dishes doesn't sound like much fun, but I guess she really enjoyed it. More than once, she called it *the time of her life*.

"He was a friend and neighbor of my aunt's. His family owns a ranch just up the road, the Little Dogies Ranch. It's not far past that roadblock."

"That's far enough," a man behind the roadblock yells through a bullhorn. "This road is private. You'll need to go around."

"Okay, Leanne, you're on," Rey says quietly.

My mom clears her throat before calling back. "We're going to Fergus Peak Lodge."

A laugh sounds from the roadblock. "The lodge is closed, lady. But there's a hotel or two in town for travelers."

I watch as my mom straightens her shoulders. A scowl passes over her face before she forces her new smile into place. "Yes, thank you. My aunt is Karla Belvedere. We're here to see her."

Several people put their heads together. Mom's about to say something else when Kimba whispers, "Give them a minute. First one who talks loses."

"Whichever one of you just said Karla is your aunt, step on up here. The rest of you, stay where you are."

Mom starts to step forward when the man yells, "Wait! Set the rifle on the ground. In fact, all of you set your rifles down."

"We don't want to do that," Atticus whispers.

"Go ahead, put them down. Rifles only." Rey's jaw is tight, his teeth clenched.

"You sure about this?" Donnie asks.

"She needs to find out about her aunt. We'll comply. Leanne, put your rifle down and then start walking forward. Everyone else, set

144

them on the ground but stay alert. Donnie, maybe they didn't see yours in the scabbard. Just relax unless they tell you otherwise.

"I don't like this," Donnie mutters, while those carrying rifles unsling them and gently place them on the pavement.

Once my mom has hers on the ground, she loudly calls out, "I'm coming forward."

"Right," the man yells back. "Keep your hands away from your pistol. The rest of you too. Just be cool and everything will be fine."

"Sadie, Sebastian, don't worry. I'm sure we'll be fine." Mom gives us a smile that doesn't reach her eyes. "We didn't come all this way— God didn't bring us all this way— "

"We're okay, Mom," I insist.

She gives me a nod, raises her chin, and walks toward the roadblock.

When Mom's about halfway there, the man says something to her. He doesn't yell like he did before, so I can't hear him clearly, but I think he says, "You don't look much like Karla."

Mom says something back, speaking loud enough I can hear. "Karla is my mom's sister. *Was.* My mom . . . she didn't make it."

He says something back, then Mom replies, "I used to work at the lodge when I was young, just during the summers. Um . . . if you get Karla, she can tell you. Or if Jack Mosher's still around, he knows me. His dad and mom too, and even his little sister. They all know me."

There's scrambling at the roadblock as Mom stands in the road and we wait. It's many minutes before I hear a small engine in the distance. Then, about a minute later, a four-wheeler comes into view. A tall man wearing a tan cowboy hat climbs off and talks to the people at the gate for a minute. Several of them are pointing at Mom.

The new man takes the bullhorn. "Those of you at the back, I want you to step back a dozen feet. Leave the rifles where they are."

"Figures," Donnie grunts.

"Everyone do it," Rey says. "Donnie, just walk your horse back, see if you can keep the offside, where the scabbard is, out of view."

Once we're back away from the rifles, the man tells Mom to remove her gun belt and put it on the ground.

"She can't go up unarmed," I say with a squeak in my voice.

"She'll be fine," Rey assures me. "If they wanted to hurt her, hurt any of us, they'd have done so already. They're just being cautious."

145

After Mom is disarmed, she puts her hands out by her side. "Now what? Are you going to get Karla or one of the Moshers for me?"

The new man with the cowboy hat moves around the barricade and toward my mom. When he's about halfway to her, Mom says, "Jack? Is that you?"

"Hello, Annie," he responds, increasing his stride. "Karla thought you might show up."

I feel my eyes narrow as my mom moves forward to meet him. They stop a few feet apart before he opens his arms. She walks into his embrace.

"Mom must know him pretty well," Sebastian mutters under his breath.

"I guess so," Donnie says, his disappointment obvious.

He and Mom may not have publicly declared a relationship, but I'm sure Donnie thinks there's one. And from the little Mom's told me, he's right. I like Donnie. Sure, he's gruff and opinionated, but he's been good to Sebastian and me. And to my mom.

He goes out of his way to make things easy for her. When she was so negative about everything, so cruel to everyone, Donnie didn't let it bother him. He'd still go out of his way to talk to her, to crush on her. It seemed almost stalkerish at times.

He reminds me of a geeky guy who went to my school and had a crush on one of the cheerleaders. The only thing is, Donnie isn't a pimple-faced teenager. He's a thirtysomething burly cowboy. And right now, he looks like his heart is breaking.

"Dude," Jameson whispers. "Not cool to have a guy moving in on your girl."

Donnie shoots him a look. "Zip it."

With a mischievous smile, Jameson mimics zipping his lips.

Donnie shakes his head.

Mom steps away from the man in the cowboy hat. At this distance, I get a good look at him. He's clean shaven with a hawkish nose—handsome in a way. She's looking up at him as he says something, but they're speaking too quietly for me to hear.

"Do you think they'll let us see Aunt Karla?" Sebastian tugs on my hand.

"Maybe." I tilt my head.

After another couple of moments, Mom turns and motions us to come forward.

The man points to the gravel road. "Go ahead and pickup your weapons, but we expect you to be smart about it. Grab Annie's rifle also."

"So does this mean everything's okay?" Nicole asks her dad.

"Better than it was," Rey answers. "Let's still be smart, cautious."

"Something feels wrong about this." Kimba's voice is low.

The guy in the cowboy hat—Jack—walks with Mom to where she left her gun belt, holding her hand.

"Howdy, folks," he says when we're closer. "Sorry for the rigamarole. Just precautions. We can't be none too careful these days."

"This is my old friend Jack Mosher." Mom looks up at him. She gives him a smile, then looks over to me. "My daughter, Sadie, is in the light blue shirt. My son, Sebastian, is next to her."

"Nice to meet you." He tips his hat.

"The rest are good friends we've been traveling with," Mom says before quickly rattling off everyone's name.

"You all have been traveling by foot? Except you with the horse? Donnie, was it?"

"That's right." Donnie nods. "Leanne and I take turns on the horse."

Donnie's chest seems to puff out a bit when talking about sharing the horse. Of course, that's not really true right now. Although she often rode during our journey, she's been riding the roan since we left Roundup. I half expect Mom or someone to correct him.

Instead, Mom says, "Donnie's been wonderful about helping us get here. I got sick along the way, and if it wasn't for Donnie letting me ride when I was too tired to walk, why, they might have had to leave me on the side of the road." She lets out a small laugh.

"Never." Donnie is all serious, puffing out his chest even more. "We're a team. I made a commitment to get Leanne and her children to her aunt's house. Where is she, by the way?"

"Aunt Karla's here!" Mom cries. "Oh, I should've started with that. I'm sorry. Jack even called on his radio to let her know we're here."

"Well, someone will let her know. She doesn't have a radio at her place, but someone will tell her."

"My aunt fell a few days ago and sprained her ankle. Jack says she'll be fine but won't be able to come and see us. We'll need to go to her. They'll let us camp in his field tonight then we'll go to the lodge tomorrow."

"That's right." Jack nods. "But I forgot to mention to Annie—um, Leanne—we have a firearm rule within our compound."

Mom stops walking, causing Sebastian to bump into her. "What do you mean *a firearm rule?*"

Jack stops and looks at Mom, as the rest of us look at him. "Only authorized personnel carry weapons. The rest are locked up. It's a safety issue with the children around."

"We know all about being safe around guns," Sebastian declares. "I know every gun is always loaded and— "

"Thank you, Sebastian." Mom touches his shoulder, then looks up at Jack. "Are you saying we need to leave our guns somewhere?"

"Oh, no, not leave them. We'll stow them for you."

"This is just for the people living here?" Kimba asks.

"And for our rare visitors. Leanne said you'll be staying a few days while you tend to your game. We'll make sure you have your guns back when you go."

"No way." Donnie shakes his head. "No way, man."

"I understand that, with the way things are, it's concerning to not be armed. But as you can see— " he motions to the roadblock " — we have a well-trained security staff. This barricade is only one of three. No one gets past them. You'll be completely safe."

"I don't care if— " Donnie starts.

Mom interrupts. "Jack, let me talk with my friends for a moment. But before I do, I want to make sure I understand. If my friends stay, they need to be unarmed for the duration of their visit? And my children and I will be unarmed while we live here?"

"That's right." Jack nods vigorously. "You won't need guns inside our perimeter. Think of it as a vacation. You'll be able to relax and enjoy yourself while you're here."

Jack looks around at the group before looking back at my mom. "And you and your children will be plenty safe. Why, within a few days, you'll forget the troubles you may have seen that made you feel the need to be armed."

Mom scoffs. "I doubt that." For just a moment, a grimace crosses her face. She closes her eyes and takes a deep breath. "Please let us discuss this privately."

"Absolutely," Jack says. "Just know, there's no wavering of the rules."

"Understood." Rey's voice is gruff and low.

Jack touches his cowboy hat before turning away.

Rey motions we should step farther from the barricade, toward where we were before. After we go about thirty yards, he motions us to stop. "We're far enough away to speak privately."

"I'm so sorry," Mom says. "I had no idea."

"There's no way you could've known." Kimba pats Mom on the arm. "I suppose you understand why we're uncomfortable with this."

"*I'm* uncomfortable with it!" Mom's voice rises. She clears her throat. "I don't know if we should stay here."

"Mom!" I gasp. "We don't have any place else to go."

"You can continue on to our ranch," Jennifer says. "You're always welcome there."

Mom puts a hand to her head, massaging her temple. "No, we can't do that. As much as I appreciate the offer, my place is here, with my aunt. Especially after hearing she's injured. But I guess you won't be able to stay and take care of the meat."

Kimba and Rey share a look.

Donnie crosses his arms. "I'm not leaving you here with those pacifists. You'll be a sitting duck."

"I'm not sure they're actually pacifists," Mom says. "It sounds like they just want to ensure anyone using a weapon is well trained. I'll probably just need to go through some sort of class and then I'll be part of their . . . um, what'd he say? Security personnel?"

"I'm not sure about that." Victoria motions toward the roadblock. "Do you see any women there? They probably keep the women doing the cooking and cleaning. At least they didn't say they'd lock up my hatchets. And everyone can probably keep their knives."

"I'm not sure we should go inside the perimeter," Rey says.

"I know." Mom lets out a sigh. "Maybe they'd let you camp outside of it? We can take care of the meat at least before you continue on?"

"That might be best," Kimba agrees. "What does everyone think?"

"I'm not leaving Leanne until I know she's safe—her and the children." Donnie crosses his arms. "I want to be sure their aunt will take them in."

"Thank you, Donnie." Mom smiles at him. "And I agree. I'm not comfortable separating from any of you until we know. I'd like to stay with you until they can get word to my aunt and I can be sure everything is . . . well, until I'm sure we can stay."

"Why wouldn't we be able to?" Sebastian asks. "God led us here, right?"

"He did," Mom agrees. "But I guess I just thought things would be different when we got here. And I'm sure Aunt Karla will want us to stay. Don't worry, Sebastian."

"I'm not worried, but . . . " He chews on his bottom lip. "It's not time to worry yet."

"So, we'll make sure it's okay to camp outside their perimeter?" Mom asks, looking around.

After a series of nods and verbal agreements, she lets out a loud breath. "Then, tomorrow, I'll walk the rest of the way to Aunt Karla's. I'll visit with her and then come back out and let you know everything is okay."

"And we'll work on the meat while you go check on your aunt," Jennifer says.

"Man, I was really looking forward to getting an elk," Jameson pouts.

"I'll let Jack know and make sure we can do what we're talking about." Mom turns toward Jack. Her stride is strong and purposeful. Even from the back, she looks fierce. Determined.

Chapter 22

Jack Mosher gave us permission to set up camp in a cleared area a couple hundred yards from their roadblock.

As we put up our tent, I ask Mom about Mosher. She lifts a shoulder before reminding me she hasn't seen him in years and really knows little more than the rest of us. Especially about what they're doing now.

I can't help but roll my eyes. "I know that. What I meant was before. I mean, it's kind of strange for you to see him here."

"Not really. His family owns the ranch, have since before Aunt Karla and Uncle Ralph bought their place."

"And you were friends?"

She closes her eyes. "Let's finish setting up."

Okay, then. I can take a hint. She doesn't want to talk about him.

We're quiet for many minutes, each doing our part, when Mom says, "I noticed you aren't limping when you walk. Does your toe feel okay now?"

"It doesn't hurt at all. I'd tell you if it did. I definitely learned my lesson on that."

"Need some help, Leanne?" Donnie asks, striding toward us.

Mom gives him a smile. "We about got it. I do have to say, it's good we're here. I'm not sure this tent has much life left in it."

"It's hard on them, with as much up and down as they get. So . . . you're thinking you'll stay?"

She tilts her head at him. "That was the plan all along."

"Even with their rules?"

"I'll talk with Karla. I'm sure— "

"I'll be going with you."

"No, Donnie." Mom raises a hand. "While I'm confident it's completely safe, I'll feel better going to the lodge alone. Being unarmed . . . " She shakes her head. "I know it's not something anyone's really comfortable with."

"You shouldn't be comfortable with it either."

"I'm not, not entirely. But I'll abide by their rules. I didn't come all this way to not see my aunt, to not do everything possible for Sadie and Sebastian to finally have safety."

"Humph. Safety. It's your God-given right to protect yourself. Why— "

"I know, Donnie." Mom's voice is quiet. "Please, I need you to support me."

He lets out a long breath. "I always support you."

As their eyes meet, I'm suddenly embarrassed to be here. The look they share is one of love.

The corner of Mom's mouth twitches slightly. "You've been good to me. I understand the concerns you have. But I have to do this. I *must* do this."

"You don't have to do it alone. I want to go with you."

"I know you do, and I think you will. But not this time."

He shakes his head. "You think I'll be too much of a hothead."

"Well . . . " She gives him a brilliant smile. "There is that."

Letting out a roar of laughter, Donnie lifts his hands in defeat. "Guilty. How about Kimba? She could go in with you. No one could ever accuse her of being a hothead. And if things get tough, she could probably kill whoever it was with her pinky finger or some such spy tricks."

Mom moves her mouth, chewing on the inside of it before giving a slight tilt of her head. "That's not a bad idea, if she's willing."

"You know she will be."

After camp's set up, everyone gathers around for supper.

Donnie crosses his arms and stretches out his legs. "I suppose you all know Leanne is dead set on going in there unarmed. Leanne and I were talking about how dangerous it is."

"I'll go with her," Kimba volunteers. "Rey and I already talked about it."

"You're sure?" Mom asks.

"Positive."

"And you'll follow the no-gun rule?" Donnie asks.

Kimba lifts a shoulder. "I suppose we'll be searched, patted down even."

"That'd be my guess." Mom nods.

Kimba raises her eyebrows. "Well, that could be interesting." She gently touches her right hand to her armpit where she carries a second small pistol. "Very interesting."

~~~~~

I wake up with the sun filtering into my tent. It's already too warm in here. Sebastian is curled against my back. I squeeze my eyes shut a moment more as I listen to the sounds around me. A tent does little to keep out the noise. Or keep it in, for that matter.

When the three of us were traveling with Ben Ferguson, we had a tent similar in size to this one. Stealth was always the name of the game. Inside the tent, we talked in low voices only, listening and straining our ears for any little sound that might be a threat.

And there were plenty of threats for sure. While the worst of it happened when we were first kidnapped and separated from the rest of Ben's family, none of it was worry free.

Squeezing my eyes shut, the memories of being locked up and then escaping wash over me.

When I first wake up, the morning after we got away, it's to the smell of a campfire. It's nearly dark, with Mom and Sebastian still sleeping.

"How'd you get the fire going?" I ask Ben.

"Friction."

"Friction?"

"Yeah, and dry tinder. Took a while. I've seen it done before, but this is the first time I've tried it. Whenever I camped before, I always made sure to have a lighter and matches."

As I smell the campfire outside this tent, here in Lewistown, I smile at the memory of Ben's excitement over making fire. He may have struggled the first few times, but he soon became a friction-fire expert and taught the rest of us how to do it too. The skill saved our lives more than once, I'm sure.

Sebastian stirs next to me. He rolls over, giving me some space. I sit up. Mom's spot on the other side of my brother is unsurprisingly empty. I'm sure she was up with the sun.

"Whatcha doin'?" Sebastian mutters.

"Getting up. Scoot over a little, and stay facing away while I get dressed."

153

I miss the privacy of my own space. Getting dressed in a tiny tent isn't easy. I don't know how Mom manages to do it when all three of us are in here. But each morning she does, rarely disturbing us as she changes from her comfortable sleeping clothes into her day wear.

Leaving our bags and anything we don't absolutely need outside the tent helps, but it's still tight. At least we haven't had rain the last few days, so my clothes are dry.

During the snowy winter and rainy spring, dry clothes were almost a luxury. The ankle area of my pants were often wet—even with wearing snow gear over the top! We'd do our best to dry them out near the small fires in the evening, but it was almost always a losing battle.

After I'm dressed, I tell Sebastian he should do the same as I work the zipper to escape the now too-warm tent. In the camp, my mom is kneeling near the firepit.

She lifts her head and gives me a smile. "Good morning, baby girl."

I cringe at the use of the nickname.

Seeing my expression, she corrects herself. "Sadie. How'd you sleep?"

"Good. Where is everyone?"

"You're the first of the youth up. Donnie's brushing his horse." She motions to Donnie at the edge of camp. "Atticus is keeping watch, walking the perimeter. Everyone else went down to the creek for water—and to have a chat, I'd suspect."

"You should let me come with you to Aunt Karla's."

Mom pats the ground near the firepit, inviting me to come sit near her while she cooks antelope strips for our breakfast. "I know you want to go. And I know the talk we had last night and knowing about the problems they had at the ski lodge with the no-guns rule bothers you."

"It should bother you too," I say quietly.

Before we arrived at the ski lodge, the town council, led by Victoria's crazy husband, passed a rule that no one could carry guns unless they were on watch. That rule was what allowed him and his followers to think they could take over the town. It didn't work the way he planned, but it could've.

"It does," Mom agrees with a nod. "But I'm still going to Aunt Karla's."

"Will we stay here?"

154

"Let me get more of a feel for the community and see if it really is safe, then we'll decide."

"Ha!"

"I know. After all we've been through, it's hard to trust others with our safety—with our lives. But maybe Jack's right. Maybe it'll be so peaceful we'll forget the past year."

"You really believe that? And can you even trust this guy? You haven't seen him since . . . when exactly?"

She moves her head slightly.

"I know you said last night you didn't want to talk about him right now, but we should. Don't you think, Mom?"

"No, Sadie. I don't think we need to talk about Jack to decide whether or not we stay here. The choice will be up to Aunt Karla and me."

I close my eyes, feeling almost as if I've been slapped. I guess I thought I'd have some say in a decision like this. My voice is tight. "But he'll have to approve it, right? It sounds like he's king of this little group—or cult, if Dewey's correct."

Mom lets out a small laugh. "I can't imagine Jack leading a cult. He's . . . religion isn't his thing."

"You mean Christianity? He doesn't have to be a Christian to run a cult, does he?"

Mom makes a face while lifting her shoulder. "I suspect Dewey exaggerates."

"But he wouldn't let us in! Not without leaving the guns behind. That sounds . . . just like we were talking about last night."

"Taking care of people isn't always easy. Sometimes it includes hard decisions. I'm sure Jack has his reasons. Let's not worry about this today. I'll talk to Aunt Karla, then we'll have more information."

I open my mouth to interrupt, but Mom raises a hand. "I'm sure it's going to be fine. We'll look back on this and laugh about how silly we were being. Besides, like I said yesterday, I probably just need some training before they allow me to carry inside their compound. We'll be fine. You'll see."

Chapter 23

Even though it's only shortly after lunch, it feels like a long day already. Mom and Kimba left yesterday after breakfast. They planned on hiking the five or so miles from our camp to the lodge, visit with Aunt Karla, and stay the night before returning to camp today.

Atticus, Brett, and Axel went hunting, and Rey, Jameson, and Donnie are monitoring the camp, walking the perimeter to make sure all is well.

Jennifer, Victoria, and Nicole were working on drying the antelope. Now that they've got it all started, they took a walk to forage for edibles. I told them I'd keep an eye on the meat and also stay with Sebastian and Naomi, who are working on spelling words.

Mom and Kimba decided a few days rest meant they could have a little schooling. Nate is also supposed to do schooling, but he's out setting box traps to try and catch birds.

I'm barely paying attention to the kids as I think about what we should do—what Mom will *decide* we should do. Sometimes I love the idea of stopping, staying here and letting Jack Mosher and his people provide for our safety. Could it really be so easy? Could this little enclave be a utopia where we won't be in constant worry of danger?

On the other hand, somehow it feels wrong. Like we need to visit Aunt Karla for a few days, just to make sure she's okay, then we should keep going, continue on with the rest of the group and make our home with the Dosens on their ranch.

The idea of living around Victoria and Jameson causes me to cringe. Both have been considerably kinder since the mud incident, where Jameson insisted he was just teasing me, but I'm still not comfortable around them.

I glance toward the rotted stump they found and set up last night for axe throwing practice. As usual, they had a great time. One would nail a good throw, and they'd high-five each other and laugh. The two of them seem so much happier.

Even Brett, who doesn't practice with them often, seems to have a weight lifted off his shoulders. He smiles more readily, and he'll even occasionally joke around. And there have hardly been any arguments among the family and few difficulties with the rest of us.

Mom said she thought part of the reason they've been better is because of Asher's death. Although Jameson could be a jerk, he was still friends with Asher. And Brett and Asher were very close. Maybe they've realized they're both grieving and that helps keep them from being at each other's throats.

Last night, Jennifer commented on how much calmer things are. I half expected Victoria or Jameson to take offense—their usual response to things—but both just nodded.

"I feel calmer." Victoria let out a loud breath. "I don't know what the difference is, but . . . I think maybe the fact that you all have been so, um, accommodating to us has helped. I know there have been times when things were difficult. I wouldn't have faulted any of you for telling us to pack up and get out."

"We wouldn't feel right about it," Rey said. "Kimba and I, our children too, we discussed leaving you on the side of the road. It may have been the easy choice, but how could we? What kind of people, *what kind of Christians*, would we be if we stranded you over a hundred miles from home?"

"The kind who got tired of Jameson's sh—stuff," Donnie said.

Rey shot Donnie a look. "Jameson isn't the only one who's been difficult at times, mate."

Donnie threw back his head and laughed. "Touché. I guess there was a time I wasn't exactly in my right mind. And I do appreciate you all putting up with me." He lifted a hand to the side of his head, rubbing a finger along the hairless groove where he was shot.

"Earth to Sadie." Sebastian pokes me in the arm, rousing me from my thoughts. "Did you hear me?"

"Huh?"

"I said Mom's back." He points toward the roadblock where Mom and Kimba are talking with someone. "I'm glad. Maybe we'll leave."

Last night, in our tent, Sebastian started crying. At first, he wouldn't tell me what was wrong, but I finally got him talking—somewhat anyway. He said he was worried about staying here. God promised him we'd get here and see Aunt Karla, but now he's not so sure. He thinks maybe Aunt Karla is supposed to leave with us.

Today, he's been out of sorts. Distracted, tired even.

"My mom doesn't look very happy." Naomi shakes her head.

"How can you tell?" I ask, squinting my eyes to better peer at Kimba. "They're so far away, I can't even see their faces."

She shrugs. "I just know. The way she's standing, I guess. She looks mad . . . or something."

Once Mom and Kimba are closer, I can see Naomi's right. Not only does Kimba not look happy, but neither does Mom.

"I'm going to run out and meet them," Sebastian says. "Okay, Sadie?"

"Let's all go." I hoist myself from the ground.

As we move toward them, Mom gives us a tired smile and a wave. "Hey, kids."

After hello hugs, I ask, "How's Aunt Karla?"

Mom releases a loud sigh. "Her ankle's bad, very swollen. Jack didn't mention she hit her face when she fell. Both eyes are blackened, and she may have a concussion. She's completely bedridden and . . . confused."

"A concussion? Is it bad?"

"Bad enough. She, uh . . . she barely recognized me. And she said some weird things. Her ankle . . . " Mom shakes her head.

"Is it broken?"

"Maybe," Kimba answers. "They don't have a doctor here. They're being extra careful, just in case."

"When will she be walking again?" Sebastian asks, his eyebrows drawn close together.

"Weeks, probably."

With a shake of his head, he says, "We'll just have to wait for her."

"What's that?" Kimba asks.

"Nothing."

Kimba and Mom share a long look.

"Well . . . " Mom wraps an arm around Sebastian's shoulders. "We're going to talk about our plans."

"Good!" Sebastian exclaims as we begin to walk back to camp. "Atticus's ranch sounds nice, and we can be happy there. It's right on a river, you know. He said they even have an area where they go swimming."

Mom stops walking and looks directly at Sebastian. "We'll talk about it. But we'll wait until the group is all together."

"The hunters should be back soon." I motion toward camp. "We haven't heard any shots."

158

Moving again, Kimba shakes her head. "I suspect the wild game is pretty well played out this close to town and the compound. At least from what we've heard. The people living here sent a group of elk hunters into the mountains."

"Do they have things set up nicely?" I ask.

"Pretty nice," Mom answers. "Lots of gardens and planted fields, cattle, chicken, goats. One of the people who walked us to the lodge said they haven't really had any trouble. And they had very few deaths over the winter."

A sad look crosses Mom's face. "Unfortunately, one of those was Jack's dad. He was a nice man, and it's a huge loss for their community. I also found out Jack's mom died the day after the EMP. No one knows why, she just collapsed. And Jack's sister moved away years ago. She lives on the East Coast. He hasn't heard from her."

"I'm sorry," I say, only because I know it's expected. So many people have died, people I actually did know and love. Strangers I've never met don't really affect me.

"I haven't seen them for years," Mom says. "Jack either, of course. But it's still sad to know his parents are gone. And I know it could've been Aunt Karla too. She's only a few years younger than them. I just hope this injury doesn't— " Mom shakes her head.

While we wait for the others to return, Mom and I are alone, and I try to get her to talk about Aunt Karla and what things were like at the lodge. Other than telling me again about the crops they're growing and how they're working together, I learn nothing new.

"Did you ask about training so you can have your gun?"

She gives a slow nod. "Seems Victoria may have been right about that. They have some gender-specific roles."

I let out a harsh laugh. "What's that mean? The women do all the cooking and cleaning, while the men tote the guns around?"

She raises her eyebrows and gives a single bob of her head. "We'll talk more when everyone's back."

"We'll stay?"

"We'll talk with everyone, Sadie. I need more time to process this."

"Mom," I say softly, "I think I should have more of a say in this than— "

"Sadie, please. I do want your opinion, and you'll be able to give it. But I also need to hear what Rey and Donnie have to say about everything."

"If we stay, will you invite Donnie to stay with us?"

A shy smile lifts her lips. "Would you be okay with that?"

"Would you marry him?"

"Well . . . " Her voice goes very quiet. "We've talked about it."

I put my hand to my mouth. "Really?"

"You'd be okay with it?"

Would I? It's not like I haven't watched them and noticed the beginnings of a romance. But do I want Donnie as a stepfather? He's so . . .

"I know he can be a little much sometimes." Mom grins. "But then again, I've been a little much sometimes too." She gives a laugh. "Oh, what a pair we were. I'm sure there were times we drove the rest of them crazy, especially poor Tamra. I was terrible to her. Donnie was too."

It's at least an hour later before our people start trickling back into camp. When Mom sees Donnie, she tells me she'll be back in a minute. They spend a considerable amount of time talking, well out of hearing distance. Even though I can't hear them, from their gestures, the conversation seems intense.

Atticus, Axel, and Brett finally return from their hunt, empty handed. "We found a creek—or maybe more of a ditch—that was beat up with tracks," Atticus says. "I think we'll go and sit there this evening, see what comes in."

"I'm not sure that's the best idea," Kimba says. "We got the impression they might take issue with us harvesting game around here."

"Really?"

"I don't know." Mom shrugs. "It doesn't sound like there's much game left this close to town, but they probably wouldn't mind. They have the cattle and other livestock."

Kimba doesn't look convinced. "I've called Rey on the radio. I'll meet him, then when we get back, we can all talk about what we know—and don't know."

Atticus watches as Kimba walks away. "Is she okay?"

"I don't think she thought much of Jack's community," my mom answers, then motions to Donnie. "Want to walk with me a moment until Kimba and Rey return?"

Once they're gone, Atticus turns to me. "Did you have fun being the schoolmarm today?"

160

"A blast."

Sebastian and Naomi, released from their lessons, have set up a makeshift game of hopscotch.

"It was fine, really. I used to think maybe I'd like to be a teacher. I've always enjoyed learning, so . . . "

"You'd be a great teacher. I guess, until official schools and colleges start up again, it'll be like it was when we lived at the ski lodge. People will apprentice to learn what they need to know and then teach others. Were you starting to think about colleges?"

I lift a shoulder. "Maybe a little. I'd just finished my sophomore year when . . . you know, everything happened."

"Yeah, I know. You being sixteen makes sense. Asher— " Atticus gulps in a breath. "He, um, he always said you were a smart one, way too smart for your age. He thought you might be some kind of genius or prodigy."

I let out a laugh. "Um, no. I'm pretty much normal for my age . . . my real age. You were looking at colleges, right? That's why you were away from home when the attacks started?"

"We were. Seems like a long time ago now. It hasn't even been a year yet since the first planes were blown up and the downward spiral began, but it *feels* like it's been longer."

We sit in silence for several minutes until Atticus says, "We found a cabin today. Shack might be a better word. It looks like there's a family living there. Good thing it's summer. With the condition of the place, I'm not sure they'd do well in the winter."

"Do you think they're living there or just resting a few days? You know, like we did in places?"

"Maybe. Yeah. But they did have things set up pretty well from what we could see. We kept our distance."

"Smart."

"As my mom would say, 'no use borrowing trouble.' We've had enough trouble as it is."

It's at least a half hour before Rey and Kimba return. Once everyone's gathered around, Atticus turns to my mom. "So, your aunt? She's okay and you'll be staying?"

"As much as I want to say yes, that this is exactly where we should be, I have some concerns." Mom looks at Sebastian.

Shortly before everyone came back to camp, he started complaining of a stomachache. I made him some peppermint tea, which he said helped, but he still looks a little pale. When Mom asked him if he was okay, he said, "I'm worried about Aunt Karla."

Donnie motions at my mom. "Leanne and I were talking. Would you all be willing to hang out here a few days? She'd like to take her children to the lodge, let them meet their aunt—have a real conversation with her, too, without prying ears hanging around."

"Kimba was telling me about that." Rey rubs his chin. "She said there are several women, teenage girls, and children living at your aunt's place."

"Right," Mom says. "They've taken in people from the area who needed a place, and others who were friends but too far away to provide the protection needed. Aunt Karla's added a few cabins since I was last here, so she has the space. The way they've sectioned off their group . . . " Mom furrows her brow. "Um, Jack calls everyone the Little Dogies. You know, after the name of his ranch, but for the meaning of the name, too, I guess."

"Doggies?" Jameson asks. "Like pups?"

"Dogies," Donnie corrects. "The o is long. It's an old cowboy term for a calf separated from his mom."

"Hmm," Jennifer says. "I do like the sound of that, in a way. And it sounds like they're taking in people who need homes. Is that correct?"

"Seems so." Kimba scrunches her face while lifting her shoulders. "One of the women at the lodge said there are more women and children than men. Because of the space she has, Karla's place is their home. The lodge is nestled up against a couple of mountains and seems protected—good thing, since they're back there all alone. It's a good half mile to the nearest house."

"Do they have security?" Atticus asks.

"There're a couple of roadblocks like this one, and those look good. There are other houses and farms too. Then there are the mountains and wilderness behind the lodge. Attacking from there would be a challenge—possible but challenging. And there wasn't any security at the lodge."

"They do have sentries and roving patrols," Mom adds. "And even someone living up on the mountain to act as a scout."

"Jack Mosher gave you all this intel?" Atticus shakes his head. "Doesn't he know loose lips sink ships?"

162

"He didn't," Kimba corrects. "We saw the roadblocks, and Leanne told me about the lay of the land. Another lady at the lodge told us about the person on the mountain. There's an old trapper's cabin up there. They rotate out each week, sending a new man from the community to be on watch."

"I do think we'd be safe enough." Mom directs her comment to Sebastian. "The security here seems close to what we had at the ski lodge."

"My stomach hurts when I think about staying," my brother says, once again looking pale and pained.

"It does sound okay, Sebastian," I say. "Plus, wouldn't you like to be able to stop? And you know how excited you've been about meeting Aunt Karla. You said we'd be safe here."

He shakes his head. "No . . . I said we'd *get* here safely. I think that's what I said."

I close my eyes as sadness overwhelms me. We, my little family of three, did get here safely. But we lost Asher.

"And you were right." Mom touches his leg. "We're here. We're safe. I know none of us like the rule of not being able to have our guns on us, but we know how rules can be. There were rules the military had in place when we were traveling through. We couldn't take our guns in when we got meals."

"But we weren't living there," Sebastian replies.

"And from what Kimba and Leanne saw, it sounds like very few people do carry," Rey says. "You didn't see anyone except for the people at the roadblocks, right?"

"Right," Kimba agrees with a nod. "We saw Jack, of course, when he was giving us our little *welcome to the neighborhood* talk. The man who was our escort and those stationed at the two roadblocks were all armed. And there were people working in the fields and gardens. I didn't see any guns on them, but they were at a distance."

"And was it only men at the roadblocks?" Victoria asks.

"That's all we saw. We didn't specifically ask, but from the lady we talked to, who told us about them rotating out at the cabin, it sounds like the men are in charge of security."

Victoria shakes her head. "You know I'm not a fan of guns, and before all this happened, before the lights went out and everything, I was a fan of traditional gender roles. I had my part to play, while my . . . " She clears her throat. "I'm just not sure I think that any

163

longer. I mean, look at you, Leanne. You've kept your children alive. I'm not sure I'd be willing to rely on someone else for my security."

My mom's eyes meet mine. It's true that she's kept us alive, most of the time without the benefit of a rifle or handgun. With just the one gun we took from our captors, Ben and Mom provided food and security for weeks. Well, just Ben at first.

Mom knew very little about guns, so Ben had to show her how to use it. And ammunition was an issue. He only had what was in the gun and a second magazine he took off the guy he overpowered.

When we found a house where a man and woman had chosen to take their own lives, we got a second handgun and a light rifle, each with a decent amount of ammo. Mom had to use the rifle when a couple of men saw us and started after us. It didn't end well for one of them. The other one yelled terrible things but didn't keep coming.

Mom sucks in her top lip and gives a slow nod. "I think we'd best."

"No, Mom," Sebastian says with considerable force. "We need to take Aunt Karla and go with Atticus."

"Aunt Karla isn't in any condition to travel," Mom replies. "With the concussion and her ankle . . . it'll be weeks."

"Then they need to wait for us." My brother motions to the group.

"A couple of days?" Donnie asks. "If you'd all be willing to stay here, keep our guns and my horse until we know more, we'd appreciate it."

Mom reaches for Sebastian. He scoots into her arms, and she gives him a kiss on the top of the head. "Okay? Then we'll have enough information to decide. I certainly won't rush into a situation that won't be okay for you and Sadie."

Dropping his shoulders, Sebastian whispers, "Okay, Mom."

Chapter 24

"Want to hunt with us this evening?" Atticus asks.

I glance around to see who he's talking to.

"Sadie? You interested?"

"Me?" I point at my chest.

"Yeah, why not?"

"Because . . . you remember what happened last time you took me hunting?"

"I remember you learned from the incident. We want to hunt the creek with all the tracks on it. I think we should plan on being in place about an hour and a half before sundown and then see what comes in."

My heart rate increases, and my breath comes in quick gasps. I chew on my upper lip as I give a slow nod. "I'll go."

He gives me a smile. "I knew you would."

During an early supper of stewed antelope, the conversation of Aunt Karla and the situation in this neighborhood continues. Mom seems impressed with the things they've done, with the crops they're growing and the way they work together.

She's concerned about Aunt Karla's injuries, which are much more severe than Jack originally indicated. When she spoke with him on the way out, he said he had no idea she had a concussion; the only thing he'd heard about was the ankle.

Kimba seems less impressed with their organization. "Like we said earlier, there's several women and children staying at Karla's lodge. The one who seemed to be the main caregiver to Karla's injuries was rather . . . uptight. She didn't want to share much about anything. But another lady—a girl really, maybe late teens or early twenties—was a chatterbox, and she's seriously in awe of Leanne's friend Jack."

My mom leans back slightly as a dreamy look crosses her face. "Jack always did have a way with the ladies."

Donnie stiffens. "Is that right?"

Something in my mom's demeanor shifts. I notice her eyes fill with tears right before she drops her head.

Watching my mom, Donnie changes too. His eyes soften as he reaches for her hand. "Hey, I'm sorry. I shouldn't have been so . . . "

Mom waves a hand. "It's not you. I just . . . sometimes the past has a way of coming back and hitting full force." With an embarrassed smile, she looks around our gathered group. "Jack and I have a history."

Victoria scoffs. "That's been obvious from the start."

Mom shakes her head. "Knowing him, I shouldn't be surprised he took control of the situation and set these things up. He always needed to be in charge."

"It sounds like he has things under control. It'll be a good place for you to live." Victoria motions back toward the roadblock. "Maybe it really will be restful for you, knowing someone else is looking over things and protecting you."

"You change your mind about keeping the women barefoot and pregnant?" Donnie asks.

"Humph. Not even. I'm just saying Leanne can finally get a break after all she's been through. Sadie and Sebastian too. Part of me wishes we were all at the end of our journey and were being welcomed here." She quickly shakes her head and makes eye contact with Jennifer. "Not that I'm not excited about being on your ranch with you."

"Understood." Jennifer nods. "I, too, can see the appeal of here. But then I remember we had that at the ski lodge with our friends from Bakerville. My boys and I, we made a conscious decision to leave their shelter and protection." Her voice breaks. "We all wanted to go home."

Atticus wraps an arm around his mom's shoulder. She rests her head on him as her tears fall.

"I appreciate you putting off your journey a few days to wait with us." My mom gives Jennifer a small nod. "I know how badly you're ready to be done with this, to finish your journey and properly grieve the loss of Asher."

Jennifer offers my mom a small smile.

Mom's eyes fill with tears as she returns the gesture. "God has . . . He has truly given me a gift in you and your sons. You and your family, too, Kimba. Even when I was too stubborn to see it." Mom's eyes travel to Victoria. "You feel it, too, right?"

Victoria wrinkles her nose. "I don't . . . I'm not sure what you mean."

166

"You feel the difference? How there's a . . . a peace, a knowing that we all needed to be together, to help each other. It's how it's supposed to be."

Victoria frowns. "Supposed to be? I'm grateful, if that's what you mean."

"Yes, grateful. Me too." Mom leans forward, meeting Victoria's gaze. "I'm grateful for you as well, and for your sons. I know things haven't always been easy. There've been times . . . " Mom lifts a hand and gives a girlish giggle. "I've been awful, and so have you."

I gasp, as do several others.

Victoria's eyes go wide. She opens her mouth, then rapidly closes it and points at my mom. Just when I think she's going to go off on my her, Victoria's shoulders give a shudder. Then she lets out a noise. Soon, she's also giggling, which gets my mom going into full-on laughter.

Kimba is soon laughing, too, and even in her grief, so is Jennifer.

Sebastian gives me a weird look and scratches his head. I'm with him and can't figure out why this is so funny to them.

"Women," Donnie grunts.

~~~~~

"You know, baby girl, you don't have to go. You have nothing to prove."

I crane my neck up to meet her eyes. "You sure?"

"Positive. No one even thinks twice about what happened before."

"Other than me." I turn back to my pack. I've emptied it out, leaving only the essentials for the hunt.

"Why do you let it bother you? Not everyone's like Atticus and is able to go out and come back an hour later with a deer slung over his back. He didn't even do that this time, you know."

"Because he didn't see any deer, not because he messed up and scared them away. I can't explain it, Mom. Other than . . . I haven't contributed anything."

She squats next to me. "You're still young."

"Mom, I'm nearly the same age as Atticus. Two years younger isn't much. And look at Nicole. She may not hunt, but she's . . . she's a warrior, just like her mom."

"*You* are a warrior! You got your brother away from a madman."

"I need to do this. It's probably my last chance to prove to myself I *can* do this."

Mom rests a hand on my shoulder. "I understand."

I stare at my pack as I bite my lip.

Mom moves a finger to my chin and gently raises my face to meet her eyes. "Baby girl, you've always been wise beyond your years. Your grandma, the first time she saw you, she said— "

"I know, Mom. She looked in my eyes and said there was so much going on there and God had blessed me with wisdom."

"She was right. You were always so grown up. Quiet but alert. Never missing a thing. Even when you were toddling around, there was something mature about you. When I made the decision to lie about your age, I wasn't sure people would believe it."

I wrinkle my forehead.

"Oh, your size was right, no doubt about that. But your demeanor . . . Ben was the first to tell me it'd be a hard sell once you opened your mouth and your wisdom showed. I guess it's a good thing you're so quiet." She gives me a half smile. "Is that some of the reason, Sadie? Me forcing you to pretend to be a young child instead of a budding adult?"

"Reason?"

"That you feel the need to prove yourself."

"Mom." I force myself not to roll my eyes. "I'm just going hunting. For a deer. Or maybe an antelope. It's not like I'm going off to war."

"Really? It sort of . . . " She contorts her mouth. "I don't know why it feels so . . . so big." She opens her arms wide.

"You ready to go, Sadie?" Atticus calls from the other side of the camp.

I lift a finger. "One minute." My eyes move back to Mom. "Are you saying you don't want me to go?"

"No, no. Not at all. Go. Enjoy the experience. Just don't put so much stock in your success. Bringing home supper has little bearing on your contribution to our group." She awkwardly duck walks toward me to wrap an arm around my shoulder. "You *are* enough."

"Thanks, Mom. I'd better go." We stand together, and I lift my chin toward Atticus.

He responds with a nod, then turns to talk with Brett. Axel, who has first watch tonight, has decided not to come but rather stay in camp and catch a nap.

168

Mom pats me again. "I'd better go see to Sebastian. His stomach's bothering him again."

"Yeah, it's been off all day."

"It'll be good to get settled. This traveling is hard, and he worries too much. See you soon, baby girl."

As I step up to Atticus, he hands me a rifle. "We'll sit together. Brett will be in another spot where we saw a game trail."

Taking the rifle, the same one from the failed deer hunt, I check to see if it's loaded and if the safety's on. I'm uber careful, making sure to follow all the gun rules. A shudder runs through my body as I think of how deadly a negligent discharge could be.

"You okay?"

My lips are a tight line. "I'm ready."

Atticus's eyes meet mine. "Let's go then. This is going to be a little different from what we've done before. Our plan is to get there, set up, and wait for them to come to us."

"You think they will?"

"Hard telling. We know they've been using the creek for water, so they could. But it's always a gamble."

"I guess that's why they call it hunting." Brett cracks a smile.

"Yeah," Atticus agrees. "Once upon a time, hunting was a fun pastime. Now it feels like a chore needed for survival."

We make our way to the creek in silence. When we're close, Atticus puts a hand on Brett's shoulder and motions for him to break off from us.

Brett gives me a smile before leaning toward me. "You'll do fine." He winks and then turns away.

Atticus beckons me to start moving. We walk a couple hundred yards before he stops. With his mouth by my ear, he says, "The trail is just ahead. It leads down to the water. We'll sit on that knob there." He gestures with his chin.

I nod my understanding. Sitting and waiting for the deer to come to us sounds like it may take a while. A buzz near my ear has my hand moving frantically. This close to the creek on a warm June evening, we'll be feasted on by mosquitos while we wait for the elusive wildlife. I smack a blood sucker from my arm.

"They're relentless," Atticus whispers. "Maybe a breeze'll come up and push those nasty things out for a bit."

We move to the spot Atticus chose for us to sit. The hillside is steep, and I wonder if the ground will give way as I carefully pick my way to the top. With Atticus behind me, I make the final stretch to a semi-flat spot. I turn and look at him for confirmation.

He answers with a nod as he scrambles next to me, then looks out over the creek. "Good view. We can see how beaten down the trail is. This brush will be good camouflage."

As I survey the creek, which is really nothing more than a wide ditch, I motion to a gentle slope behind us. "We could've come up that way. It would've been much easier."

"Oops. We'll go down that route. Won't be nothing but an easy stroll." He gives me a wink. "Get yourself in a position you feel comfortable shooting from. We've practiced sitting flat on your bottom. Do you feel good about that, or would you rather go prone?"

I answer with a shrug. On my bottom is much more comfortable than on my stomach, especially if we may be here awhile. And even though he says we've practiced, I've only live fired in each position one time, and that was with the .22 rifle. We've practiced moving to the different positions and holding them, but with cartridges at a premium . . . "Sitting, I guess."

"Make yourself comfortable." He motions with his hand.

I move into sitting cross-legged, just like I used to do in kindergarten during story time.

Atticus gives me a nod. "Test it out. Pretend like you're ready for your shot. But, um, Sadie, leave the safety on."

I roll my eyes in response.

"The trail opens up at the bank. I think that's where they'll come out, so pretend your target is there and position accordingly. Remember, move your body instead of twisting at the waist. You need to be stable."

I'm sitting on my butt, with my left leg on bottom and my feet connected well to the ground for extra support. I place my left elbow on my thigh so I have a good base for holding the rifle with my nonfiring hand. I pull the rifle tight against my right shoulder, resting my right elbow on the right thigh, making sure to keep my finger well away from the trigger.

After looking through my scope to ensure I'm where I think my target will come out, I look to Atticus.

"It looks like you have a good, solid base. Maybe pull the buttstock in a little more. And your right elbow should rest more toward the inside of your thigh, away from your knee."

I reposition before looking at him for approval.

"Good. Now relax a minute and then do it again."

I practice getting into position several times until the movements feel natural. We're quiet, watching and waiting. The singing from the birds and the gentle rumble of the creek are soothing but contradicted by the buzz of mosquitos.

I can almost imagine this is a normal day out in the wilderness, not the end of the world where we hunt for our food. The sound of a twig breaking causes both of us to sit up slightly. Atticus slowly turns his head to look up the trail.

I follow his gaze but see nothing.

He leans into me. "Keep your movements minimal. I can't see anything yet, but there may be something coming toward us." Another crack of the brush punctuates his words. He gives me a smile and a lift of his shoulder.

With my eyes glued to the trail and my heart beating loudly, I think about what I need to do. Get into position first. Once the muzzle is on my target, then I'll take a deep breath and silently click off the safety. Another deep breath while I take the slack out of the trigger. Then I'll—

"Don't move, scum bags," a hoarse voice demands. "I've got a gun aimed at the back of your head."

Chapter 25

My eyes go wide as I take in a noisy breath. *What's happening here?*

I move my head to look behind me when the voice growls, "I said don't move."

"No problem," Atticus answers. "We're, uh, holding still."

"Why are you here? You people said you'd leave us alone. That was the deal."

I squeeze my eyes tight as I try to comprehend what he's talking about.

"We're not who you think we are," Atticus says. His voice is calm, almost soothing.

"Oh yeah? Put the rifle down, girlie."

I shoot my eyes to Atticus. My head naturally follows. I stop midmotion, afraid of what the man will do.

"Go ahead. Do what he says."

"Y-you're sure?"

"Put down the gun!" the man roars. "And both of you get rid of your pistols."

"I don't have one," I answer, my voice a whisper as my fingers itch to feel the knife on my belt. I may not have a gun, but the knife gives me some comfort.

"Fine then. I'm surprised to see you with a rifle. Y'all must have reconsidered your methods, huh? Decided on equality? Get rid of your backpacks too. Toss them aside."

The deer rifle is off to the side with the packs next to it. The man has Atticus put his handgun on a bit of brush an arm's length away. It's close, but too far to reach in a hurry without getting shot.

"What now?" Atticus asks.

"Now I send a message your people won't forget. You think you can mess with me? Threaten my family?"

"I'm telling you— "

"Shut up! Turn around, both of you. I want to see the look in your eyes."

Unwanted tears sting my eyes. This guy is going to kill us.

"Wait," Atticus says. "Let Sadie go. She'll deliver whatever message it is you want delivered, just tell her who to contact."

He lets out a harsh laugh. "That's rich. You people take our livestock, our supplies, leave my wife and young 'uns to starve. Now you're acting all innocent?"

"We are innocent!" I cry.

"Enough! Turn around. You first, girlie. Then the big guy."

"Go ahead, Sadie," Atticus whispers. "Remember— "

"Shut up!"

I turn my head, getting my first look at the disheveled man. He's skinny and filthy, standing only about ten feet from us. A small handgun is held loosely in his left hand, while he motions wildly with his right.

My stomach drops as I think of how close he was able to get without us hearing him. The snaps of the twigs . . . was that him instead of a deer?

As I move my body, he lifts the muzzle of the pistol. "Keep your hands where I can see them."

Chewing on my lip, I answer with a nod.

I slowly turn, moving from a full sitting position to kneeling, with my left knee on the ground and my right foot flat.

After I face him, his eyes go wide. "Why, you're nothing more than a child. How old are you anyway?"

"She's twelve," Atticus says in a rush.

"They really have changed their ways then. All right, Big Guy. Keep your hands up and turn around. I want you looking me in the eyes."

"We're not with them," I say, purposely keeping my voice young and shaky—not that I need much help to add a quiver to it. I'm scared, and my cheeks are wet with tears.

Moving slowly and cautiously, Atticus says, "She's telling you the truth. We're just passing through."

"And you thought you could hunt in my area?"

I lift my hands. "We didn't know."

The gun bobs as he narrows his eyes. A shudder runs through his body. "Get up. On your feet."

"Both of us?"

"Just you, girlie. I want you on your feet and moving toward me. Big Guy will be smart, won't you?"

173

"Absolutely." A sigh escapes Atticus.

I glance over to him. He raises both eyebrows and tilts his head slightly. There's a slight flicker to his hand—the signal we use as an indicator to *go*, the same one Nicole gives me when she's ready for me to attack when we're sparring during combat training.

At least I think that's the motion he's making. It's abbreviated and slight so the man doesn't see.

I purse my lips and open my eyes wide. This crazy man is holding a gun. And not holding it the way Kimba taught me. His one-handed grip is loose and careless instead of steady and firm.

Yet, Atticus wants me to go up against him? Go up against a man with a gun?

The training we've had during this journey crowds my brain, images of moves and phrases from Kimba and Rey. Their phrases run through my head. "Eliminate the threat," "Most fights are over within thirty seconds, so make every second count," and, "Fight until you can't fight."

I'll *go*, all right. Go hard and go fast. I take a wobbly step toward the man.

"Calm down. I get you're scared. I'm sorry it has to be this way, but you'll tell them. Tell them not to mess with me and mine. They've pushed me too far this time."

"W-what are y-you going to do to us?" I take another step forward.

"I told you! Deliver a message. Now, Big Guy, you just stay still. Don't be getting any bright ideas. Move it, girlie."

I'm about three feet from him. I take another tentative step. "W-we keep telling you, we're just passing through. Pl-please, let us go."

He moves the muzzle of the gun toward me. It jerks with his movement. "Persistent thing, aren't you?"

As his eyes dart back to Atticus, I drop my stance and tighten my right foot. Making my foot like a knife, I sweep his left ankle. He staggers as I continue to pivot and then lift my right leg higher into a side kick. I aim for his sternum, but with his body in motion, it lands on his shoulder, causing him to stumble backward.

I'm almost shocked to see the pistol fly off to the side. As he works to regain his footing, I step into him. Using the palm of my right hand, I thrust upward, landing a solid hit to his chin, then swing my elbow into his face.

"Hold it!" Atticus yells, directing the muzzle of his sidearm to the man's temple. "Sadie, in my backpack are a couple of zip ties. Get them out."

I'm breathing hard, gasping for air. "Zip ties? Why do you have those?" I stumble toward the packs, my body shaking from not only exertion but also adrenaline.

"We carried them in the militia. Seemed smart to keep a few for this trip."

"Whatcha gonna do?" the man asks, his words slurred.

I glance at him from my squatted position by the backpacks. His nose is bloody. *Did I do that?*

"Right now, I'm tying you up. Then . . . then I guess we'll decide what to do with you based on what you planned to do to us."

"I-I was just going to send a message, like I said. Have her tell them I had you and wouldn't release you until y'all promised to leave me and my family alone."

Atticus sets his jaw. "I'll tell you again. We're. Not. Who. You. Think!"

Once Atticus has the man secured with his hands behind his back, he turns to me. His eyes are hard. Angry. "Why didn't you do what I said?"

I crinkle my forehead.

"I gave you the signal to leave. You could've been hurt. Shot even."

I cross my arms. "You gave me the signal to *go*, the same one we use when we're sparring."

"What? No. Go means go. You— " He lets out a loud breath through his nose, and his shoulders drop. "You did good, Sadie. Real good."

Atticus hoists the man to his feet. "Keep the rifle on him while I hold him."

"Just let me go. My family, they need me."

"Where are they?" I ask.

"The house down the way." He motions with his head.

"The place that looks like it's about to fall down?" Atticus asks.

Atticus mentioned they saw a shack when out hunting, said he thought it was being lived in and hoped they found someplace else before winter.

"It's not that bad." The man straightens his shoulders. "I've been working on fixing it up. Finding materials isn't easy."

"No, I guess not."

"Humph. Maybe y'all shouldn't have stolen my house, then we wouldn't be forced to live in a shack."

"Maybe you shouldn't go attacking people who are innocent!"

The man's body deflates. "In retrospect, I guess it wasn't too smart. Didn't exactly think the plan out like I should've. I just . . . I saw you hunting on my knob and couldn't take it anymore."

As we near the trail Brett took, Atticus hoots like an owl. He motions me to stop as we wait. After a minute, he hoots again.

I lean in. "Why don't you just call to him?"

"Brett!" His eyes meet mine as he smirks. "C'mon out to the main trail."

"On my way!"

In less than a minute, Brett comes into view. As soon as he sees us, he skids to a stop. "Who's this?"

"Some guy playing Rambo."

"I've told you— "

"I know, you put a gun to our heads for your family."

"He thinks we stole his house and are forcing his family to live in a shack." I catch Brett up on the situation. "He held us at gunpoint and said he was going to send a message."

"A message? To whom?"

"Mosher, of course!" the man yells.

Brett's eyes meet mine, his eyebrows shooting to the top of his head. "Jack Mosher?"

"Of course! You know another Mosher?"

"You sure let him have it, Atticus." Brett's voice is full of awe.

"Wasn't me. That was all Sadie."

Brett's head turns quickly toward me. "Wow. That's . . . that's amazing. Good thing my brother stopped picking on you."

I snort out a laugh.

It's close to sundown when our camp comes into view. The man jerks against Atticus. "What's this?"

"Knock it off." Atticus yanks on the guy's arm.

"Who's camping here?"

"We are, for a few days anyway while we sort things out."

"Mosher's letting you camp?"

Sebastian points toward us as everyone in the camp looks our way.

Rey immediately grabs his tactical rifle and must start barking out orders because my mom and the others move into defensive positions. When we're within a hundred yards, Rey lifts a hand, telling us to stop. He turns and says something to Kimba before moving toward us.

Rey moves swiftly but cautiously. I have little doubt he's using all his senses to ensure this guy is alone and there aren't any additional threats.

At twenty yards away, he stops. "Who's your friend?"

"Didn't ask his name." Atticus pulls on the guy's arm. "What is it?"

"Hyde. Ledger Hyde. Look, I made a mistake."

"He pulled a gun on Sadie and me," Atticus says. "Said he was going to send a message."

"To Mosher," I add. "Only, he didn't tell us that until afterward."

"I thought you guys were from the compound. I can see now I made a mistake. Let me go so I can return to my family. I won't bother you again."

Rey takes a few more steps toward us. "What's your beef with Jack Mosher?"

"He kicked me, my wife, and kids out of our place. Said we weren't following the community rules and had to go."

"What rules did you break?"

The guy vigorously shakes his head. "That doesn't matter. Besides, it was a lie."

Rey lets out a sigh. "Bring him into camp."

My mom meets us halfway. "You okay?" She looks me up and down.

"Fine."

"Sadie did great," Atticus says.

"She beat me up!" Ledger cries. "Look at me."

Mom lets out a chuckle. "Sadie?"

I lift a shoulder, willing myself not to smile. I shouldn't be happy about bloodying the guy, but . . . well, I am. I'm proud. And shocked. I can't believe I actually did that. The things we've practiced actually work.

In the camp, there's a brief conversation about how we "met" Ledger Hyde. Nicole gives me a thumbs up after Atticus brags on my saving us.

Kimba motions to the barricade Jack Mosher has set up. "Take him to them."

"No, no, no." Hyde shakes his head. "Just let me go. It was a misunderstanding, that's all."

She steps close to his face. "You put a gun on our people. I'm not misunderstanding *that* at all. Your beef may be with Mosher and his community, but you are a threat to us."

"Look, just let me go. I won't bother you again."

"Too late." Jameson motions toward the barricade, where several armed men are starting in our direction. While they're not exactly running, they're moving quickly.

"Let me go." Hyde pulls against Atticus.

"Knock it off," Atticus growls.

"Please! Taking you hostage was my leverage, the only way to keep us safe. Now— " He shakes his head as he bucks against Atticus. "They'll kill us."

Sebastian stares at the man with wide eyes. "Mom?"

"Come over here, honey. It's okay."

"My stomach hurts again."

Jack Mosher is the first to reach us. "Hyde! What've you done now?"

Ledger Hyde narrows his eyes and pulls his mouth tight in a grim line.

"Did he bother you?" Jack asks my mom.

"My daughter. But she took care of herself."

Jack looks Ledger Hyde up and down. "I guess she did. Sorry that was necessary. Hyde's been a blight on our community for far too long. When we caught him stealing— "

"That's a lie!" Hyde yells.

"We had to banish him. He and his family settled nearby, and he harasses us every chance he gets."

"Humph. More lies," Hyde sneers.

Jack motions to two of his men. "Take Ledger home."

"What are you going to do?" Hyde asks again, bucking against Atticus. "Beat me? Kill me? Take my wife as your own like you planned to do all along?"

Jack steps close to Hyde, his face inches away. "You are crazy. If you didn't think everyone was out to get you, if you wouldn't have stolen from our community, from our family, you wouldn't be an outcast. And your wife knows that, when she can no longer take your insanity, she'll be welcomed back with open arms. By all of us."

Hyde pulls back his head a few inches and lets loose a stream of bloody spit, landing it smack on Jack's cheek.

My stomach curls at the sight.

"*Ewwww,*" Sebastian moans. He grabs his stomach and throws up.

Chapter 26

"Your boy feeling better?" Jack Mosher asks when Mom, Donnie, Sebastian, and I arrive at the roadblock.

Last night, after Sebastian vomited, Mom had me take him to our tent. We heard Hyde screaming and cursing as Mosher's men took him away. He kept saying not to let them take him, that they'd kill him and murder his family.

I asked Mom about it later. She said Jack feels bad for the guy and his family. He used to be a friend, but his mind is gone. They've done what they can for them, and they even leave food where the wife knows to find it. But Ledger Hyde is a menace and a danger to the community. Possibly even a danger to his family, but his wife won't leave him.

Mom shook her head before saying, "Those poor kids."

Before Jack left last night, Mom and Donnie arranged for the four of us to visit Aunt Karla. Mom and Donnie have already been searched for weapons. Even though guns aren't allowed, we're able to keep our knives.

Mine's still on my belt, where I've made sure to wear it every day since Becky and her crazy friend kidnapped us back in Roundup. I didn't need the knife yesterday when taking down Ledger Hyde, but it was reassuring to know it was there—and that I know how to use it if needed.

"He's better, thanks." Mom rests a hand on Sebastian's shoulder. "Something must not have agreed with him. No fever or anything, just . . . well, you know."

Jack responds with a half-smile. "I thought I'd walk in with you. I haven't seen Karla since she fell, so it'll be good for me to visit."

Donnie visibly stiffens.

Mom reaches for his hand and cocks an eyebrow. "Sure, Jack. We'd welcome the company. Wouldn't we, Donnie?"

"Sure." Donnie's tone leaves little doubt that Jack walking with us is anything but fine. Mom and Donnie may have plans for a future together, but Jack and Mom's history is certainly an issue. At least for Donnie.

Last night, after Sebastian fell asleep, Mom kept saying how proud she was of me. Though Ledger Hyde insists the message he planned to send was just to hold Atticus hostage, there's some doubt, especially from Atticus. The way Ledger kept saying he needed him looking at him led Atticus to believe he planned to kill him.

"You were amazing, Sadie." Mom said with a proud smile. "I know you've been working hard on your skills. And I'm so glad you weren't hurt, so glad God protected you."

"Ha." I snorted. "I'm not sure it was God as much as Nicole always being willing to work with me."

"You sure about that? Perhaps God sent Nicole to work with you."

I shook my head. "I don't know. I'm not— "

"I'm not pushing, Sadie, just reminding you God loves you. And He wants you to love Him back."

"Okay, maybe."

Though I didn't admit it to Mom, I've been thinking more about God, especially considering the changes I've seen in her lately. Donnie too. I think, maybe, he's also realizing his need for whatever it is Mom has. Maybe I need it too.

With Sebastian snoring softly beside us, Mom and I talked late into the night. Not much more about God, but about Ledger Hyde, Aunt Karla, Donnie, and Jack Mosher. Especially Jack Mosher.

I stare at the man as the memories of what she said rush over me. They were a couple. Although they'd known each other for several years, they didn't start dating until the summer after Mom turned eighteen. Jack was twenty then, and it was a whirlwind of a romance. Mom told me about a few of their dates and how she was sure she was in love with him.

Then she slammed her jaw tight and said, "But I was wrong. Jack wasn't the man I thought he was." I asked her what she meant, but all she said was, "Not tonight, Sadie. I'll tell you, but not yet. Let's get things sorted out first."

At first, our walk to Aunt Karla's is tense. Both Donnie and Jack try to dominate the conversation.

At some point, I catch Mom's eye. She gives me a wink, then makes a funny face. I hide my laugh with a cough. I'm really glad my old, fun Mom is back. Even though she's more religious than she used to be, it's okay. There's something genuine about her.

When the deaths and destruction of the apocalypse made her so miserable and she went out of her way to make others miserable, it felt wrong. It definitely wasn't the Mom I knew. Her recent transformation has even helped Donnie mellow.

Even though it's hard to see right now, with Donnie trying to one-up Jack for Mom's attention, he's been much more pleasant to be around.

It does help that even Jameson seems to be less of a jerk too. He really knows how to push Donnie's buttons. I can't help but, again, wonder if part of the reason everyone's getting along so well is because we're all grieving over Asher.

As we walk, I realize that, as much as I want to be here at Aunt Karla's and have our journey finished, I'm going to miss my friends. Well, maybe not Jameson or his mom much, even though they're easier to be around, but the rest are like family. These months we've been traveling together, and now grieving together, have brought us closer.

I never did tell Mom if I'd be okay with her and Donnie getting married. I probably should let her know I just want her to be happy. And if marrying Donnie is part of that happiness, then yes.

"There's sure a lot of trees here," Sebastian says as the road winds through a wooded area.

"Fergus State Forest. It starts here and goes up into the mountains." Jack motions with his arms. "Your aunt's place is surrounded by woods, probably part of what made it so popular when it was an operating lodge. And now it gives us the firewood we need to stay warm during the winter."

"Is it much farther?" There's a weariness in my brother's voice.

"Are you feeling okay?" Mom asks him. "Do you need to stop?"

"I can keep going. I just wondered how much farther."

"Maybe a mile," Mom answers. "Can you make it?"

He lets out a soft sigh. "My stomach feels better. I can keep walking."

A rush of memories come back when Aunt Karla's lodge finally comes into view. Mom and Dad brought me here several times before Dad got sick. Aunt Karla always had a nice room on the top floor for us. I loved visiting, especially since my bed was in a little loft accessed by a spiral staircase with big windows looking out over the forest. It felt like my own little treehouse getaway.

Aunt Karla and Uncle Ralph lived on the first floor of the lodge. Their apartment was a tiny one-bedroom on the main floor separate from the guest rooms. She always said they didn't need much space since they had the entire lodge to stretch out.

Their apartment was way different than the rest of the place. Where there was a dude ranch feel to the lodge, with photos of wildlife and fishing, plus lots of greens and browns, their room was very modern with bright, vibrant colors and funky decor. She had a large beanbag in the living room where I'd take naps.

The last time I was here was before Uncle Ralph died. Before my dad died too. Although the exterior of the main lodge looks much the same, the cabins around are all new. Just like Mom said, these have been added. One's a big two-story with a deck. There's laundry hanging off the railings, showing it's obviously occupied. There're four more much smaller cabins, connected by decking, between the large one and the main lodge.

Jack waves at two women standing near a firepit by the large deck. "Karla added those smaller cabins recently. We've been housing all of the single and widowed women plus children here."

"Only three of the cabins are finished though, right?" Mom asks. "The young lady we spoke with the other day said one wasn't completed before the EMP and you're scrounging materials to get it ready before this winter."

Jack lifts a hand toward another group working in the garden space. "These four are done. Karla started another section of cabins down the creek, just past the gazebo. She planned on three there, honeymoon cabins or some such thing. Only one was started, it's unfinished. We did have a woman and child in there last year, but once the cold hit, it was too uncomfortable. They kept what few things they had in there but slept in the lodge."

"It's bigger than I thought it'd be," Sebastian says.

"Humph," Donnie grunts. "Smaller than I thought. The way your mom talked about it, I thought it was a hundred-room place. At least a hundred beds since she said that's how many she made each day."

"Quit now." Mom lightly taps Donnie on the arm while shaking her head. "I loved working here. Even if making beds wasn't my favorite thing to do."

"I'll say it wasn't!" Jack snorts out a laugh. "You complained every single day."

"There's horses!" Sebastian says excitedly. "And a dog!"

"Yep. Aunt Karla and Uncle Ralph used to take their guests on trail rides up the mountain." Mom motions to the forested mountain behind the lodge. "That's when I first started loving horses. They'd let me help sometimes."

"In the past few years, Karla hired wranglers," Jack says. "They'd come from all over for a chance to live and work in Montana for the summer. A couple of them are still here, stranded after the EMP. That dog is one of the guardian dogs. There're a few pets around too. You like dogs?"

"Sure! Who doesn't? I like cats too."

"We have those around also. Plenty of other livestock and such too."

As we near the main building, I take in a deep breath. There're flowers growing in several small gardens: roses in one section, lavender elsewhere, several patches of wildflowers, and a beautiful lilac hedge making a barrier between the lodge and the parking lot. I inhale deeply, trying to capture their sweet scent. When they reach full bloom, their fragrance will waft over everything.

Aunt Karla loves them; Grandma Jackie also loved lilacs. She's the one who gave Aunt Karla the cuttings to start her hedgerow. I take another deep breath as the memory of my grandma washes over me.

The front door of the lodge opens with a squeak, and a stern-looking woman steps out. "Jack? I didn't know you were coming over today."

"I brought Leanne, Karla's niece. Did you two meet before?"

The lady crosses her arms and glares at Mom. "I thought you were going to give Karla some time to get well before you came back."

Mom gives the crabby woman a pleasant smile. "Aunt Karla asked me to bring my children to see her. This is my daughter, Sadie, and my son, Sebastian." She rests a hand lightly on Sebastian's head. "And this is my friend Donnie. I don't think you told me your name when we were here before."

"Ah, well . . ." Jack steps toward the woman. "Annie, please allow me to formally introduce you to Ms. Daniela Reynolds."

The woman's cheeks color as she looks to Jack. She gives him a fleeting smile before turning to the rest of us.

Mom reaches out her hand. "It's nice to meet you, Daniela."

"I prefer to be called Ms. Reynolds." She limply reaches for Mom's hand.

A shadow crosses Mom's face, quickly erased by a composed smile. "Sure, of course. I go by Leanne. Jack's the only one who's ever called me Annie."

"Humph," Ms. Reynolds and Donnie both snort simultaneously.

Jack looks amused. "Well then, is Karla up for visitors?"

"I'll let her know everyone's here. She can decide for herself." Ms. Reynolds returns to the lodge through the door, leaving it ajar for us to follow.

"After you." Jack grabs the knob and motions to my mom.

Chapter 27

Inside, the restaurant of Aunt Karla's lodge is much the same as I remember. There's a fireplace to the right, a small bar straight ahead—now stripped of the bottles of alcohol that used to fill the shelves—and lots of tables and chairs filling the space.

Ms. Reynolds is near the door to the kitchen when she yells over her shoulder, "Wait here."

"This dining room is nice." Sebastian strokes the wooden table.

Mom puts her hand on the table. "It's been redone since I was here last. Aunt Karla's done a lot of updating in the past ten years."

"She had these custom made." Jack touches a chair. "The tables and chairs were built by a man she met at the Big Sky Grocery."

"The Amish store at Eddie's Corner?" Mom asks. "Aunt Karla told me about it."

"It's a good one. I rarely drove to Great Falls without stopping there for a made-to-order sandwich. You ever stop there?"

"I don't remember it being open the last time I visited."

"There's an Amish community in Montana?" Donnie asks.

"A few." Jack nods. "The one near us isn't very large, only a dozen—maybe two dozen—families. Not nearly as many as the Hutterite communities."

"Hutterites, sure." Donnie says. "I know some people who used to buy chickens from them. Similar religion, I think, but different from Amish, right? They use electricity and cars?"

"Right. But they know how to work together, just like the Amish."

"I guess they're probably doing okay—the Amish, I mean, with being used to not having electricity and all."

Jack lifts a shoulder. "Maybe. I think they might be more worldly than the back east communities. The grocery store has electricity and everything."

"Well, this is beautiful work." Mom rubs a hand across the tabletop again.

"Karla's ready for you," Ms. Reynolds calls from the door. As we approach, she puts up a hand. "Keep it short. She needs her rest." She glares at Mom before spinning on her heel.

"Wow." Sebastian is wide eyed as he takes in the large commercial kitchen. Even with everything that's happened, the stainless steel is shiny and bright. "Do they use this?"

"Most of the cooking happens outside, especially during the summer," Jack answers. "There's still propane, but it's best to save it for winter use."

"What about water?" Donnie asks. "Do you pull it from the creek we crossed on the way here?"

"For most of the community, we use creek water and captured rainwater. A few of us, including Karla, have skinny buckets to access our water wells."

After making our way through the gleaming kitchen, we reach a small, dark hallway with an office to the right and a bathroom next to it. I remember this from the last time I was here and know we'll go to the right, pass through another office, and then find the door to Aunt Karla's apartment.

Ms. Reynolds doesn't turn to see if we're following, just walks stick straight as we trail along. With her hand on the door to the private quarters, Ms. Reynolds turns. With another glare, she juts her chin. "Keep it short."

Once the door opens, more light streams into the room, thanks to the full bank of windows along the western wall. I breathe in. The smell is still the same, a wonderful light flowery scent—a mixture of roses, lavender, lilac, and more—that always reminds me of both my aunt and grandma.

"There you are!" Aunt Karla reaches her hands toward us from her recliner. "I almost thought your visit was a dream. God delivered you, just as I knew He would!"

Aunt Karla is tiny like me, her body barely a speck against the dark maroon fabric. Her left eye has a cut above it and is terribly bruised all around. The right eye is also discolored, but not as much. Her smile is brilliant, lighting up the entire room and beckoning us forward.

"You look so much better today." Mom rushes toward her. She takes both hands in hers, then bends to kiss Aunt Karla on the cheek.

"I'm feeling better. Daniela and Samantha have been taking excellent care of me." Aunt Karla smiles at the stern-looking woman.

Ms. Reynolds dips her head in response. "Samantha had the night shift. She's resting now."

"Oh mercy, Sadie! You've grown into such a lovely young woman. And Sebastian, you're even more handsome in person than in your pictures." Aunt Karla motions toward us. "Please, come over."

I move to Aunt Karla, kissing her on the cheek just like my mom did.

After I pull back, she looks into my eyes. "Still the knowledge of the world in there." She points to my head. "I bet you keep your mom on her toes."

"Sadie's a blessing to me." Mom touches my back. "She's been amazing at . . . well, everything. I don't know if we . . . anyway, here's Sebastian." Mom turns and smiles at my brother.

"Hello," he says, stepping next to Mom. "I'm glad you're feeling better."

"And I'm so glad you're here. I remember bits and pieces of your mom's visit. I think she said you walked most of the way."

"From Oregon to Wyoming, but we did find a car once and rode in it until it ran out of gas. Did she . . . do you know my grandma and grandpa died? And Uncle Wes?"

Aunt Karla's eyes fill with tears. "I guess I do . . . it's all a little fuzzy."

"Sorry, Auntie." Mom reaches for her. "I should've realized you weren't understanding everything I told you."

Aunt Karla lets out a sigh. "Samantha helped clear up a few things I wasn't sure about. And I guess, in my heart, I knew about your mom. I had a feeling. But you and the children, I always knew you'd show up. I felt God had given me a promise you'd join me. And here you are." Her eyes travel to Donnie. "Is this your man?"

Mom's cheeks color. She reaches a hand for Donnie. "This is Donnie McCullough. Donnie, this is my aunt, Karla Belvedere."

"Ma'am." Donnie steps forward.

"You'll be staying with Leanne and the children?"

"Yes, if we can work it out. I've, um . . . I've asked Leanne to marry me."

A snort sounds from Ms. Reynolds. Glancing in her direction, I notice a look cross over Jack's face. Anger? No . . . it's disappointment.

Aunt Karla looks at Mom, who gives a slight nod. "I said yes."

"Then welcome to the family. Jack, this is the answer to our prayers!"

"What's that, Karla?" Jack steps closer to the recliner.

"You know how I've said over and over how wonderful it'd be to have a man around here? Here we go."

"Karla, we've agreed this is a refuge for the women and children, a safe place for them away from negative male influences."

"Pshaw. I trust my niece to have good judgment in her man. I'm sure he'll be an asset. And this way, any time we need heavy lifting done, we don't have to wait for one of your men to make their way here."

"We don't need a man here," Ms. Reynolds states, her arms crossed again. "If your niece is going to live in the community, then Jack will find a family home for them. This is our place."

"No, Daniela, dear. This is *my* place, my *home*. Leanne and her children are my family. She's my heir, even. She, her children, and her husband will be welcome here."

"Thank you, Aunt Karla." Mom reaches for her again. After a long hug, she steps back, tears streaming down her face. "We're so glad to be here, to find you safe." Mom reaches for my brother, pulling him close. She plants a kiss on the top of his head. "What do you think? Are those butterflies clearing up?"

Sebastian glances to me, his eyes questioning. I bob my head. "I think it's good."

Mom smiles. "So, it's just up to you, son."

He looks around the room before retuning his gaze to Aunt Karla. "You like it here, huh?"

"I love it here. It's been my home for many years. Even with all the troubles, we're making do, coming together and trying to survive." She furrows her brow. "Not just that. We're doing better than just surviving. Jack's put some important things in place."

"With your help." Jack reaches for Aunt Karla's hand. "When I lost my mom, Karla was the one who took care of things then. Then, when Dad died . . . " He shakes his head. "If it wasn't for Karla, we'd be in a world of hurt."

"Enough with you." She gives his hand a playful swat. "I'm just an old broad, usually causing troubles."

Ms. Reynolds gives another one of her snorts. "You're an injured woman who needs her rest."

189

Aunt Karla waves her away before motioning to Sebastian. "Do you want to share your concerns?"

He lifts a shoulder. "I feel better now. After meeting you and seeing your house . . . maybe we're okay here."

"Then it's settled?" Mom's voice is bright. "You and Sadie will be so happy here. With the horses and the flowers and . . . just everything. It's such a magical place."

My mom's being silly, but it still makes me smile. I'm not sure any place is magical any longer. At least it does seem safe. That's what's important anyway.

Jack turns to Donnie. "When will you wed?"

"What's the procedure here?" Donnie asks. "Do you have something set up for record keeping and such?"

"We've had a couple of births, but no marriages yet," Aunt Karla responds. "I suppose we'd do something similar?"

Jack cocks his head. "I guess we'll just keep the record, like we do for the births . . . and the deaths. Someday, a government of sorts might start up again, and they might ask for the info. They'll probably come around collecting taxes and marriage license fees."

Donnie snorts out a laugh. "Undoubtedly."

Mom gives a slight shake of her head—a warning, maybe, to prevent Donnie from getting started on his conspiracy theories. From Jack's slight comment on taxes, I wonder if the two of them might have a dislike for the government in common.

"What's the process to join your community?" Donnie asks. "To be able to be a full-fledged member with all the rights?"

"Are you asking what you'll need to do to carry your guns?"

Donnie tilts his head in response.

"There won't be any issue with that," Aunt Karla says. "Will there, Jack?"

Jack lets out a loud sigh. "We'll work it out."

Donnie looks from Aunt Karla to Jack. "Leanne too?"

"Women do not handle firearms here," Ms. Reynolds declares.

Mom glances at Aunt Karla.

With a nod, Aunt Karla says, "That's a concession I agreed to."

"Even though you're back here, a good half mile from the nearest house, with just women and children?" Mom asks, her voice soft.

"Especially because of the children." Ms. Reynolds lifts her hands. "They've been through enough. They don't need to see weapons.

Frankly, I'm appalled you let your young daughter carry a big knife on her hip."

"Oh, give it a rest, Daniela." Aunt Karla shakes her head.

"I'm just saying the entire fascination with firearms and giant knives seems rather fetishistic is all. It was bad before, but now . . . " Ms. Reynolds lifts her hands. "The way Jack runs things is smart. He understands not everyone's a threat and not everyone should be a defender, only those well trained and capable. Personally, I don't feel at all comfortable with an armed man living here."

"Well then, Daniela dear," Aunt Karla says in a calm, patient voice, "we might need to find alternative lodging for you."

Ms. Reynolds's face goes white as she straightens her shoulders. "That's fine, Karla. I'm sure Jack will have room for me at his home."

She huffs out a noise and quickly leaves the room.

"Don't bet on it," Jack mutters.

Mom touches Aunt Karla's arm. "I'm sorry. I didn't mean to— "

"It's not you, Leanne. Daniela often has a bee in her bonnet. She . . . things were rough for her before she found us, for many of the women here. And she's right, most of the people here have seen some terrible things.

"Even so, Jack and I agreed we'd have a family move back here before winter. Whether any of us want to admit it, there are things we need a man for. And not just the heavy lifting. We're too isolated, and even with the mountain behind us, I worry we could be attacked and our defenders won't get to us in time."

"Why don't you at least have a radio?"

"There aren't enough of them," Jack answers. "We have just enough for our patrols and blockades."

"They won't be much good for long anyway."

"Karla . . . " Jack cautions.

"It's true. We're on the last of the batteries. Then what? Having Leanne and her husband here will help us. Maybe even move another family or two in." Aunt Karla leans back in her chair, closing her eyes.

"We should let you get a nap." Mom pats Aunt Karla's arm, causing her eyes to open. "We'll need to see our friends again, let them know our plans."

"You'll stay over tonight? It's too much of a walk for the children to go back in one day."

I can't help but smile. It was a long five miles, but going back would be a normal day's walk for us.

"We'll stay tonight," Mom agrees with a nod. "Then we'll return to tell our friends goodbye. They're anxious to get home also."

Home. I glance around Aunt Karla's eclectic room, still decorated in its bright and cheery way.

We've made it home.

After reaching the safety of Aunt Karla's lodge, and Donnie's promise of a marriage proposal, have the Monroes finally found their happily ever after? Sadie's story continues in Cruel Havoc: Montana Mayhem Book 4.

While Sadie and her family rebuild their life at the lodge, their friends continue walking.

Victoria Dawson and her sons, Brett and Jameson, used to have it all—a beautiful home, prestige in the community, and what appeared to be perfect lives. Then it all came crashing down. Now that she's walking her way to a new start at the Dosens' ranch outside of Great Falls, Montana, a nugget of hope and a promise of happiness help Victoria carry on. But will that be enough?

Also by Millie Copper

Montana Mayhem Series

Unending Havoc: Montana Mayhem Book 1

Ruthless Havoc: Montana Mayhem Book 2

Havoc in Wyoming Series

Wyoming Refuge: A Havoc in Wyoming Prequel

Havoc in Wyoming: Part 1, Caldwell's Homestead

Havoc in Wyoming: Part 2, Katie's Journey

Havoc in Wyoming: Part 3, Mollie's Quest

Havoc Begins: A Havoc in Wyoming Story (Part 3.5)

Havoc in Wyoming: Part 4, Shields and Ramparts

Havoc in Wyoming: Part 5, Fowler's Snare

Havoc Rises: A Havoc in Wyoming Story (Part 5.5)

Havoc in Wyoming: Part 6, Pestilence in the Darkness

Christmas on the Mountain: A Havoc in Wyoming Novella

Havoc Peaks: A Havoc in Wyoming Story (Part 6.5)

Havoc in Wyoming: Part 7, My Refuge and Fortress

Nonfiction Books

Stock the Real Food Pantry: A Handbook for Making the Most of Your Pantry

Design a Dish: Save Your Food Dollars

Real Food Hits the Road: Budget Friendly Tips, Ideas, and Recipes for Enjoying Real Food Away from Home

Stretchy Beans: Nutritious, Economical Meals the Easy Way

Find these titles on Amazon:
www.amazon.com/author/milliecopper

Acknowledgments

Thanks to:

Ameryn Tucker, my editor, beta reader, and daughter wrapped in one. I had a story I wanted to tell, and Ameryn encouraged me and helped me bring it to life.

Dee from Dauntless Cover Design.

My husband, who gave me the time and space I needed to complete this dream and was very patient as I'd tell him the same plot ideas over and over and over.

Three more daughters and a young son, who willingly listen to me drone on and on about story lines and ideas while encouraging me to "keep going."

My amazing Beta Readers! Thanks to Barbara, Becky, Delia, Glen, Judy, Tammy, Tonya, and Tracy for your help in creating the final story. Your insights and abilities to see the things I miss are very much appreciated! And a special thank you to Tim, specialist in all things that go boom, for always answering my questions and pointing out things I wouldn't even think about.

And to you, my readers, for spending your time with our band of weary travelers. If you have five minutes, you'd make this writer very happy if you could leave a review. I appreciate you!

About the Author

Millie Copper, writer of Cozy Apocalyptic Fiction, was born in Nebraska but never lived there. Her parents fully embraced wanderlust and moved regularly, giving her an advantage of being from nowhere and everywhere.

As an adult, Millie is fully rooted in a solar-powered home in the wilds of Wyoming with her husband and young son, milking ornery goats and tending chickens on their small homestead. In their free time, they escape to the mountains for a hike or laze along the bank of the river to catch their dinner. Four adult daughters, three sons-in-law, and three grandchildren round out the family.

Since 2009, Millie has authored articles on traditional foods, alternative health, homesteading, and preparedness-many times all within the same piece. Millie has penned five nonfiction, traditional food focused books, sharing how, with a little creativity, anyone can transition to a real foods diet without overwhelming their food budget.

The twelve-installment *Havoc in Wyoming* Christian Post-Apocalyptic fiction series uses her homesteading, off-the-grid, and preparedness lifestyle as a guide. The adventure continues with the *Montana Mayhem* series, scheduled for release in the summer of 2021.

Find Millie at www.MillieCopper.com
Facebook: www.facebook.com/MillieCopperAuthor/
Amazon: www.amazon.com/author/milliecopper
BookBub: https://www.bookbub.com/authors/millie-copper

Made in the USA
Middletown, DE
23 January 2022